P9-DEK-833

Praise for *Waking Lazarus*

"This taut inspirational thriller will keep readers guessing. . . ."
Library Journal

"Readers who consider most faith thrillers too tame should find this satisfactorily chilling."
Publishers Weekly

"This book is compelling as well as spell-binding . . . an excellent murder-mystery . . ."
Alan Paul Curtis, Who-Dunnit.com

"From the opening sentence, Hines delivers. *Waking Lazarus* is a twisting, thrilling, and satisfying ride. With a deft hand, Hines weaves supernatural and human mysteries into a colorful tapestry. Keep an eye on this guy."
Scott Nicholson, bestselling author of *The Farm*

"What's better than a fast-paced, edge-of-your-seat, insanely original thriller with deep characters and lots of heart? One that's well crafted by a true wordsmith and raconteur. That's what you get with *Waking Lazarus*. It's a riveting novel you won't soon forget, and T. L. Hines is an enormous talent with a bright future."
Robert Liparulo, author of *Comes a Horseman* and *Germ*

"*Waking Lazarus* provides the reader with a rare treat, a supernatural thriller managing to be spiritual, intelligent, and imaginative while consistently maintaining page-turning, heart-racing suspense."
William Hjortsberg, author of *Falling Angel*

"*Waking Lazarus* is a thought-provoking seat-of-your-pants thriller of personal redemption; like Lazarus himself, this book rises to the occasion."
Craig Johnson, author of *The Cold Dish* and *Death Without Company*

"T. L. Hines probes characters' thoughts and motives to give readers a psychological thriller that is both suspense-filled and spiritually complex."

James BeauSeigneur, author of THE CHRIST CLONE TRILOGY

"T. L. Hines is a fresh voice in the field of suspense, balancing dark moods with moments of emotion and redemption. . . . With flawless pacing, Hines leads us to a final twist which is startling, yet satisfying."

Eric Wilson, author of *Expiration Date* and *Dark to Mortal Eyes*

"Rarely anymore do I read something and immediately think . . . 'I wish I'd written that.' With *Waking Lazarus* the thought kept recurring constantly. . . . I had despaired of finding another suspense writer to love. Now I don't have to."

Chandler McGrew, author of *In Shadows* and *The Darkening*

"*Waking Lazarus* has it all! An exciting, intelligent plot with layers of meaning and truly unforgettable characters. Readers looking for a first-rate novel of suspense will want to put this tale at the top of their must-read list. No doubt about it—T. L. Hines is an author to watch!

Margaret Coel, *NY Times* bestselling author of *The Drowning Man* and *Eye of the Wolf*

"*Waking Lazarus* is a spooky, creepy, engrossing supernatural suspense novel in the tradition of Frank Peretti, Bill Myers, and Brandilyn Collins. Don't read this book late at night! Strongly recommended for the reader who thinks he can't be scared."

Randy Ingermanson, Christy-award winning author of *Double Vision*.

"A good read for those who enjoy thought with their thrill. T. L. Hines handles his characters with confidence and compassion and invites readers to keep turning the pages through the twist at the very end."

Jill Morrow, author of *Angel Café* and *The Open Channel*

WAKING LAZARUS

Books by T.L. Hines

Waking Lazarus

The Dead Whisper On

T.L. HINES

WAKING LAZARUS

BETHANY HOUSE PUBLISHERS
Minneapolis, Minnesota

Waking Lazarus
Copyright © 2006
T. L. Hines

Cover design by Gearbox Studios

All rights reserved. No part of this publication may be reproduced, stored in a retrieval system, or transmitted in any form or by any means—electronic, mechanical, photocopying, recording, or otherwise—without the prior written permission of the publisher. The only exception is brief quotations in printed reviews.

Published by Bethany House Publishers
11400 Hampshire Avenue South
Bloomington, Minnesota 55438

Bethany House Publishers is a division of
Baker Publishing Group, Grand Rapids, Michigan.

Printed in the United States of America

ISBN-13:   978-0-7642-0344-2
ISBN-10:   0-7642-0344-4

The Library of Congress has cataloged the hardcover edition as follows:

Hines, T. L.
   Waking Lazarus / T. L. Hines.
        p.   cm.
ISBN 0-7642-0204-9 (alk. paper)
1. Supernatural—Fiction. I. Title.
   PS3608.I5726W35   2006
   813'.6—dc22

2006007776

To Nancy and Jillian,
for always believing.

If any man walk in the day, he stumbleth not, because he seeth the light of this world. But if a man walk in the night, he stumbleth, because there is no light in him. These things said he: and after that he saith unto them, Our friend Lazarus sleepeth; but I go, that I may awake him out of sleep.

—John 11:9b–11

WAKING LAZARUS

The first time Jude Allman died, he was eight years old.

It happened after a day of ice fishing with his father, William. Mid-January. Duck Lake. Twenty degrees above zero on the thermometer, and something far below that on the wind-chill scale. Jude sat on an overturned pickle bucket most of the day, occasionally threading a hook through fresh corn or salmon eggs before dropping his line into the inky hole at his feet. A few times, when he was impatient for a bite, he put his face over the hole and cupped his hands to peer at the watery world beneath. He saw a few sunfish, but no perch—none of the perch his father considered such "good eatin'."

"Should be headin' back," William finally said. The comment startled Jude, partly because he himself had been ready to leave for hours, partly because it was only his father's third sentence of the day. (The first two, respectively, had been "Ready to get goin'?" and "Hungry?") Jude slid off the bucket and reeled in his line. His hook had no salmon egg. Maybe an unseen good-eatin' perch had nibbled it, or maybe the egg had shriveled and slid into the chilly water, resigning itself to fate.

They gathered their gear and started toward the pickup. Jude counted each footfall: from memory, he knew it would be 327 steps.

For several steps, all Jude could hear was the steady crunch of their boots, amplified into a hollow echo by the ice. Every so often, a forced cough from his dad, one of those quick huffs to clear the lungs. Jude stared down at his boots, watching as he continued to count. *Fifty-six, fifty-seven, fifty-eight.* He lifted his gaze again to stare at William's broad back, wishing he could match his father's long, loping strides. It was 327 steps for him; how many would that be for his father? *Seventy-two, seventy-three, seventy-four.* He pictured his mother, waiting at home with a steaming cup of hot chocolate, maybe a cookie or two. Chocolate chip. *Eighty-seven, eighty-eight, eighty—*

For a moment, he felt as if he were on the roller coaster at the county fair as gravity's pull licked at his stomach.

Instantly he knew what was happening. The lake was swallowing him, pulling him in, whispering his name.

He opened his mouth to call for his dad, to scream, to do anything, but the water was alive as it raced down his throat, and the bitter cold was a red starburst as he closed his eyes, and the world was a dark, fading memory as he felt himself sinking.

Sinking.

William heard a whisper, a sudden gust of wind, followed by something even more unsettling: silence. The steady *chunk-chunk-chunk* of Jude's footsteps behind him had disappeared.

He turned, wondering why Jude hadn't cried out if he had slipped on the ice.

Jude was gone. Only a dark patch of water, swirling like a drain. It was an auger hole (*Jude fell through*) left by previous fishermen (*Jude fell through*), and it wasn't possible, wasn't possible at all for Jude to—

Jude fell through.

Following this thought, another idea came to William, an unsavory idea he chewed on for a moment while looking at the black hole of water. He glanced at his old Ford pickup parked at the lake's edge, his mind caressing the idea's rough, brutal edges.

Then the liquid sucking sound of the hole at his feet pulled him out of the thought. Pulled him to his knees.

William plunged his arm deep into the gaping hole, and the frigid waters of the lake made him suck in a deep breath, a ragged gasp of protest from his sinew and muscles.

Images of his son began to haunt his mind. Jude's thin body sliding through the ice. Jude's mouth stretching into a small 'o' as the last gasp of air escaped his lungs. Jude's limp body floating beneath the ice, forever out of reach just inches from his fingers.

William's hand found nothing. Nothing at all.

He pulled his arm out of the water, trying to banish the terrifying pictures that muddied his thinking. Cold and snow swirled around him, but his throat became a desert of grit as panic slid into his stomach. Jude was drowning.

He plunged his head into the hole, not really knowing why, but driven by a need to do something else, *anything* else. He tried to open his eyes under the water, really tried, yet his body refused to cooperate. He pulled his head from the water, gasped for air, and felt rivulets of trickling water beginning to freeze as they traced lines down his forehead.

A few more seconds. Rushed panting. Thinking.

William thrust his arm back into the murky water, stretching it as far as possible and willing his fingers to touch something, anything other than ice and liquid. Although he'd never been a religious man, he subconsciously begged God to—

His finger brushed something. Then, not just his finger, but his whole hand. He grasped and pulled, closing his eyes against the exertion.

The dull purple of Jude's winter coat surfaced, now slick and shiny with water. William used both hands to reclaim his son's motionless body from the lake.

Streams poured from Jude's clothing as if he were a sunken treasure lifted to the surface after centuries in the murky depths. William rubbed at Jude's face, tried to open the eyes, find a breath, a heartbeat, anything.

Jude was still.

William looked to the pickup again, tore off his own coat, and wrapped it around the lifeless form. He picked up the body and turned toward the shore, then slipped and sprawled across the ice after a few steps.

But he wasn't going to lose his grip on Jude. Not now.

William crawled to his feet and started shuffling toward shore once more. He listened to the slow drizzle of water draining away from Jude's clothes. Or maybe it was the sound of time draining away from him. For a second—just for a second when Jude slipped through the ice—he had thought about . . . Again he pushed the idea from his mind. Couldn't think about that now. Couldn't think about that *ever*. Had to get to the hospital.

He opened the passenger door and pushed aside a jar of pickled beets as he slid Jude into the cab. He ran to the other side of the pickup, put the key in the ignition, and turned it. The old Ford roared to life, and William had it in gear before it was hitting on all cylinders, spraying snow and ice from the tires as he turned and started the twenty miles back to town.

As his pickup and his heart raced each other down the icy county road, an odd realization settled into his brain: *Dead.* His mind didn't reject the thought but instead embraced it. *Dead, and ain't nobody gonna change it.* He knew they were easily half an hour from the nearest telephone, maybe twenty-five minutes from the hospital. Jude's last breath had been something like ten minutes ago. So, Jude's body would be almost forty minutes gone before . . .

William skidded around a lazy corner, chirping across the road and toward the ditch. At the last moment he regained control of the pickup and straightened its path again. The adrenaline circulated in his veins, and the word returned to his mind: *Dead.*

The hospital's automatic front doors slid open. William blinked a few times before stepping inside. Pink, the lobby was pink. What were they thinking? He pushed the irritation from the front of his mind and took in more of the scene. A woman sat behind a large desk. Evidently she hadn't heard him, because she was still reading.

But how could that be? Couldn't she hear the deafening roar of water leaking from Jude and spilling onto the floor? He shifted his weight to his other foot as he looked at Jude's dull blue face again. Okay, the water wasn't really coming out in a stream now, more like a steady drip, but the cursed drip was deafeningly loud. *Drip.* He could hear the sound bouncing off the harsh pink-tinted walls. *Drip.*

The nurse still didn't acknowledge him, so he took another step toward her oak-finished desk and cleared his throat. She finally looked up and focused tired red eyes on William. Then, her eyes widened.

Drip.

William didn't have to say anything after all. The nurse shifted gears, dialed a phone, said something he couldn't quite decipher, then rushed around the counter. Running footsteps approached, bringing a woman and a man—a nurse and a doctor, he guessed—to take Jude from his arms.

It wasn't difficult to let go. It was a relief, really, to feel the wet body being lifted from him. Now it really was out of his hands, ha ha, had always been out of his hands, hadn't it?

"I said, you his father?" The doctor's question brought him back into focus. Guy didn't have one of those white lab coats, but he had to be a doctor. He was obviously in charge of the situation, directing the two women to cover Jude's body with some kind of blankets. Blankets. Yeah, those would help a boy who's been dead over half an hour.

The doctor must have sensed William's thoughts. "Need to bring up his core temperature," he said.

"Sure," William answered.

The doctor and the nurses started to push Jude's cart down the hall, toward a pair of large steel doors with small windows. He looked back toward William again. "What happened?"

"Fell through the ice," William answered.

The doctor looked as if he wanted to hear something else when the front of the gurney crashed into the doors. "Just wait here," he said. "We'll—" He kept on barking something, but the steel doors whisking shut behind him swallowed the words. Not that it mattered. Jude was dead. William knew that. Even the doctor knew it.

He walked down the hallway to the steel doors, peeked through one of the windows, and saw nothing. A large sign told him HOSPITAL STAFF ONLY BEYOND THIS POINT.

He didn't move. He stood at the door for what felt like five hours, occasionally looking through the small glass window.

No sign of the doctor.

He tried to ignore the gaping, insistent thought his mind had birthed on the ice, the thought that now continued to grow inside and threatened to devour every other thought.

"Sir?" The voice echoed off the tiled hallway behind him. William whirled around and couldn't help feeling as if the doctor had known what he was thinking.

"I'm sorry," the young doctor said. "We couldn't save him."

William stared for a few moments, half expecting the doctor to add something, to say *I know what you were thinking out there on the ice*, but he simply returned the gaze. William nodded, thinking the doctor would take that as a cue to leave. The doctor *had* to go first; if William did, it would seem shallow, callous.

"We tried to raise his temperature," he offered. William noticed the doctor studying his own face now, gauging his reactions. "I'm sorry," the doctor finished abruptly. "We tried everything we could."

William nodded again, hoping that would be enough to send the doctor on his way.

It was. The doctor backed through the steel doors and disappeared into the bowels of the pink-tinged hospital.

Now it was time to go home and tell his wife their son was dead.

When Jude awoke, he didn't move. Didn't even open his eyes. He felt the crisp linen of a sheet pressed against his face, pressed against his whole body, and the sensation made him realize his clothes were missing. Buck-naked, as Mom always said when he popped out of the bathtub. And something was tied to his toe. A piece of string? What kind of game was that? Not one he liked, he decided.

Where was he? He concentrated. He could remember doing something with his dad. Grocery store? Movie? Wait. Ice fishing. Yeah, ice fishing and . . . that was all his mind would give him right now. That, and a sense he couldn't quite explain, something like the way he'd felt when Mom had dropped him off at kindergarten the first time. Yes, it was that: the feeling of *missing*—not missing Mom, exactly, but missing all the same—and it tasted like a mouthful of pennies.

He stifled a gag, trying to swallow the awful taste of copper, and froze when he felt the sheet brushing his face. Yes. He was in a strange place. Maybe an unsafe place. He wanted to throw off the sheet, but he was afraid to move. He had spent many nights under the protective cover of a sheet in his own bed, hiding from the creaks and moans that blew through the farmhouse where they lived. Even now, he told himself that's where he was: home in his own bed, huddled under his own sheet, just a few feet down the hall from Mom. Yet he knew this wasn't his bed. The cold metal biting the bare skin of his back said as much.

A sound came to him from the terrifying world on the other side of the sheet. A repeating sound in a steady pattern: *click-click-click-click*. Footsteps. Moving toward him. Jude closed his eyes again. No, this wasn't his home, wasn't his bedroom. And that meant the person walking across the floor wasn't his mother.

Maybe, if he stayed very still, he wouldn't be seen. He held his breath and listened, feeling the dull beat of his own heart pounding in his head.

Suddenly the sheet lifted from his face. He felt it but kept his eyes closed, not wanting to see whoever, or whatever, had come for him.

Silence. No movement, no voice. After a few seconds, Jude ventured a peek, thinking he had perhaps imagined all of it. The harsh fluorescence of the hospital morgue's lighting attacked his pupils, forcing him to squint against the glare.

As his eyes adjusted, he saw a woman staring at him. Though he didn't know the woman, her warm smile seemed . . . safe. He waited for her to speak, but she didn't. Instead, she simply held out her hand. He returned the smile and reached out, guided by a need to touch the offered hand. To make sure she was real.

Jude Allman was back from the dead.

The Hunter moved quickly, putting away the chloroform-soaked cloth while lifting the child's limp body and rolling it into the black Dodge's trunk.

In precise terms, the Hunter was not human.

Certainly the Hunter had once started as a human, but had progressed, evolved even, to a higher plane. Now the Hunter was something much more, a being of a higher order, unconstrained by human emotion.

The Hunter had simply *become*.

Of course, the Hunter still needed to interact with others; that's what the Normal's role was. The Normal presented a typical presence to other people, mixed in with them, made them believe it was one of them. *Hi, how ya doin'? Nice day, ain't it? How are the kids?* These were the kind of pithy things the Normal had to say, the kind of blather lower beings disgorged in conversation. The Normal was good for that sort of thing, actually seemed to like idle chitchat occasionally. On some levels the Normal perhaps tried to ignore the existence of the Hunter, maybe even feared the Hunter's roles. Stalking. Trapping. Killing.

Not that the Hunter really liked killing. Killing was, in fact, the Hunter's least favorite part. It had been enjoyable once, a very long time ago, in the early stages of *becoming*. But not now.

The stalking. That's what brought the sweet taste of anticipation to the Hunter's tongue, what made the back of his head crackle and spark. When hunting, he was quiet and careful, almost invisible.

Definitely scentless. The trick was to never let the Quarry smell excitement. Before he started, he always rubbed dirt—dark, loamy dirt was best—on his exposed skin to mask the scent of excitement. If he didn't, the strong, citrus smell of his excitement would over-power carefully laid plans, alerting the Quarry.

The Hunter didn't look around, concentrating only on the imme-diate tasks. Wandering gazes invited suspicion, and suspicion made people notice. This didn't really matter, though, because no one would recognize him. When he was the Hunter, he walked with a practiced limp. He gained forty pounds, thanks to a padded body suit. He even cocked his head to the side and imagined himself as a hunchback. That was all his Quarry would ever see: the Hunter, not the Normal. They were two separate figures, two separate lives.

The Hunter opened the front door of the car, slid into the seat, and sat motionless. Killing. Killing was too messy, making the Hunter feel hollow. The way he had felt after breaking toys as a child. He always regretted breaking the toys, making them worthless bits from the past. But even worse, he hated ruining the future: a broken toy was useless, empty.

The Hunter sighed and retrieved a cigarette from the pack on the car's dash. He didn't smoke, not when he was the Normal. But he was careful to do so when the Hunter, to do everything differently.

He inhaled the dry, crisp tang of the tobacco and let a tendril of smoke slide from his lips, wondering if there might be someone like-minded wandering the streets out there. An opposite doppelganger who loved the actual kill, for instance. Maybe, if he could find such a being, they could complement each other, work together, confide. Perhaps, here on God's green earth, he wasn't the only one who had *become*.

He stubbed out the cigarette after just a few puffs, stubbing out thoughts of similar beings along with it. Of course there were no oth-ers. He was special, a unique creation all his own.

He looked at the watch on his wrist, watching as the analog second hand ticked its way around the face. Time to lock up the Quarry.

Two smells always comforted the Hunter: root cellars and burlap. They made him think of his father, a worthless drunk who had riddled his liver with cirrhosis by age fifty. In fact, drinking was one of two things his father had seemed to do well. That, and gardening.

When the Hunter had been a child, he had figured gardening must be easy. Had to be for his dad to be so good at it. But he only had to try gardening once to figure out the task was considerably more difficult than hoisting a bottle of Aces High whiskey.

He had planted carrots, corn, and potatoes. Then the weeds took over. No matter what he did, the weeds infested his small garden patch, mostly a low-growing viny thing that sprouted white flowers. And the more he hoed, the more he dropped to his knees and yanked vines, the more he sprayed the leaves of the weeds with chemicals, the more the weeds laughed in his face, taunting him.

A mason jar of gasoline and a match had solved the weed problem permanently. True, that meant torching the corn and carrots, but such was a small sacrifice to watch the weeds shrivel and burn. The weeds didn't laugh then. They screamed. A beautiful, vibrant, orange-colored scream filled with flecks of purple.

His father's penchant for gardening, almost as strong as his penchant for cheap whiskey, meant they had to store vegetables. Every autumn was spent canning the garden's bounty: beans, pickles, carrots, beets. For three solid weeks their home was filled with the low, chattering whistle of a pressure canner. Somewhere underneath that shriek, if you listened closely, was a faint clinking made by the jars bouncing together inside the canner. So many times as a child he had resisted sneaking into the kitchen and unsealing the canner's lid. In his childhood mind, releasing the lid would surely cause an explosion of shattering glass and boiling water. Even reflecting on it now, years later, he still wished he had opened the canner once, just once, to see the jars inside detonate in a poetic ballet of splintered glass.

His father had converted the basement of their home into a root cellar, where they stored jar after jar of canned treasures from the garden. And next to all those jars sat burlap sacks filled with potatoes. Late at night, after his dad passed out, he often liked to sneak down into the basement root cellar, breathe in the smell of fresh dirt and burlap.

Mice liked the root cellar, too. They couldn't do much to the canned vegetables, but often the mice chewed through the burlap to get to the potatoes. Sometimes the Hunter himself chewed on the burlap. He wasn't sure why, but chewing burlap was comforting. *Right.*

Other times he just liked to catch the mice and choke them. Their whitish-gray forms wriggled, squealed in his hands as the life drained from their bodies and into his own. Sometimes the mice would even bite, though he didn't mind this. He savored the sensation, embracing the pain and watching the blood trickle from his fingers. And really, the pain of the biting mice was nothing in comparison to the pain his father inflicted with belts. Or cigarettes. A shovel, once. He had learned to stay away from his father when the late afternoon rolled around, when the beer or liquor took hold. Father couldn't control his behavior, which was part of why Mother—

Never mind that. Burlap and dirt. Comforting scents.

The Hunter opened the door to his current home, similar in so many ways to the childhood home that still haunted his thoughts. The house had a deep root cellar, stocked with a fresh supply of burlap bags. He liked to store things in root cellars, too.

His Quarry had been very loud, squirming and screaming after the chloroform wore off. But now, a few hours later, the Quarry didn't move much. The fun part was ending.

Soon the toy would be broken.

When he was young, yes, the Hunter enjoyed killing the mice. But when he matured—when he *became*—the thrill of killing wore off. Now he really didn't like killing.

Killing was his least favorite part.

The man who called himself Ron Gress awoke, as he did every morning, in a sweat-stained panic. He always spent the first few minutes of each day sitting in the recliner where he slept, gulping deep breaths and trying to slow the jackhammering of his heart.

Keep it secret, keep it safe. He said it in his mind, over and over, a kind of mantra that calmed his body, stilled his nerves. *Keep it secret, keep it safe.*

Ron looked at the table next to his recliner. The arms of the old-fashioned alarm clock were nearly touching as they pointed down: 6:27. 6:28, maybe. He liked having the old clock with hands; it was gentler, more trustworthy than its digital cousins. Not that he really needed an alarm clock—he managed to wake within five minutes of 6:30 A.M. every morning without one—but it was still comforting to have the clock there, just the same.

A control center for an elaborate alarm system sat below the clock. He pressed a button on the system, changing the crimson LED from "Status: Armed" to "Status: Disarmed" with a short beep. He sat in his chair a few more minutes, remaining absolutely still, holding his breath as he listened for noises in the house. A squeak. A scrape. Anything indicating an intruder. Of course, he knew there couldn't be any intruders inside his home, especially with the alarm system. But it was comforting to listen, just the same.

He stood and began his usual morning ritual. First, he walked through every room in the house, opening closet doors, looking in dark spaces, searching for electronic bugs. He knew he wouldn't find anything.

But it was comforting to check, just the same.

When Ron felt certain he was alone in the home, he followed his gnawing stomach to the kitchen. Along the way, he turned on the television and flipped it to the local morning news. The set percolated to life, blaring something about a local kidnapping.

Inside Ron's cupboard was a place setting for one: one plate, one bowl, one glass, one fork, spoon, and knife. He reached for the bowl and spoon as he listened to the television. The newscast wasn't really about *a* kidnapping; it was a report on the recent string of child abductions. Within the past six months, kids had mysteriously disappeared in Bozeman, White Sulphur Springs, Harlowton, Miles City, and even a few hours south in Cody, Wyoming. None in Red Lodge, where Ron lived, nor nearby Billings. But the reporter wasn't afraid to suggest such a thing could happen. After all, in that ratings-happy, give-'em-something-big world, the sensational was perfectly normal. It had to be. Ron himself knew something of that world, once upon a time when . . .

He let go of the memory. *Keep it secret, keep it safe.*

At the refrigerator, Ron checked the milk's expiration date—still four days out, he should be safe—and splashed some on his Grape-Nuts. The television faded into the background as he wandered to the single chair at his small dining table.

The town of Red Lodge had a long reputation as a refuge, a place to escape the physical world. In the late nineteenth century, outlaws such as "Liver-eating" Johnson and the Sundance Kid often came to the remote wilderness of the area to hide from their growing infamy. Keeping it secret, keeping it safe.

Red Lodge was still a fine place for someone with a past to hide. Buck pines and cottonwoods intermingled along the banks of gurgling Rock Creek, while the granite peaks of the Beartooth Mountain Range—every bit as rugged as their name suggested—were the ancient sentinels protecting the town from the twenty-first century.

How long had he been in Red Lodge now? Seven years? Something like that. He couldn't quite remember; when he tried to wipe out memories of who he'd once been, he also wiped out memories of other things. At times like this, when Ron tried to take old thoughts off the shelf and examine them in isolation, he failed. His mind had thrown a thick, heavy blanket over all of it. If he tried too hard to think about details, the blanket lifted, letting a ray of recognition light up whole memory banks.

He took another bite of Grape-Nuts. Better to leave that blanket undisturbed.

The sun marched into the twilight of late afternoon when Ron returned to his home. After putting in eight hours at the school, he was ready to be cocooned safe inside, away from all the prying eyes.

He didn't mind being a school janitor. In a fitting way, it was pure. Honest. He showed up on time and did his work without complaining; in return, no one hounded him. Or asked questions.

But occasionally, he knew he was being watched at work. Especially after school hours. When all the kids went home, and the halls echoed every clank of the mop bucket, he sometimes felt *their* eyes boring into him. Waiting. Encouraging him to do . . . something. But he had figured out long ago to act unaware of the staring. Just go about his business, pretend he was oblivious. After all, if he let on, *they* would surely send more people to watch him. Or maybe do something even more drastic.

That was why he had to lock his home, beginning with the knob on the handle. Then the chain. A dead bolt. And another dead bolt. He turned the action on each of the locks to make sure they were all engaged. You could never be too careful.

Satisfied the door was properly secured against the outside world, Ron turned and walked toward his bedroom. The security system needed to be armed.

A knock came on the door before he'd gone more than two steps. His heart shrank, shriveled, and refused to contract for a long moment. Had he been followed? He stood still, listening.

Another knock, accompanied by the muffled voice of a woman. "Hello?"

A third knock, louder, more insistent. Ron stood in place, held his breath. *They* had probably sent her, and that would mean she might have an infrared monitor to let her see inside his home. But if he stayed still—absolutely still—

"Jude Allman? I know you're in there."

His stomach somersaulted, and he felt his legs turn to oatmeal. Jude Allman. He hadn't been called that name in years. Not since he'd been in Red Lodge. Not since he'd left Jude Allman behind and become Ron Gress, trustworthy school janitor. This was trouble. Serious trouble.

Ron (*Jude*) cleared his throat and moved toward the door. For the first time, he wanted a peephole in the door to let him see the person outside. He knew, of course, that if he ever installed one, *they* would sneak into his home and reverse it so *they* could see him in the magnified fisheye. But he still wished for the peephole, just for a moment.

Keep it secret, keep it safe, Ron (*Jude*) reminded himself.

"I just want to talk," the voice said.

He would have to respond if he was going to get the faceless stranger off his front step.

"What did you say?" he yelled through the door.

"I said I just want to talk."

"No, before that."

"I'm looking for Jude Allman," the voice answered.

"Never heard of him."

A slight laugh from the other side of the door. "Everybody's heard of Jude Allman. You're not a very good liar."

Okay. She wasn't going to leave. He had to stay calm, especially if she was one of *them*. Unless . . . maybe, just maybe, she was a reporter. He had always figured some ego-tripping journalist would finally track him. And if she was just a reporter, he could handle her.

He'd handled them before. He could probably even convince her he wasn't Jude. (*Ron, he was Ron.*) Sure. He'd fooled a lot of people, stayed under the radar for several years. He could deflect some news jockey sniffing down a dead trail.

He had to. If he didn't, the report might get back to *them*.

The man who called himself Ron Gress, and who had once called himself Jude Allman, reached for his first dead bolt. "Just a minute," he said as he fumbled with the knob, then worked the other dead bolt and locks with increasing urgency. He wanted to see the person who waited on his doorstep, the person who had managed to track him across several years and lifetimes.

He cracked open the door, then peeked outside.

He wasn't sure what he had expected. Someone different. Someone who loomed large, and who gazed at him with icy steel eyes. Instead, the woman who stood there was rather small, with chocolate eyes and light hazel skin. Maybe she was Indian. Or Hispanic. Or a light-skinned African-American. Or a mix.

She smiled, as if they were old pals reunited after years of being apart. In her hands she held a book. Even before she held it up for him to see, he knew what it was. A tome entitled *Into the Light*, written by one Jude Allman.

"Yeah, it's you," she said. "I can tell from the photo." She spun the book around. The man in the photo was younger, thinner. Less scraggly. But also recognizable. The photo penetrated deep recesses in his mind, bounced around for a few seconds, and dislodged white-hot memory flashes. The blanket, despite his best efforts, was lifting. He looked from the photo back to the woman.

"I'm Kristina," the woman at the door offered. "I need to talk to you about your book. About—" She paused. "About everything."

"Everything," he said. "Not my strong subject."

She blinked, smiled again.

"How did you find me?" he demanded.

"Let me in and I'll tell you," she answered.

Jude (*Ron. It's Ron!*) considered for a moment, then looked beyond her, up and down the length of the street. Quiet. No one had followed her, and he *was* getting uncomfortable standing here with the door wide open. He was sure, at some point, *they* had sprayed the exterior of his home with unknown pathogens. The longer he held the door open, the more pathogens would leak in. Just what *they* wanted. He backed up and waited for her to enter.

Kristina stepped through the doorway, stopped, and backed out again. She studied his windows. Or rather, where his windows used to be. The previous year, he had gone to Renton's Hardware and Home Center for a special sale on Sheetrock. In one weekend he'd been able to seal off the windows with fresh dry wall. It was little protection from the infrared scanning technology *they* could use to scan his home, and probably even less protection from the pathogens. But it was something.

Kristina looked at the glass windows outside the home, then poked her head back in again to see the smooth surface of Sheetrock. "Love your window treatments."

He shrugged, waited for her to enter. She glanced around the room, then stepped in and made her way to the lonely easy chair in the center. He re-engaged the dead bolts and locks before turning around. She was already sitting.

It felt uncomfortable having someone inside his home, like having an itch in a place he couldn't reach.

"So I'll ask again," he finally said as he pulled his dining room chair into the living room, "how you found me."

"How did I find the elusive Jude Allman? The greatest disappearing act since D. B. Cooper?"

She was toying with him. Cat and mouse. He didn't like being the mouse, never did like anything about mice in general. He shivered. Any moment, he expected, she would launch into some self-congratulatory soliloquy detailing how she, the most brilliant among journalists, had picked up his trail.

"I looked in Montana," she finally continued. "You know, the place everyone goes when they want to hide."

Jude knew it was a joke. He was supposed to smile, maybe even offer a polite chuckle. He didn't. A rusty headache was forming directly behind his eyes and slowly oozing its way throughout his brain.

A long sigh escaped from his lips. "My dad moved into a nursing home near here. That's when I came." And it was true. His father, William Allman, was only fifty miles away at a nursing home in Billings. "Retirement community" was the politically correct euphemism so popular these days, but Jude wasn't fooled by the high-minded name. To him, it was still a nursing home. And he imagined that was exactly what his father would call it, as well. Maybe he'd ask William, if he ever went to see him.

Kristina shifted in the chair a bit and nodded. "What about your mother?"

His mom. His dear mom. "She died. Long time ago."

Kristina nodded again. No sense trying to stall her. She'd already pulled the nice, comfortable blanket off his memories, and now those memories were shining before him like bright shards of glass, ready to cut him open. Jude's headache deepened, but he knew he'd have to stumble through this somehow. Maybe he could convince her to hold on to this story. Maybe she'd feel sorry for a paranoid janitor.

"Look," he began. "Before . . . before I changed my name and got away from all the nonsense—"

"Ron Gress."

"Huh?"

"Ron Gress. You changed your name to Ron Gress."

"Yeah. Before I was Ron Gress, I was . . . I don't know." He stopped and tried again. "Do you have any idea what it was like to be Jude Allman?"

Kristina shook her head slightly.

"Like being a piece of steak. Everyone wanted to cut off a piece. All the weirdos."

"What kind of weirdos?"

"You name 'em, I had 'em. Lots like you."

"Like me how?"

"Newspeople. Journalists."

"I'm not a journalist."

His eyes narrowed. He was pretty sure she wasn't one of *them*, and he'd been almost positive she was a writer or some such thing. Once, he had been so good at seeing these things. He was out of practice. Still, maybe she was lying, just trying to get him to trust her.

Her smile returned. "Nope, I'm not a journalist. So what kind of weirdo am I?"

Jude felt as if Rumpelstiltskin was sitting in his room. *No, that's not my name.* "Well, other than reporters," he said, "there were UFO junkies, conspiracy freaks, New Agers."

"None of the above."

"Paranormal researcher, something like that?"

"Nope."

He continued to look at Kristina, and suddenly everything dropped into place. The answer appeared on the markerboard of his mind, drawn in large red letters. "You're dying," he said.

Kristina returned his gaze, looked to be deep in thought for a few moments. She scratched her forearm as she spoke. "Well, let's just say I won't be around very long," she answered.

"How long?" he asked, finding himself caring. A bit.

"Long enough to get a few things done."

His cynicism slid back into place, fueled by the buzz-saw headache. "Looking for your higher purpose, huh? Let me break it to you: there isn't one."

"Oh, there certainly is, Jude," she said with a continued hint of familiarity that made him flinch. "Yours, for instance. Some people receive special gifts from God, and—"

He laughed. So that's what this was. "You spent all this time tracking me down just so you could convert me, huh? I got some news for you: I ain't buying." If only this woman knew what her so-called God had done. To his mother. To *him*.

She continued to stare at him, seemingly undaunted by his words. So he went on. "I know how this goes," he said. "First, you'll want to know what happens. Then, you'll want to know why it happens. Then, you'll end up mad at me because I don't have any of the answers you want."

"I saw you once on Sally Jesse or something," she said, ignoring his comments.

He leaned back in his chair and crossed his arms in front of him. "Maybe. Yeah, I suppose. I was on a lot of those shows."

"You were talking about the second time."

The second time. Yes.

The second time Jude Allman died, he took a friend with him.

As a teen, when the thoughts of most young men in Nebraska turned to girls and Cornhusker football, Jude's thoughts turned to the forest. On weekends, he followed his feet down tree-lined paths, absorbing the crisp scent of pine on the whispered forest breezes.

Jude made most of these excursions alone. But on this particular late summer day, when the next school year was closer than the last, he brought along Kevin Burkhart.

Kevin, Jude thought, looked a lot like Barney Rubble. He was short and squat, with a thatch of blond hair growing from his head. Even Kevin's eyes fit the part: wide and vacant, as if they couldn't really focus on anything around him. But Kevin was one of Jude's few close friends, and he also felt the siren call of the woods. In the wilderness they could hike for hours without speaking, losing themselves in the journey.

The day started out bright and blue, pregnant with promise. Jude's father dropped him off at Kevin's house in town. The two of them shouldered packs (even though they were only going out for the day, they preferred taking along packs "just in case," and a day hike could always be seen as conditioning for longer, multi-day excursions) and made their way to nearby Soldier Ridge Forest.

Years later, after Jude had moved away from Bingham, Nebraska, he found people were always surprised to hear him talk about Soldier Ridge Forest near his hometown. People, it seemed, felt Nebraska had no trees—especially no pine trees. But for Jude, it had heaven: a patch of evergreen that stretched from the northern edge of Bingham to parts of Wyoming and South Dakota.

About fifteen minutes from Kevin's house, they reached the trail-head; after another fifteen minutes, they were in heavy timber. They hiked at a steady pace, unhurried by a specific destination or time-table, but driven by a simple need to explore. They passed through thick stands of ponderosa, then open meadows as they pushed deeper and deeper into their journey. Scents of sweet wild flowers and musky underbrush mingled and meandered around them as they walked.

After about five miles, they stopped for a break. They sat on a large boulder, ate a bit of gorp, and exchanged ideas about which girl was the prize beauty of Bingham—Kevin voted for Carol Blades, while Jude was more partial to Kim Oakley.

That was the only day Kevin ever asked him about dying.

"What was it like?" Kevin ventured after he put his head back and shook the last bit of trail mix into his mouth. He munched steadily as he eyed Jude.

"What was what like?" Jude asked, even though he knew Kevin was talking about the drowning. The Drowning. Jude had been a minor celebrity in their small Nebraska town since The Drowning. The local media gave it plenty of coverage. A few regional papers and television stations had even picked up the story.

Jude had returned to life after being clinically dead more than an hour—all with no apparent ill effects—but he was uncomfortable with the local celebrity status it brought. He knew it didn't make him a celebrity in the same sense James Dean had been a celebrity. More like Typhoid Mary.

Even though he came back to life, a certain part of him, perhaps the most normal part, had died when he drowned. People were wary of him, and a few kids were actually afraid to touch him. Thoughts of junior high gym class made him wince even years later. One of the boys, Bobby Evans, had said he wouldn't shower with a freak. Soon, other boys followed Bobby's suggestion like the lemmings they were, and Jude found himself showering alone three times a week, always after the other boys were done. Mr. Johnson, the bald-headed gym teacher who was more interested in sitting on his can than actually educating anyone, acted oblivious. But in his heart, Jude knew that wasn't true. He was sure Mr. Johnson *knew*, and enjoyed the torture as much as Bobby Evans and the rest of the idiots. The memories of gym class, along with a thousand other memories of people avoiding him, were still fresh, wet, and painful.

If he hadn't drowned, none of that humiliation would have happened. He would be anonymous. Normal.

The Drowning had always been a taboo subject between Jude and Kevin. Without ever speaking about it, both of them understood this. And both of them had always abided by that unspoken rule.

Until now. Amid the safety of the forest, Kevin obviously felt sure enough to wonder aloud. Jude, in turn, was also relaxed by their surroundings, and Kevin *was* his best friend. "I don't remember a lot of it," Jude offered.

"Did you see anything?"

"Yeah." He looked up, gauging the reaction; Kevin's face was rapt, so he continued. "A bright light—like a huge spotlight, you know?—but it didn't hurt to look at. Not at all. It was hard *not* to look at. I wanted to go into the light."

"So did you? Go into the light, I mean?"

Jude nodded. "I started. I mean, I knew this was where I was supposed to be. And then I saw someone standing in front of me. Other people who have had, um—"

"Life-after-death experiences?"

"Yeah. Life-after-death experiences, I guess. Other people say they see someone they know. A grandfather or a friend or something. But not me. I think, maybe because I didn't really know anyone who had died. So it was just this person, standing there in the light. And I couldn't get a good look at him anyway. He was just a dark shadow, with light all around him. But he knew my name."

"You're kidding."

"No. He said: 'Jude, it's not your time. You have to go back.' And I didn't want to, you know? It was like I was really tired, and he was telling me I couldn't sleep. I asked him why, and he said, 'Your purpose.' So I asked him about my purpose."

Kevin leaned in closer. "Yeah? What was it?"

"He said, 'You have to let Kevin Burkhart know he doesn't stand a chance with Carol Blades.'"

Kevin blinked, then reached across the gulf between them and punched Jude's shoulder. "That wasn't funny."

Jude was doubled over, partly because he was laughing, partly because Kevin's punch was harder than he expected. He looked up again, and he could see genuine disappointment in his friend's eyes.

At that moment his perspective on dying slipped into perfect balance, and he understood it would always haunt him. He realized he could never outrun it. Or the questions it elicited. He saw how he would always have to handle these questions, whether from strangers, family, or friends. He would have to be reverent. And he would have to avoid the truth. He would never tell anyone what really happened on the other side (make that Other Side), because people didn't want the truth. They just wanted the hope. That was why it could never be a joking matter, not even with his closest friend.

Jude had hurt Kevin, and he felt like an idiot for not having understood all this sooner.

"Look. I'm sorry. Really, I was just dinkin' around with you."

"Forget about it," Kevin answered as he started picking up his backpack.

"No, really." Jude put his hand on Kevin's shoulder, the kind of physical contact normally uncomfortable between sixteen-year-old boys. It had its desired effect: Kevin stopped and looked at him.

Jude took away his hand quickly. "I wasn't kidding you about the rest of it. The light, the man, all that. He told me I had a purpose. Everyone has a purpose. And look, I'm gonna tell you something I've never told anyone before. Not even my mother."

Kevin was listening again.

"He said it's much better than this life."

"Really? He said that?"

"He said it."

That was when the first peal of thunder rolled toward them.

They hadn't noticed the clouds moving in, the kind of bruise-colored clouds that throw bolts of lightning in long, hot, jagged flashes. The thunder caught them by surprise, and they both looked heavenward at nearly the same moment. Instantly they knew they were somewhere they shouldn't be.

They shouldered their packs again and started back down the trail, just shy of running. But the thunder ran faster, rolling over them like giant ocean waves. Then they didn't just hear the storm. They saw it. Flashes illuminated the forest floor as lightning stepped across valleys, striding ever closer.

The forest trail opened into a small meadow, and they stopped to look at each other. They panted as they studied the meadow and considered their unspoken thoughts. Staying near trees was a bad idea. The giant pines reached toward the sky and begged for lightning strikes. At the same time, neither of them wanted to be the highest point in a flat meadow when the lightning decided to stomp.

"Maybe we should try to crawl," Kevin finally offered. Jude swallowed hard, feeling as though he could taste the hot, dry lightning in his mouth. He nodded.

Because it was Kevin's idea, he went first, moving on all fours but keeping his body off the ground; if lightning hit them, they knew it would cook the parts of their bodies touching the ground. Hands and legs could sear and the body might survive. Internal organs were another matter.

Kevin moved quickly, despite the mud and roots beneath him and the heavy external frame pack perched on his back. As soon as he'd gone a few yards into the clearing, a finger of lightning sliced deep into the patch of forest ahead of them, almost as if uttering a warning. They heard the crackling of the electricity sucking the air around them, and they both froze. A smell like burning rubber floated in their nostrils.

Jude saw Kevin look back over his shoulder at him. Jude hadn't yet gone into the clearing, wanting to keep some distance between them. He nodded, and Kevin began moving again.

After a few more moments, Jude dropped to his hands and knees, then started into the clearing. He traveled about twenty yards before everything went to white static: the whiteness swam in his eyes, and the static buzzed in his ears.

And then, nothing.

Jude hated hospitals. True, he hadn't been in a hospital many times in his life—couldn't think of any trips there after drowning at age eight, in fact—but he hated hospitals all the same. Everything was drab, gray, lifeless. No, not just passively lifeless, but dead. Hospitals even *smelled* like death.

When Jude awoke, he knew he was in a hospital. That much was certain from the sounds and smells. He didn't want to open his eyes yet. Even eight years later, memories of the morgue hounded him, forcing him to keep them shut. To put off the inevitable a bit longer.

"Are . . . are you awake, Jude?"

It was Mom's voice. Jude willed his lungs to breathe deeply, and when the air hit his mouth, the taste of burning copper overcame him. A memory, like a broken, interrupted dream, danced at the edge of his consciousness, leaving behind the bitter aftertaste.

He swallowed, trying to clear the metallic residue, then slitted open his eyes and saw his mother at the side of his bed. She was a thin woman, but her face was a mismatched round circle with chubby cheeks. Jude recalled many nights from his childhood when his mother's smiling face, topped by warm coffee-colored eyes, bent down to kiss him after a bedtime story.

She smiled as she stood beside his hospital bed, although it wasn't the smile of joy he knew from his younger days. It was forced, difficult, a smile that said more about pain than happiness.

"Feel okay?" she ventured.

He nodded his head, moved his hand toward her. She seemed grateful for the distraction and made a show of taking his hand tightly, then grasping it between both of hers like a sacred offering. She ran one of her hands up his forearm briefly, as if to confirm the arm was in fact there. When she looked back to his face, Jude saw a small tear trickling down her cheek.

"Remember much?" she asked.

"No," he said.

"You and Kevin—"

At the mention of Kevin's name, he *did* remember. The door of his mind opened, and the whole afternoon came rushing in.

"Is Kevin. . . ?" he asked, not wanting to ask the whole question.

"He's fine. A little scared, but perfectly fine. He carried you out."

Kevin carried him out? That had to be five miles or so, with one hundred sixty pounds of dead weight. Newfound respect for Kevin started forming in his mind.

"So Kevin saved me."

He wasn't looking at his mom, so when no answer came, he glanced back her direction. Her face seemed a bit whiter, nervous.

"What's the matter?" Jude asked.

She looked down at their hands, still tightly clasped. "Well, you had another . . . episode."

Episode? For a moment, he thought she might be talking about some strange television program. But then he realized what *episode* meant.

"Do you remember anything?" she asked again. But this time she wasn't just asking about the death; she was asking about the Other Side. Even his mother needed to voice the question.

"It's a bit fuzzy, but I think it will come back," he offered. She seemed satisfied with his answer, so he continued. "What exactly happened? I think, I'm pretty sure, we got hit by lightning."

She nodded, wiped at another tear on her cheek. "I don't know why you have to go out there all the time. What's so interesting about those woods?"

Jude waited.

She exhaled, nodded again. "Okay. Yes, it was lightning. Kevin said . . . well, he said it melted your pack, knocked off your shoes."

Jude nodded slightly, then tried to wiggle his toes. They moved. He fought the urge to peel away the sheet and look at them.

"So he got you down to the end of the trail, flagged down help from some guys loading up horses, and they brought you here to the hospital."

"How long ago?" he wondered. At first, he was sure he had only thought it, but his mom answered.

"About three hours. You were, clinically, you know . . ."

"Dead."

"Yes. They tried CPR and machines and everything. The doctor I talked to said you were probably killed instantly."

She sobbed a little bit, and Jude waited patiently for her to regain control.

"Did they send me to . . . the morgue?"

She shook her head, seeming relieved. "No, but they were getting ready. One of the nurses was cleaning the room, and you just suddenly, um, I guess you just moved."

Jude smiled. "Probably scared her into next Tuesday."

His mom put on another pained smile. "I think they let her go home early."

After his mother left, Jude lay back and stared at the ceiling, thinking. Trying to remember. Wondering. Soon his head felt like one big abscessed tooth in need of a root canal.

He raised the hospital bed to an upright position, then fumbled with the attached remote control. He turned on the television and flipped through a few channels until he came to a local newscast. A reporter was standing outside the local hospital. He let his finger hover over the channel button a few moments, wondering what the story at the hospital was about.

"In a unique twist, the young man struck by lightning was involved in a separate drowning accident eight years ago," the reporter said.

Jude felt blood rushing in his face. Of course. *He* was the story at the hospital. He hadn't really thought about it, but if he'd now died and come back to life twice, well, that made him like a human lottery ticket. What were the chances? Jude found the volume button on the remote and pressed it.

"According to the experts we consulted, this young man may be the first repeat survivor of a near-death experience. And so Jude Allman, now a patient here at St. Francis, is also a local celebrity."

"Time for your dinner."

Jude jumped. He hadn't seen or heard the nurse come into his room.

"Sorry," she said, acknowledging his startled look. "Guess I have a way of sneaking up on people."

"'Sokay." He watched her as she set plates and platters in front of him. She was pretty, almost exotic in some way.

Maybe that was what he needed to pound down this splitting headache: a bit of food. Hospital food, which mostly consisted of cold mush or warm mush, wasn't his first choice. But his stomach rumbled a welcome anyway.

On the television, the camera revealed a crowd of people outside the hospital. Not a throng of thousands, to be sure. But there were a good hundred or so, which represented a fair percentage of Bingham, Nebraska. Signs dotted the crowd, including one held by someone he recognized: Kim Oakley, his dream girl, holding a placard that read

Get well soon, Jude. He smiled, half wondering if Kevin had put her up to it.

The scene cut to the reporter interviewing Kevin.

"So you knew it was lightning right away?" the reporter asked Kevin.

"I don't think we both got hit. I think Jude took the hit, and, I don't know, the blast or something knocked me down."

"And you carried him all the way out?"

"Well, yeah. What else could I do?"

"Were you surprised to hear Jude Allman seems to be fine after this ordeal? Did you ever think in your wildest dreams this could happen?"

Kevin paused a moment. "I don't know. But I guess, in the back of my mind, I thought about how it happened to him before."

The story cut to the reporter interviewing another person, a middle-aged man Jude didn't recognize.

"Why did you come here today?" asked the reporter.

"I just want to meet him," the man answered.

"Why's that?"

"I dunno, something special, I guess. Like a television star or something, when you think about it. Better than that, because it's not like he just acts on a soap opera."

Jude flipped off the TV, watched as the phosphorous dot in the center of the screen faded. He leaned toward the window, trying to get a glimpse of the crowd outside, but couldn't quite see to the lobby area.

The nurse finished putting out his dinner, then finally spoke again. "He's right, you know."

Jude jumped again, and she smiled this time. "You're awfully jumpy," she said.

"Yeah, well. I've had a couple thousand extra volts today," he said, "so I guess I have a little extra energy to burn off."

She laughed, then turned to go before he remembered what she'd said and stopped her.

"Who was right?" he asked.

"The man in the interview," she said. "There's something special about you." She left the room, closing the door behind her.

Jude stared after her for a minute, then turned his attention to dinner.

Jude pulled his mind from the past and focused on the painful present: his Spartan home, closed in on all sides by walls of Sheetrock. Kristina was still staring at him. He didn't want to look her direction, certainly didn't want to look her in the eye, but he felt her stare. A small trickle of sweat traced a wet line down his forehead, and his palms were starting to itch. Maybe *they* had sent her, maybe *they* hadn't; he still wasn't sure either way. But it didn't really matter, because it was wrong, terribly wrong, to talk about deep things.

Buried things.

You didn't bury bodies and then dig them up years later. It was best to take the same approach with memories.

He stood and mashed the heel of his hand into his right eye. "I need to get something. I have a killer headache."

Kristina immediately opened her purse and rummaged through it for a few seconds. "Here you go," she said, holding out a white bottle of ibuprofen.

Jude shook her off and headed to the bathroom for his own medication. He fumbled with the safety-proof cap, then popped it off and shook two tablets into his hand. He hesitated before shaking out two more.

Jude popped all four tablets into his mouth, arched his head and dry-swallowed, then headed back to his *guest* and took his chair again. Silent.

After a few moments, Kristina finally spoke. "So whatever happened to Kevin?"

"Hmmm?"

"Your friend Kevin. You keep in touch with him?"

He leaned back in the chair and crossed his arms. "Nah. Haven't talked to him in, I dunno, ten years."

She leaned forward as he leaned away. Stalker and prey. "So what about the third time?" she asked.

He sighed, shook his head as he ran his hands across his face. "I can't right now. I . . . I have to be somewhere."

She grinned a bit. "You mean you actually leave this house sometimes?"

Jude said nothing, found the floor in front of his chair suddenly very interesting. His tongue felt thick, as if it were covered in long shag rug. He hadn't spoken this much in years; he had moved to Red Lodge to avoid conversations, and while the people of the mining-town-turned-ski-town were always ready with a "How ya doin'" or a simple wave, rarely were they prone to prying. If a man walked down the street with hunched shoulders and a steady gaze fixed at the sidewalk, the people of Red Lodge knew he wasn't the sort of person to stop and chat about the weather. And if a man boarded over the windows of his home with Sheetrock, well, that was his God-given right. He could do whatever he wanted inside his own home.

But now this woman—this woman, who wasn't from Red Lodge, but somewhere else—had invaded his comfortable world, stabbed at him with her questions, haunted him with past lives.

"So what exactly are you doing now? What's Ron Gress's life like?" Kristina pressed.

"Janitor."

She huffed a bit. "Jude Allman as: Ron Gress, the resurrected janitor."

"Like I said, I don't have the answers you want, and now you're ticked." Jude looked up at her, secretly hoping his words would hurt. He saw no reaction as she stared back, forcing him to break eye contact first.

Kristina stood, brushed the front of herself, then turned and walked toward the door. The sound of her footsteps bounced off the sheetrocked walls. Kristina reached for the chain, slid it out. She twisted both dead bolts, then unlocked the door and swung it open. Jude felt uncomfortable with someone else touching his locks—it seemed too personal—but he made no move to stop her.

Suddenly she turned to face him. "For a janitor, you don't seem too worried about your messes."

Her comment rubbed him like eighty-grit sandpaper, and he lashed back. "Well, I wasn't really expecting visitors, so I didn't get a chance to clean up."

Her lips became a thin line for a moment. "I wasn't talking about your house." She walked out the door and swung it shut behind her.

Jude looked at the door briefly. His pupils refused to dilate. Or maybe it was his mind. As he sat, a large white bloom of light spread before his eyes; when he tried to blink it away, a ghost image stayed, floating in air. He closed his eyes, but the ghost image remained, now outlined in an electrical red current. Maybe it was his headache, pushing steadily against the backs of his eyeballs. Maybe it was a cancerous tumor in his brain, attacking the parts that controlled his vision.

Cancer. Was that what was killing Kristina? She didn't look too bad, but then, she probably wouldn't wait until the very end to travel.

Jude took a deep breath and wished . . . He was too tired to even know what to wish for. After all these years, the jangly, jagged thoughts he had put in the attic were dusting themselves off, and they were knocking on the old attic door. He didn't have a lock on *that* door, and he knew it would be open soon.

He needed a drive, a long drive to clear his mind. He felt for keys in his pocket, then cautiously opened his front door and peered outside before leaving. The white, static ghost still wavered before his eyes.

Late that night at home, Jude sat watching the local newscast. Sometime—he wasn't quite sure when—he had returned home and melted into the single chair in front of his TV. Where had he been? What had he done? It was there, perhaps, if he wanted to strain for it. But he didn't. These memory lapses, these blackouts, were just a side effect of the old paranoia. Somewhere deep inside was his huddled psyche, trying to turn off all sensory information and lock out the world.

He knew this, and he accepted it. Still, the blackouts seemed to be getting worse. And more frequent.

Jude ran a hand over his face. He *wanted* to black out the visit from the woman who had knocked at his door and pulled him back into the skin of Jude Allman (what was her name, anyway?), but her image kept rattling around inside his head. *"God gives some people special gifts,"* she'd said. Right. Her God had given him nothing; instead, He'd taken everything away. Starting with his mother.

Jude tried to run a mental eraser over it, tried to throw that soft, comforting blanket over all the memories again. But now those memories were ablaze, and every blanket fueled the flames instead of smothering them. His headache was a constant roar in his ears.

Keep it secret, keep it safe.

The news blared a breaking story about a missing girl in Big Timber. She'd been at the city park playground with a few other kids, just half a block from her house, when she suddenly disappeared. The image of a tear-filled mother filled the screen. She could see her daughter at the park, she said, and had been looking out to check on her every few minutes. One checkup, she was there. The next checkup, not more than five minutes later, she was gone. Vanished.

Jude watched, trying not to think. He wanted to clear his mind of strange visitors, of Jude Allman—he was Ron Gress now, after all—of everything.

The phone rang.

He hurried toward the phone and looked at the caller ID. The readout told him it was *Rachel Sanders* of *Red Lodge, Montana* calling.

He watched the readout, making sure it didn't change. His machine picked up after four rings.

Rachel's voice blared. "Ron. It's me. Pick up the phone."

He grabbed the phone and put it to his ear. "Hello?"

"Why do you always wait for your answering machine to pick up, Ron?"

"I . . . I just want to make sure it's you." Jude looked back at the TV. A graphic on the screen showed a map of Montana and Wyoming, with white dots appearing where children had gone missing.

"Yeah, well, that's what Caller ID is for," Rachel said. "And I know you have it. If you hear the phone ringing, and you see my name on the Caller ID, it's a pretty safe bet it's me."

"I guess." Jude looked at his front door, wondered if all the locks were secured. He quickly went over, phone between his ear and shoulder, and started checking them.

"Anyway, I've been trying to call you for a couple hours now. Where you been?"

"Out."

"Out where?"

"Just out."

"Okay, well, I guess it's none of my business anyway. Good for you for getting out. I just promised Nathan we'd call to remind you about dinner tomorrow. He wanted to talk to you himself, but he's in bed now."

"Tomorrow?"

"Dinner? Your son? About four feet tall, five years old, blond hair. You've met him."

"Yeah, yeah. Okay. I just . . . is everything—"

"I'll sterilize everything three times and make sure the secret service has the place under surveillance. Give it a rest."

Jude frowned. He wanted to ask about Nathan, make sure no one had been around to bother them. If what's-her-name had found him, she could also find his son, and (*Kristina, her name was Kristina*) he was sure there was something more going on. Something that made his stomach slowly roll, like the drum on one of those giant cement trucks. Still, this wasn't the time or place to go into all of it with Rachel, who was obviously in her usual bad mood.

"Okay. I'll be there," he finally said. He hung up the phone without waiting for an answer.

When Ron hung up the phone, Rachel immediately felt like a witch. She sighed, gently replaced the receiver in its cradle, then sat down and began to pray. She couldn't control her emotions with him. He was like the pathetic little puppy who'd been kicked around. Sometimes she felt sorry for him. She could tell he had stowed away deep, dark secrets from his past, unwilling to unlock the chest even to look at them himself. And in a lot of ways, she was fine with that; everyone had a few sins tucked away.

At other times—usually any time he was around for more than five minutes—she just wanted to shake him, slap him on the face, and tell him to pull himself out of the pity party. "Life goes on," her grandmother had always said after any setback. "So should you."

She knew she shouldn't feel that way about Ron, of course. She'd changed dramatically since first meeting Ron; she had accepted God's grace and forgiveness, so she should be able to extend that acceptance to others in her own life.

By and large, she could. Except when it came to Ron.

Rachel sat quietly, trying to clear her senses and open herself to God's direction. Why was she always this way with Ron? Every time she thought of him, a tight ball wrapped in fear, anger, revulsion, pity, and other emotions sat at the top of her chest. Was God trying to say something to Ron through her? Maybe. But if He was trying to use her, she was being a poor vessel.

Even now, in this time of prayer, she felt herself resisting. She relaxed, willing her body to overcome those feelings and release the pressure.

She had met him in a previous life, of sorts. A life in which she looked for her salvation in the bottom of a glass tumbler.

The night she'd spotted him in the bar, tucked safely into a dark corner, she'd already had five margaritas. Not a record night, to be sure, but enough to keep the dull, disconnected buzz humming steadily in her brain. He had seemed so helpless, so much in need of someone. And she remembered her first thought: *He's even more pathetic than I am.*

Looking back now, she felt maybe it *had* been the sad-puppy syndrome that first made her walk around the bar and sit next to Ron. He had been abused by his previous owner, and now all he needed was a bit of love to make things better. That sort of thing. Yeah, that had been part of it. But she also had to admit something else was there. A part of her searched for the people who were so obviously haunted by demons. Being with someone worse made her feel better about herself, if only for a night.

She shook her head and brought herself back to the present. She whispered an "amen," then went to Nathan's room, cracked open the door, and peeked inside. His towhead lay on the pillow, his mouth open as he slept. She smiled and went into the room to turn out the light on his night table.

Sometimes, of course, mistakes could be turned into something unexpected and wonderful. She and Ron had made a mistake that long night some six years ago. But God had used the mistake and brought her Nathan.

Nathan, in his perfection, had also brought her out of that hazy realm of drunkenness. Once she had found out she was pregnant, the clouds cleared from her mind. It wasn't just her own miserable life anymore; it was another life, and she wanted to do everything right for that other life. She stopped drinking, started opening her eyes to the world around her. Started opening her eyes to eternity and realizing there was much more to life than, well, this life.

Now, a few short years later, she was a respected member of the

Red Lodge community and such a regular churchgoer that the pastor knew her name. She owned a small jewelry shop—Rings n' Things—in a charming brick building along historic Main Street. She had a wonderful son who filled her life with light and color.

Still, there was Ron. He troubled her, without even trying. Maybe he was just too painful a reminder of her past. Maybe he brought to mind sins she couldn't quite leave behind. Maybe he needed something from her, and she was just unwilling to do anything about it.

Or maybe God wasn't using her to teach Ron at all. Maybe He was using Ron to teach her.

Rachel closed her eyes and breathed deeper, telling the knot in her chest to loosen its grip.

Mike Odum, chief of the Red Lodge Police Department, sat at his desk and stared at the front page of the *Carbon County News*. "Child Missing in Big Timber," the headline proclaimed. "Red Lodge Next?"

It was a question he'd asked himself before, but it still infuriated him that James Flynn, the local editor, had the nerve to put it in the paper. No, not in the paper, *on* it: good old James had put this right up front. *If it bleeds, it leads.*

Odum knew James well. One of those people who preferred the proper "James" to the more informal "Jim," a bit of pretense that usually bothered him. But he could cut the man some slack. James had actually been the first person to welcome Odum to Red Lodge the previous year. The town had interviewed several candidates for the Chief of Police position. For most folks in town, a local boy already in the department was the sentimental favorite, but Odum managed to get the position. James Flynn had been unabashedly in the local boy's corner, although that didn't stop him from showing up at the office the first day with a nice bottle of Scotch. James even did a flattering interview for that week's edition, a fine piece asking folks to welcome the new Chief of Police.

Red Lodge was a good move for Odum. He had needed to get out of North Carolina. It wasn't that he disliked North Carolina— quite liked it, in fact, with its lush green undergrowth and the mountains—but Mike Odum was a travelin' man. He didn't stay in any one place and cool his heels for long. That made a police officer soft, mushy. Pretty soon you started worrying about yourself, and it was all over then. He didn't plan on worrying about himself for a good long time yet.

Odum picked up his coffee cup, read the lead-in paragraph for the story again. Man alive. James would have everyone in town panicky, convinced their children could be snatched at any moment. Of course, in this day and age, that was certainly a possibility. But people didn't need to be reminded of it all the same. Especially people in *his* town. Maybe he'd have to call James and chew him out a bit. Couldn't hurt.

Still, it wasn't really James bothering him. Odum was misplacing his anger by directing it at James, an easy and convenient target. Odum had been thinking about the child disappearances quite a bit himself. He knew the pattern of the disappearances, the towns, the dates. All of it was committed to memory. Once he heard or saw something, he never forgot it. Never.

Odum put down the paper after reading the story for the fifth time, then grabbed the coffee. He had, of course, already memorized all of the text, filing it away in his head. But something compelled him to keep rereading. He put down his coffee, brought his hands to his face, and rubbed his eyes. Not even ten o'clock in the morning, and he already felt tired.

Odum had been tracing the kidnapping patterns for several weeks now. Again and again he pulled the names and faces of victims into the foreground of his mind, examining them from every angle. He didn't share any of his work with the Feds out of the Billings office, who of course were working the case because of multiple disappearances. The Feds hadn't bugged him yet, because no children had disappeared in his town.

But they would, he was quite sure of that. He was in the mind of the killer. None of the bodies had been found, so no one had really named the perp a killer. But Odum knew. He *knew*.

It was terrifying, in some ways, knowing how the killer thought.

But at the same time it was crucial and energizing. So Odum embraced it—had to embrace it, knowing that doing so would keep him on the edge and ready.

Right where he wanted to be.

Jude mopped the floors of the school in the morning, playing thoughts of Kristina over and over in his mind. Normally Jude didn't mop during the school day, but today he wanted to be near other people. Be near the students. So he mopped the hallway while students sat in classes no more than twenty feet away.

He flipped his mop out of the bucket, ran it back and forth across the white and green linoleum. He tried to make himself think of other things, anything.

Keep it secret, keep it safe.

He called an image of his son to mind, reminded himself of dinner at Rachel's after work. But after a few minutes, the image of Nathan dissolved, displaced by the face of Kristina. Overnight she had become the five-hundred-pound gorilla battering through his waking thoughts. And, although he rarely remembered his dreams, he was pretty sure she'd rampaged through his subconscious mind the night before, as well.

He wheeled the mop and bucket down the hallway. One of the sticky wheels moved grudgingly, sounding something like a rusty hinge. Frank, his supervisor, had asked him to fix it numerous times, had even taken a can of oil to the wheel himself once. But still the squeak persisted. Every time Frank heard the wheel, he told Jude it was a sound that "made the monkeys moan." Jude wasn't quite sure what that meant—wasn't quite sure what a lot of Frank's colorful little quips meant—but the general gist was clear enough: it aggravated Frank. The sound didn't bother Jude at all, but he really wished it would stop squeaking just to keep Frank happy. If Frank was happy, Jude was happy.

Jude stopped the bucket, then went back up the hallway to retrieve the Wet Floor sign. Just as he grabbed it, the bell rang. Recess time. Kids seemed to materialize out of nowhere, making a quick sprint for the doors and the playground beyond.

Jude stood mute, holding his Wet Floor sign as the kids milled about. He thought of Kristina, sitting in the chair, looking at him the whole time. Yes, she really *had* stared at him the whole time, hadn't she? Whenever he had chanced a peek in her direction, she was looking right at him, and her eyes weren't afraid.

The hall emptied as quickly as it had filled. Jude stood, alone again, with his sign.

He placed the sign back in the same place, then returned to the mop and bucket. He wheeled the squeaky-wheeled contraption to the section of floor he'd just finished and began mopping to cover the fresh footprints.

Ron Gress was a head-scratcher for Frank, one of those things (and there were a few) he couldn't quite figure out. Like those blasted word puzzles in the newspaper, for instance. He could fill in the right answers here and there, but never all of them. Never. Each time in frustration he told himself he'd never do another. Yet he always did, because a different part of him inside demanded it.

So maybe that's what Ron was, too: one of those word puzzles with a five-dollar word for the answer. The guy wasn't your average village idiot, Frank could tell that. Ron was pretty smart, a lot smarter than himself, though that wasn't saying a whole lot. The bottom line was, Ron shouldn't be here, because . . . well, he just shouldn't. Ron should be doing something else, something that qualified as True Work.

Frank, himself, had some True Work. Something he was born to do. He'd always hidden the results of his True Work in the basement.

But maybe he could, maybe he *should*, show Ron. Inspire him a bit. It would be a good deed, and the truth was, he *wanted* to show someone else his True Work. Lately he'd been having trouble keeping it locked up inside his home, locked up inside his brain. The time was coming when he'd have to let the world see what he'd been doing down there. After all, it needed to be seen to be appreciated. Ron, he'd probably be a good place to start. And it would show him there was more to life than just janitorin'.

Of course, if Ron wanted to be a janitor, well, that wasn't Frank's biscuit to butter. It wasn't as if he himself had set out to be in this position; so many people end up in places they never dreamed they would. And Frank had to say that being a janitor wasn't all bad. Better than a poke in the eye with a sharp stick, as his dad always used to say. Janitorin' gave him time to clear his mind, because these days, with everything on the TV, with the newfangled cell phones and gadgets and computers, even with those godforsaken newspaper puzzles, well, there was too much to fit in your mind, wasn't there? Janitorin' gave him a chance to let loose all those jumbled thoughts. That, and his True Work.

Most people hated their day jobs, but Frank wasn't one of them. It gave him a chance to be around kids. Especially the young ones, kindergarten age or so. A janitor was just as fascinating to them as an astronaut, and they were always full of smiles and questions. And Frank, for his part, made sure he was full of answers. Oh, sure, he acted as if he didn't care for the kids when he was around Ron and other adults—it was so much easier to do that, because adults never trusted anyone who genuinely loved being around children—but deep down he was drawn to the young kids. They were, after all, what his True Work was all about.

Overall, being a janitor had a good beat, and you could dance to it. Frank gave it an 87.

Ron, on the other hand, didn't seem to be happy anywhere. He walked through life in a cloudy daze, like that kid in the Charlie

Brown cartoons who always had the storm of dust swirling around him. Frank knew a lot of kids picked up on that kind of thing, but he doubted Ron did. Or cared. Sometimes Frank would just sit Ron down and tell him the way things worked. In a small-town school such as this, you had to deal with kids of all ages.

And while Frank genuinely loved the small children, the older ones were a pain in the pants. Once they got up around middle school age, an orneriness leaked into their personalities. With these older kids, you couldn't be friendly. You had to be firm, in control. Frank knew that; any blooming idiot would know it. Ron, on the other hand, was always in some world far away, and the middle school kids liked to take advantage. If Ron heard his name, the haze lifted for a few moments; once the conversation at hand was done, the haze always returned.

Frank watched as Ron emptied garbage cans, obviously nose-deep in his own little dream world. A group of middle school boys—that snotty, uncontrollable age—walked by Ron, and one of the boys kicked over a full, as yet untied, garbage bag. Refuse scattered in every direction. The boys snickered as they walked on, and Frank waited a few seconds. Maybe Ron would say something. Maybe he'd take control of the situation. Had to happen some day, didn't it?

Instead, Ron simply bent down and started picking up the garbage, then stuffing it back into the bag.

Frank sighed. "Earth to la-la land," he said, a bit torqued that Ron had let the middle school kids get away with their stunt. That meant they might try other stunts. Maybe even with him.

Ron's eyes focused briefly.

"Sorry, Frank. Just . . . uh, thinking."

Frank smiled. Yeah, thinking. Maybe that was Ron's True Work. He grinned, picturing Ron's head on that famous Thinker statue.

That thought, in turn, made him think of his own True Work again.

And his smile grew.

That night, Jude stood on Rachel's porch, unsure of what to do. Rachel invited him over frequently—he was thankful for the chance to see Nathan, even if he'd never told Rachel so—but he always felt so awkward just before knocking on the door. Every time he felt like he should just turn and run. And keep running.

He knocked. He expected to wait for a few minutes before Rachel answered, but the door swung open almost in mid-knock.

Rachel stood in the doorway, looking surprised. "Oh, it's you," she said. Jude couldn't quite tell if she had been expecting someone else or if she just couldn't think of anything else to say right away. "You're early."

"First time for everything," he said, trying a joke. She looked somewhat puzzled by his statement but then smiled before swinging the door open and inviting him to enter.

Rachel retreated to the kitchen while Jude found his way back to Nathan's room. He peeked around the door and saw Nathan on the floor playing with toys from his own childhood: good old Lincoln Logs. Jude smiled as he watched his son. Every time he saw Nathan, a warm wave of pride always washed over him; he could scarcely believe he had been a part of something so beautiful. But soon after the pride came the shame. He wasn't much of a father.

Frightened, weak, and yes, paranoid. He knew he was paranoid, knew he *felt* he was being watched more often than he actually *was*. But he couldn't just turn off those feelings at the spigot; even if he could, some of the paranoia would still leak through, anyway.

Tonight, however, another emotion came as well. Call it resolve. Jude vowed he was going to change for Nathan. After Kristina's confrontation, he somehow felt . . . freed. Soon she'd probably let the world know that Jude Allman lived, ha ha, and he'd have to face the constant hounding once again. But until then, in this brief afterglow, he was free from a chain he'd been dragging around the last six years.

And maybe, just maybe, this was what he needed to turn the corner. Recently he could feel he was getting stagnant, the paranoia steadily worsening. The blackouts, he felt, were part of a deeper sickness, something he didn't want to face. When he was younger, he had always assumed mentally ill people couldn't *know* they were sick. After all, if you were sane enough to recognize you were crazy, how crazy could you really be? But now he knew that wasn't the case. He had always been able to feel the paranoia creeping into his own brain. Felt it crawling like a low slug, and yet he was powerless to stop it.

"Hey, squirt," Jude said to Nathan. Nathan immediately turned and grinned; he jumped to his feet, then ran over for a hug. Jude was always uncomfortable being touched, but he never stopped Nathan. Never. As they embraced, Jude thumbed through his memory banks, trying to find similar images of his own father. Memories labeled "father" were there, part of the buried trash he'd tried so long to abandon. He knew that much. But he didn't want to dig deeper and risk launching another headache. Not tonight.

They heard Rachel call to them from the other end of the home. Jude looked down at Nathan. "Ready for some chow?"

Nathan nodded. "It's your favorite, Daddy. I asked Mommy to make it."

"What's my favorite?"

Nathan furrowed his brow. "Spaghetti, acourse."

Jude smiled and rubbed the top of Nathan's head. "I think that's *your* favorite, if I remember right."

"Acourse." Nathan had recently discovered the term "of course" and found it to his liking for most situations, but he always pushed the two words into one: *acourse.* Jude wasn't sure if Nathan heard it as one word himself, or if he just liked the sound of the words together.

Jude bent down to pick up Nathan, and they made their way to the dining room. As they entered, Rachel froze when she saw them. "What's the matter?" Jude asked.

She blinked, then the moment passed. "Nothing," she answered. "Sit down, sit down. What do you guys want to drink?"

"Milk, Mommy," Nathan said as Jude put him in a chair.

Jude looked at her and smiled. "Me too," he said. She smiled back and disappeared into the kitchen again.

Jude sat and started to ask something about kindergarten but stopped when Rachel came back into the room with two glasses of milk. As much as he wanted to be gregarious and attentive for his son, he was still a long way from it.

Rachel sat, then Nathan immediately chimed up. "Can I say the blessing, Mommy?" he asked, the eagerness dancing in his eyes.

"You bet," she said.

They closed their eyes, and Nathan delivered his prayer in an unmistakable singsong cadence. "Dear God. Thank you for Mommy and Daddy, and for Poppa and Gramma Sanders, and for kindygarden. And bless this food, in Jesus' name. Amen."

"Amen," Jude added as he opened his eyes. Both Nathan and Rachel were staring at him. Uncomfortable, Jude looked down at his plate, found the salad in front of him, and started dishing it into his bowl. Obviously he'd made a mistake. It must have been the amen thing. Maybe they resented him saying it; he knew Rachel was a bit of a Holy Roller, even though she'd never tried the "God loves you" lecture on him. She and Nathan went to church regularly, and he was okay with that. Let Rachel believe what she wanted. Like his mother had.

And wouldn't he, Jude Allman, the Incredible Dying Man, know more about that than most people? He had died three times, come face-to-face with . . . Best not to think about that.

Jude decided he should just shut up for the rest of the dinner. He'd once seen a bumper sticker that said *A closed mouth gathers no foot.* Now, there was something he could say "amen" to. Just not aloud.

Jude played with the mound of spaghetti on his plate, avoiding eye contact with either of them. Who was he kidding, anyway? Rachel couldn't wait to get him out of the house. And Nathan would soon be old enough to figure out his father was more idle than idol. Maybe he could move again, start over. Leave behind the sham life he'd set up for another sham, add another blanket of secrecy. That would also solve the newly discovered Kristina problem.

Nathan broke the long silence. "Are you ready for your surprise, Daddy?"

Jude looked nervously at Rachel. She smiled (a forced smile, he thought), then he looked back to Nathan. "Yeah. Sure."

"Can I get it?" Nathan asked.

Rachel touched Nathan's hand, caressed it a bit, and nodded. Nathan jumped out of his chair and ran from the room.

Jude admired how she could touch their son so casually, without a thought. Each time he touched Nathan—the one person he actually *would* touch—he had to make himself do it. Not because of Nathan. Nathan was perfect.

But touching other people was so foreign to him now; doing it overloaded his senses and sent shock waves into his mind. He had hugged Nathan and brought him to the table that evening, and the feeling was wonderful. But before the hug, before picking up Nathan, he had to tell himself: *touch your son.* Rachel didn't have to do that, and Jude was jealous.

Nathan came back, slid into his chair. "Close your eyes, Daddy."

Jude did as instructed. Closing his eyes was easy, comforting. As long as he was sitting up.

"Surprise!" Nathan squealed. Jude opened his eyes and saw a picture: an outline of Nathan's hand turned into art. Scribbles of color raced across the page, displaying a creative disregard for the boundaries of the handprint.

"My hand, Daddy. I did it in kindygarden today."

Jude smiled, forced himself to pick up the paper. "It's great, Nathan. It's really great." Nathan beamed at him.

"I can almost remember doing something like that," Rachel said, "when I was in kindergarten or first grade or something. It was . . . wait, it wasn't quite that. It was a handprint in that plaster of Paris stuff. And I remember my teacher—Mrs. Zieske, that's right, it was second grade—painted it gold." She looked at Jude. "You ever do anything like that, Ron?"

He returned Rachel's gaze for a second. It was too much for one night, trying to talk as well as touch. One sense at a time, no more. And to top it off, there was the "amen" mistake. Jude's head was starting to itch, and despite his vows to avoid a headache, he knew one was in the neighborhood. Soon it would be pounding on the front door of his brain, demanding to come in. "I'm not sure. I don't remember too much about school. Maybe."

Rachel turned her attention back to the spaghetti.

Maybe next time they could talk. But not tonight. The batteries were too low.

During the rest of the dinner, Jude listened to the old-fashioned clock on the wall pound out the seconds, then minutes. Jude counted the ticks to himself, a comforting action that staved off the waiting headache: *one thousand three hundred twenty-seven, one thousand three hundred twenty-eight.*

He wanted to be home, safe in his recliner behind locked doors. *One thousand three hundred thirty-three, one thousand three hundred thirty-four.*

Nathan, for his part, seemed not to notice. Spaghetti was indeed his favorite dinner, and he happily slurped it into his mouth as he chattered on about school, puppies, his best friend, Bradley

Whittaker, and every other thought that floated through his mind. Jude was glad to have Nathan's incessant questions and giggles to fill the void that he couldn't.

And time clicked by. *Two thousand one hundred sixty-two, two thousand one hundred sixty-three.*

Rachel eventually stood and started to clear dishes. Jude thickly offered to help. She looked at him with that same odd sparkle in her eyes, then told him to tuck Nathan into bed.

This thought electrified Nathan, and he jumped up and down in front of Jude, begging to be picked up. *Pick up your son.* Jude lifted him for the second time that evening—this time didn't seem as draining, but more natural—and retreated down the hall.

In Nathan's room, Jude watched as Nathan peeled off his clothes, then wriggled into pajamas decorated with blue bunnies. Jude was amazed by his son's seemingly endless energy, and he watched Nathan bounce up and down on the bed a few times.

"Wanna read me a story?" Nathan asked.

Jude nodded. Nathan crawled to the brightly colored bookcase at the end of his bed to retrieve a book. He handed it to Jude and then lay back down on his pillow. Jude opened the book, something about a mouse named Marigold, and turned to the first page. Jude started to read when Nathan's voice interrupted, asking, "Aren't you gonna lay down with me?"

Jude stared into his son's eyes, wanting to say yes. Wanting to simply put his head down on the pillow and read a fun little story about a mouse who builds a yellow house. Maybe. Maybe. What was so hard about lying down, anyway?

"Okay," he said. Jude hesitated, then did it quickly. He put his head on the pillow, and his son snuggled against his shoulder, ready to listen before going to sleep. So far, so good. Jude took a deep breath, opened the book again, and started at page one.

He made it all the way to page five before the panic tightened his lungs. It always happened this way whenever he tried to lie down. His body stiffened, and his chest tightened like an iron clamp. Lying down was like . . . well, it was like dying—*really* dying, not the "dying" Jude Allman had become famous for doing—and the thought of that scared him. He bolted upright, gasping for air.

Nathan sat up with him, then put his hand on Jude's back and rubbed. Jude looked at Nathan, dimly thinking how he himself felt so young and terrified while his son seemed so old and wise.

"You're scared of laying down, Daddy?"

Jude paused, then nodded.

"'Sokay. I'm scared of some things, too."

Nathan continued to rub his father's back, and a tear formed in Jude's eye for what felt like the first time in forever.

After Rachel finished putting the dishes in the washer and cleaning up—it really didn't take much time at all—she walked silently to Nathan's room. She wanted to check, make sure everything was all right. Not because she thought anything would be wrong, nothing like that. It was just . . . Ron really hadn't been alone with Nathan very much. She didn't have any reason to feel that Ron was a danger to her son. *His son, too,* she reminded herself. But then, she didn't have any reason to feel that Ron *wasn't* a danger, either. He was now, as ever, mysterious and unknown. And she wasn't about to distrust her God-given maternal instincts.

When Rachel was a young girl, the family next door owned a wolf/dog cross. The dog had always been happy and friendly, ready to slobber all over anyone who came within a mile, and he had the very unfrightening name of "Sunny." But Rachel was terrified of Sunny, all the same.

She knew some part of him was wolf, and wolves ate children.

Rachel felt the same way about Ron being alone with Nathan. No, Ron wasn't a wolf, but he was . . . something. That was perhaps even more unsettling.

Rachel paused at Nathan's mostly closed door when she heard someone sobbing. Alarmed, she wondered what Ron had done to make Nathan cry. But that thought quickly faded when she realized it wasn't Nathan. She'd heard Nathan cry plenty of times before, and it was quite obvious this wasn't her son sobbing.

She cracked open the door, ventured a peek inside. Nathan was tightly hugging Ron as Ron's head rested on Nathan's shoulder. An odd picture. Her radar kicked down to zero. She pulled the door shut and went to the sofa in the living room, her mind full of questions. What had they talked about? What had made Ron cry? What was suddenly so different about him?

A few times that evening Ron had done things that shocked her, things she never would have expected. First, he went to Nathan's room right away. Never happened before. Even though she invited Ron over to see Nathan regularly, and even though Nathan genuinely loved his father, Ron had never seemed that . . . interested. He'd always been more like a lobotomized patient than anything else. He showed up, you told him where to sit or stand, he did it, then he left. But tonight, when she opened the door, she could tell right away he seemed more . . . awake, maybe.

Then, when Nathan finished his prayer at the dinner table, Ron uttered a quick "amen." What did that mean? Was God softening his heart? Did it mean she was supposed to talk to Ron about God?

Yes, that signal was crystal clear, now that Ron was crying in Nathan's room. Ron obviously needed someone to confide in, and Nathan had been the only one to show him unconditional love and acceptance. Her five-year-old had been there for Ron, while she herself had acted like the five-year-old. She felt the ball of pain starting to thrum a bit at the top of her chest.

She sat on her sofa and waited, unsure what else to do, until she heard Ron coming down the hallway. He stopped as he entered the living room, apparently surprised to see her.

"Oh," he said. "Hi."

"Everything okay?" she asked with a tinge of hope in her voice.

"Yeah. Sure. He's asleep. I mean, not really asleep, but he's in bed."

She nodded. "You want to sit down? Want some coffee or something?"

He looked at her for a moment. "I'm . . . I'm sorry. I'm no good at being—" he stopped and looked at the floor, and Rachel could tell he was searching for the right word—"no good at being real, I guess."

She smiled. "None of us are."

Ron shuffled. "I do want to thank you for dinner. Not just tonight, but every time. I appreciate you letting me see Nathan."

"He's your son."

Ron pointed toward the door. "I should get going."

Rachel followed him. Ron unlocked the dead bolt, relocked it and unlocked it again, then turned as if to say something to her but didn't.

He turned back to open the door, and she reached out to touch his shoulder. He flinched and stopped, actually stopped, in mid-motion. "I'm sorry," she blurted. "I didn't mean to—"

"It's okay. I'm just not used to, uh, that."

Was he this bad the night she first met him? She didn't think so. Ron seemed more withdrawn, more paranoid now. And she felt even more shame at this thought, knowing in her heart she could have prevented some of the slide. "I just wanted to tell you, Ron, that you can talk to me anytime. About anything. Really. I know I've never said that before, but there it is."

He looked down at the wood floor of her porch. "Thank you," he answered. "I'll remember that."

He stepped into the night. Rachel bit her lip as she closed the door, quite sure he wouldn't remember it.

Jude didn't park in front of his home. Not at night. It was much better to park a block away, turn off the lights, and watch. He scanned the home and the surrounding area, looking for any kind of movement. He knew it was odd to act this way, but it felt right. It was warm, comforting.

Satisfied everything was safe, Jude opened his car door and walked down the block to his home. He unlocked his front door and dead bolts, then stepped inside. It was dark, impossible to see inside the home at night without any windows. But he could hear a steady, low whine coming from the back of the home: the security system, waiting to be disarmed. He moved quickly through the home, knowing the way without the aid of lights, and keyed the override code into the keypad. The whine stopped.

He turned to walk out of the room again when a blinking light caught his attention. It was the message indicator on his answering machine. Odd. He had the answering machine because it was built into the most recent phone he purchased (it was nearly impossible to find a basic phone anymore, almost as impossible as a basic analog clock), yet he rarely received any messages. Maybe Frank at school? Rachel? He hoped not; if Rachel left a message, that might mean something had happened to Nathan since Jude had left their house.

Or maybe it was worse. Kristina had found him; someone else probably could, too. Once the dam was breached, it wouldn't take long for a torrent of water to start forcing its way through.

Maybe it was even one of *them*.

Jude turned on a light, looked steadily at the blinking '1' on his machine. He pushed the button on the caller ID. The call was identified as a Red Lodge, Montana, number, but no name accompanied it. It wasn't Rachel's number or the school number.

He pushed the New button and listened. The machine whirred a second, then found the message.

"Hi, it's Kristina. Look, I'm sorry about just barging in on you like that. So how about a coffee to make it up to you? My treat. I'm staying at the Stumble Inn—how's that for a fine motel name?—room 305. Give me a call."

Jude was relieved to hear Kristina. Mostly relieved. That meant it wasn't an accident involving Nathan, or some other amateur sleuth sniffing down his trail. No additional fires to fuel the headaches in his mind. Still, he was a bit troubled. A part of him had hoped Kristina would just fade away, discouraged he wasn't the eloquent saint she had pictured in her star-struck mind. Now it was obvious she wasn't about to do that. And—Jude was ashamed to admit he was thinking this, but it was true—she would be dead soon, anyway. Cancer, or whatever it was. She hadn't given him specifics, but she didn't need to, not with her veiled *"Let's just say I won't be here long"* reference. His location was a secret that would die with her, and then he'd fade back into obscurity. So if he just kept her happy and kept her quiet, he would be safe. He could retreat under his nice, warm blanket.

The bigger issue, of course, was: what was he, Jude Allman, aka Ron Gress, going to do next? Would he call Kristina? She needed some help, some reassurance, and if he could swallow his own miserable fear, he could give that to her. (And so keep her quiet, helping himself in the process.) The way he'd given it to his best friend, Kevin, so many years ago. The way he'd given it to thousands of people before he disappeared.

Or would he throw a few things in a bag and hit the highway? The thought had been simmering in the back of his mind since Kristina's visit. It would be so easy and painless, and he could sink back into the murky depths of his own thoughts without letting in anyone else.

As Jude sat and debated, an image of his son appeared. Nathan, a boy who was wise beyond his years, a boy wise beyond his father's years, for that matter. He thought about what Nathan would do, and the answer became very clear.

Jude pressed the caller ID button and memorized the number for the Stumble Inn.

Jude and Kristina met at the Red Lodge Cafe, perhaps the easiest place to find on the town's main street. Its sign was a large tipi, with orange neon Indian figures dancing around it.

People who weren't exposed to Indians, he knew, were always offended by the term *Indian*. They wanted you to use the euphemism *Native American*. But growing up around Indians in Nebraska, and living near the Crow and Northern Cheyenne reservations in Montana, Jude knew there was nothing wrong with *Indian*. Most of the tribal members called themselves Indians and had no problem with the word. It only made outsiders uncomfortable. In a lot of ways, death was a similar thing. People who hadn't faced death, hadn't experienced it, wanted to think warm, comforting thoughts about it. People who knew death up close and personal, people such as himself, were more pragmatic. There was nothing touchy-feely about the experience.

Jude looked at the tipi sign as he walked under it. Yes, it was politically incorrect by contemporary standards. But it was somehow correct on a deeper, more meaningful level. It didn't shy away from reality.

The glass front door *whooshed* open, then swung closed behind them with the soft chime of a bell. Immediately smoky smells drifted toward them. Onions, eggs, potatoes, and other things he couldn't quite identify. In the center of the cafe waited an old-fashioned lunch counter with built-in stools; behind the U-shaped counter the grill hissed and rumbled. Booths lined the walls, with nondescript tables and chairs filling the wide floor of the middle. Even though the front of the cafe was plate glass, the whole place always seemed a bit dark, cavelike. Maybe that was why Jude liked it. It had dark creases where he could hide.

Kristina asked where Jude wanted to sit. He picked a booth in the corner, keeping his back to the wall.

The waitress approached them, a young woman with short-cropped blond hair and a flinty edginess. She tapped the end of a pen nervously against her pad as she stood facing their booth. Jude came in occasionally, mostly late at night, but he didn't remember seeing this particular waitress before. She didn't even ask for an order; she merely stood there waiting for Jude to speak. He looked at Kristina, who shook her head, then back at the waitress.

"I guess a coffee is about all we need." He wasn't much of a coffee drinker, but he felt he needed to order something. The waitress wrote on her pad and started to turn away, but Jude stopped her. "You know what? Do you have any peach pie left?"

"Yeah, I think so."

"Gimme a piece of that."

The waitress scribbled on the note pad again, turning away as she did.

Jude glanced toward Kristina. She was staring, but he pretended he didn't notice and busied himself looking around the room. "I like their peach pie," he said simply, feeling as if he needed to fill the dead space with some sort of idle chatter.

"So, do you know why I'm here, Jude?" she asked.

He stiffened, then leaned across the booth a bit. "How about you just call me 'Ron' when we're . . . you know." He nodded his head to indicate the two other people in the cafe, both seated at the counter and oblivious to their presence.

Kristina didn't follow his gaze but nodded. "Okay, Ron. Do you know why I'm here?"

"Didn't we already go over this?" he said.

She looked at him and shook her head, almost imperceptibly. "I'm here because . . . because I think there's something more to you. More than you can admit. Maybe even more than you know."

"Such as?"

"That's a question for you to answer."

"I'm a janitor. We've been through this before, too."

"Yes, you're a paranoid janitor. But that's just your day job."

Jude studied the booth's tabletop, the flecked pattern on its surface. He knew where she was going with this.

"Maybe you've just locked it away," she continued.

"What is 'it,' exactly?"

"Your gift."

"This again, huh?" he said.

She stared at him with bleary eyes. "Dying three times . . . you think that doesn't mean something?"

He rolled his eyes, sighed. "Look, I—"

At that moment the waitress returned with his coffee and pie. As she slid the cup and plate toward him, Jude felt a sharp, acidic taste in his mouth, a taste he faintly recognized and couldn't identify until . . .

Copper. That was it. The bitter tang of copper filled his mouth, as if he were sucking on pennies. The taste of death. But this was wrong, all wrong; he'd only ever tasted that after returning from the Other Side, and that hadn't happened for years now. He'd hidden from it all here in Red Lodge.

The waitress was staring at him.

"Everything okay?" she asked.

He glanced up at her. "Yeah, yeah," he said. "Just a little . . . light-headed or something."

"You want something else to drink? Milk?"

He shook his head. "No, I think I'm fine. Thanks."

The waitress retreated, and as she did, the coppery taste subsided.

"Sorry," he said to Kristina. "I don't know what happened there." He took a drink of coffee, then picked up a fork. The hot, bitter taste of the coffee seemed to wipe away the last lingering effects of copper, and he woodenly started eating the pie while thoughts of dying began to jumble inside.

"Anyway," Kristina said, "I was saying you need to do something. *Be* something."

He stopped a forkful of pie midway between the plate and his mouth. He definitely wasn't in the mood for this now. Not after the copper taste, already unearthing even more buried feelings. "I guess a janitor isn't enough for you, huh?"

"Whatever you are, Jude—uh, Ron—you're not a janitor."

Jude took the bite of pie and studied the rest of the slice sitting on his plate. Here it was again, the whole death thing. Back in his face. Back in his mouth. People like Kristina, when they encountered it, wanted it to be some kind of mystical experience. A complete circle. An answer. Death as a mere question was much too scary for them.

Careful. He thought of his conversation with Kevin, the same conversation he'd had with so many people over the years. He needed to give her something she could hold on to; the truth, as always, was too . . . barren. The truth would have to stay hidden deep inside of him. Forever.

"I understand where you're coming from," he began gently. He looked in her eyes. "And you don't have to be scared of anything. It's nothing to be frightened—"

"You think I'm scared of dying?" she said. She smiled. "That's not it at all. I'm not here for me; I'm here for you."

Well. This certainly was a new twist. Someone coming to him, not with Questions but Answers. He shrugged, ate his pie as if it were suddenly the most important thing in the world.

"I've read your book," she said. "I've done some research. There are things, patterns, about your life."

She waited, and Jude took another bite. He wasn't overly interested in his life patterns at the moment; he had peach pie to eat. "Ah, and that's where you come in," he said, the condescension dripping from his voice.

"Maybe you don't believe it now. But I think you will."

He sighed. In spite of his best efforts, he was getting a bit angry. Who was she to be telling him what he should do with his life? "So you've got it all figured out, do you?"

"What I'm saying is: *you* need to figure it out."

He shoveled in his last bite of pie, ignoring her.

"So just try," she continued.

He looked around for the waitress, hoping she would come around for a coffee refill.

"Try what?" he asked Kristina without looking at her.

"Figure out who Jude Allman is."

"And how do I do that?"

"Look for signs. You've already had some. And you'll have more, I think."

He took a sip of coffee and said nothing. This was verging on the border of more God Talk. And once the conversation went there, he knew he wouldn't be able to control himself.

"I have some ideas. I've made some notes based on your book and other things, and—" she stopped, as if searching for words—"I have some ideas," she repeated. "But I think maybe you're supposed to see it all for yourself."

"Great, I'll get right on that."

She fell silent, and Jude eventually looked back at her. She was studying him, waiting.

"What?" he asked.

"You said you'd get right on it."

"Oh, you mean now?"

She shrugged. "Why not?"

"Where is that waitress?" he asked in frustration, mostly because he didn't want to deal with Kristina and her mumbo jumbo. He glanced back at Kristina again, then waved his hands dismissively. "Okay, okay already. Signs, you say. Maybe I could get a big old sign right now, huh?"

She shrugged again.

He closed his eyes, took a deep breath. Concentrated. After a few moments, his brow softened, and he began to speak.

"Wait. Wait a minute. I'm seeing . . . I think I'm seeing the sign."

"What is it?" she asked. He could hear the anticipation in her voice.

"It's . . . it's rectangular, and green, and it says . . . 'Welcome to the New Jersey Turnpike.'" He opened his eyes and looked at her, then loudly slurped his coffee.

They walked out the front door of the Red Lodge Cafe and started down the street in silence. After a few minutes of smug euphoria, Jude now felt miserable for being so flip with Kristina. He knew why she was here, and he could understand. One thing Jude had learned from people in general and the terminally ill in specific: when a person approaches the end of her life, she needs to feel her existence has served a greater purpose. Kristina wanted him to be part of it.

Unfortunately it was easy to let the old anger and fear drain back into his thoughts whenever someone brought up his past. Jude knew things about his past no one else knew. Things no one else would ever know.

Finally he spoke. "Look, I'm sorry about back there. It's just that . . . it was scary being Jude Allman. It's a lot easier to be Ron Gress."

"I understand," she said softly.

"So if you'll just give me—" The sudden taste of copper filled Jude's mouth again, this time so strong that he gagged. He opened his mouth and tried to spit, but the hot, hard taste slid down his throat in a molten river.

"What's wrong?" she asked.

"I don't know," he said, feeling like his tongue was too thick with metal for his voice to be understood.

Jude heard the screech of brakes. On the street, no more than twenty feet away, the headlights of a pickup—its brakes chattering—framed the silhouette of a man in the street. The image moved, but in Jude's eyes it was a photo: a black outline, bathed in a bright glare of halogen.

The pickup's front bumper hit the man's legs, launching him into an effortless cartwheel, an impossible acrobatic display that seemed to last for an impossibly long time. The man's body finally ended its gravity defying stunt with a sickening thud on the pavement.

Right next to Jude.

He looked at the man, whose eyes were vacant, unresponsive. *Dead.* But after a few seconds the eyes blinked, focusing on Jude. The man's mouth lolled open, moving spasmodically, as if he were trying to speak but had no voice. Jude stooped down, touched the quivering man, and . . .

The world swam. Colors reversed. Reversed. Jude shook his head, thinking he must be blacking out, but the odd colors stayed in his line of vision. It was as if he were looking at film negatives, everything tinted a sick orange, the sky dark and shadows white.

Then he saw something that wasn't happening. Something that wasn't happening but *had* happened. Inside the negative frame, images of other people flared and flickered in a giant slide show. A woman, a young girl, an older girl. Grade school. College. Children being born.

As Jude watched, names and memories flashed in his mind, illuminating his consciousness in a bright fireworks display.

The colors shifted to normal again. He heard himself panting, as if he'd just finished running a marathon. After forcing his lungs to slow, he spoke to the broken man whose head he was now cradling.

"You had a wife and a daughter. You loved them, really loved both of them. But your marriage split up, and you were ashamed. So ashamed that you lost all contact with them."

The man had no discernible reaction, but his gaze stayed fixed on Jude. "They're both fine. They're both happy. Leslie remarried. Your daughter, Susan, became a nurse. She's married, and she has a daughter of her own now: Corinne."

Jude stopped, feeling his breath and pulse quicken again. He wasn't sure what was happening to him, wasn't sure where these words were coming from, but he was sure he couldn't stop it. These things needed to be spoken.

"What you need to know is, they've both forgiven you."

The man closed his eyes tightly, opened them again, and smiled. His hand grabbed Jude's arm and squeezed. Finally, his eyes fluttered shut again, and a last breath crawled from his lungs in one long rasp.

Jude didn't move. He sat, considering what had just happened. He re-ran the entire scenario, trying to wrap his mind around a logical explanation. It was complete understanding, complete knowledge of the other man's life. A word came to him: *revelation*. Best not to share that one with Kristina.

Jude turned his eyes away from the dead man's face and looked across the street. Another man sat on the curb, staring at him. The man was soft and puffy, on the verge of being chunky, but his face somehow stayed angular and chiseled; atop his head was a fine mane of pure white hair. He realized this had to be the pickup driver—the man who had hit the pedestrian.

The man's stare made him uncomfortable until . . . until he realized the man wasn't staring at him at all. He was simply staring into space, a space Jude happened to be occupying. The eyes were wild and vacant, focusing but not registering. As Jude watched, a paramedic brought the white-haired man an ice pack, which finally broke the hundred-yard stare; he accepted the ice pack and put it to his forehead.

Sights and sounds began to filter through Jude's consciousness. He turned his head and noticed a couple of parked police cars nearby. Their cherry lights swirled, throwing a murderous glow on the downtown buildings. Jude heard the metallic *tick-tick-tick* of the lights cycling on the closest police cruiser.

"I said, are you okay?" a voice above him asked. Jude looked up and saw a policeman standing over him, slightly bent at the waist.

He stared at the officer for a few moments, then simply nodded.

A new voice joined in. "Quite a way to perk up your Tuesday night, eh, Grant?" The voice was deep, authoritative, impossible to ignore. Jude turned his eyes to look at the other officer. Close-cropped dark hair, a leathery face with a cleft chin, and impenetrable eyes so dark it was hard to determine where the pupils ended and the irises began.

Officer Grant also turned and stood up straight. "Chief Odum. I didn't know you were . . . I can handle this."

Chief Odum slapped a hand on Officer Grant's shoulder. "You're doing great, Grant. I'm not here to rattle your cage; I just happened to be driving by."

Officer Grant looked like he was about to say something else but then stopped. Odum turned his face toward Jude, looking down without bothering to bend. Looking down with those eyes of tar. "You see what happened?"

Jude nodded.

"Think you can tell us about it?"

Jude nodded again.

"Hang tight." The two officers retreated to the police cruisers, leaving Jude alone with Kristina. She stood over him, watching. He wanted to say something, anything.

She spoke instead. "Looks like you just got a sign."

Jude sprang awake in his usual sweat-drenched terror. But this time, something was different. This time, he remembered part of the dream. Not much, but a little. It was a memory from his early childhood, a memory he hadn't thought of in years. In the dream, he and his father flew a kite—a box kite, bright and yellow, hanging in the sky like a second sun.

He got out of his recliner and hit the button to disarm the security system, then padded to the bathroom instead of checking the house for intruders. Today, that didn't seem as important as it usually did.

He went to the bathroom mirror and studied the reflection staring back at him. He leaned closer, looking for something, anything that would explain last night to him.

Nothing was there.

He dressed for work and went to his kitchen to get cereal. As he ate, something nibbled at the back of his mind, a loose end he was missing, a connection he hadn't made.

But nothing came to him by the time he walked out the door and headed to work.

Rachel opened her shop half an hour early that morning, wanting to get a quick start on some new items from a jewelry designer in Billings. Her shop, Rings n' Things, was typical of the many boutiques that lined Red Lodge's main street: wood floors, brick walls, and a lingering sandalwood scent. It was a shop, and a building, caught between two opposing yet symbiotic 'times: one, the rough-

and-tumble early days of coal mining, the other, a modern crush of tourists trying to recapture the flavor of Red Lodge's early days.

People wandered in and out of Rachel's shop all morning, an equal mix of tourists on the way to and from Yellowstone National Park, and locals who wanted to drop in and chat about the accident the night before.

At about 9:30 A.M. Nicole Whittaker walked through the front door and offered a little wave. Nicole had been Rachel's unquestioning supporter for more than five years. They had met in a class for expectant first-time mothers and had instantly bonded. After their boys were born, the friendship continued to grow, and today it was harder to say if Rachel and Nicole were closer, or their sons, Nathan and Bradley.

"The little monsters at school?" Rachel asked as she put a sterling silver necklace with a turquoise pendant in her counter display case.

"Yup. Dropped 'em off, then thought I'd stop by the City Bakery for some carbs." Nicole held up a bag. "You're an apple fritter gal, if I remember correctly." She smiled, a bit of radiance surrounded by the wiry hair she shared with her son, Bradley.

Rachel smiled. "My hips love them, unfortunately."

Nicole shushed her with a wave of her hand as she walked toward the counter. "We'll start the diets tomorrow. Today," she said as she opened the bag and pulled out a giant fritter, "we eat whatever we want."

"The good old Tomorrow Diet," Rachel said, taking the treat. "I've been on it many a time."

Nicole took a bite of her maple bar, made a face at Rachel, and smiled. Then she wiped glaze from the corner of her mouth with a finger. "I'm sure you probably heard by now," Nicole said as she studied the jewelry Rachel was sorting.

"The accident?" Rachel asked. Nicole nodded. "Yeah, I've heard from three or four people this morning."

"So what was your Boo Radley doing there?" asked Nicole before taking another bite.

Rachel winced. Boo Radley. She herself had called Ron that, an inside joke with Nicole and a few other friends. At the time it seemed spot-on funny. Now it just seemed mean-spirited. But that wasn't the only reason she winced. Of the people who had been in to chat about the accident, none had mentioned Ron's involvement. This was news. "Ron was there?"

Nicole caught the look and narrowed her eyebrows. "Oh, I thought you knew. I mean, you said you knew."

"About the accident, yes. About Ron being there, no."

"He was."

"Was he . . . you know, part of the accident?"

"No, no, nothing like that. In fact, he was helping."

Rachel sighed. Before last night, Ron had made sense. He had always been aggravating, but at least he made sense. She always knew what he was going to do, and she was comfortable with what he was: a scared, paranoid has-been. Or, more properly, a never-was.

But as of last night, her crystal-clear image of Ron was starting to blur at the edges. She didn't like this new current of unpredictability. It made her feel like she was trying to navigate logs bobbing in a river. "Helping?" Rachel said, realizing she was having a hard time breathing. She had no idea why. "Like doing CPR or something?"

"Something."

Rachel bit her lip as she thought, a habit from her childhood that still persisted.

"You're biting your lip again," Nicole said. "That's never good."

"I know. It's just, last night, Ron was acting kinda strange."

Nicole covered her mouth, trying to hide her grin. "That's hilarious, Rachel," she laughed.

"Okay, yeah. What I mean is, he was acting *not* strange. And that's the strange part, you know?"

Nicole shrugged. "If you say so." Nicole switched gears, talking about the new Ultra Man toy Bradley wanted and how *expensive* it was. But Rachel found her mind wandering, occupied by the newly evolving mystery known as Ron Gress.

Chief Odum's fear continued to build and simmer in his stomach: *sometime soon, it's going to happen here.* He knew it. The abductions crisscrossed south-central Montana and northern Wyoming, and it was obvious Red Lodge had to be on that path of violence sometime.

Odum looked at the accident report from the previous night again. It was a straightforward case with no need to issue a citation to the driver. The pedestrian was jaywalking at 11:00 P.M., and the driver was at least five miles per hour under the speed limit. Still, something about it set off Odum's internal alarms. Something happened he didn't know about, or it didn't happen quite the way the witnesses explained it, or . . . something. His intuition told him it centered around the first guy on the scene—he picked up the report again and looked at the name—*Ron Gress. Janitor. Just passing by. Mr. Gress had no idea who the victim was, had never seen him before.*

Odum felt those things were probably true enough. But he also felt a key piece was missing, something that would put a whole new spin on the accident and open new doors. That spin was somewhere beneath the surface, if he could just do a bit of digging.

And digging was something he was happy to do.

Odum pushed away the report. It was only ten o'clock in the morning, but he needed to get out of his office for a few minutes. Inside the station, even in autumn, the air could become thick, heavy, stale. He needed to step out, clear his mind, refresh his perspective a bit.

So he left his office, walked down the hallway and out the front door. He realized he'd been holding his breath since leaving the building, waiting to breathe in the air tinged with pine and mountain breeze.

The moment he stepped outside, he felt his body starting to relax.

His gaze caught the coffee cart across the street. A nice double latte would clear the cobwebs more than a few quick breaths outside. He went down the steps and walked across the street, a slow, practiced amble he'd perfected over the years as a cop. Odum knew that actually *being* a police officer was only part of the battle for respect on the street. One had to cultivate a certain swaggering presence, a confidence that made people think you always knew more than you really did.

As he approached the cart, he casually looked down the street at the small landscaped area in front of the bank. He saw two kids playing, crawling on one of the concrete benches and then jumping off.

"What can I get for you?" It was the girl at the coffee cart, asking for his order. A sign on the cart said today's special was the KILLER BEE LATTE. Whatever that was.

He held up a finger, asking her to wait, then turned his attention back to the kids. No adult was around that he could see, and the kids weren't more than eight or nine years old. One boy, one girl. Likely brother and sister. The mother or father was probably in the bank, but why? Why would a parent go into the bank and leave the kids outside? Especially now.

He turned back to the coffee cart girl. "Those kids been alone long?" he asked, cocking his head down the street. She looked toward the kids, then turned back to Odum and shrugged. "First I've seen 'em."

Odom stepped from the cart, headed toward the children, and bent down to talk to them. Both kids saw his uniform, then relaxed. He knew the uniform was an important part of the total effect— much like the practiced swagger—and he liked wearing it.

"Where's your mommy?" he asked. On cue, the door of the bank swung open, and a harried woman came out. When she saw Odum, a bit of shock registered in her eyes.

Then, recognition. She knew him, of course. In a small town like Red Lodge, everyone recognized the Chief of Police, even if they didn't know him personally. "Chief, uh, Odum. Is everything okay?" she asked.

He wanted to rip into her for leaving her kids outside, but he knew it was much more effective to play Officer Friendly. "No problem at all, ma'am. I was just checking on your kids here," he said with a smile.

"Did they do something?"

"No, no. Not at all. It's just that—" he glanced at the kids and could tell that both of them were listening to what he said—"I'm sure you've been reading the paper and watching the TV lately. I think you know what I mean."

Her face was a scramble as she tried to figure out Odum's cryptic message. Understanding then clicked in her eyes, and she—unconsciously, Odum was sure—pulled both of her kids close. "Yes, yes. I know what you mean, Officer."

He smiled broadly and held out his hand. "No harm done," he said. "I'd just like to make sure it stays that way."

She took his hand and shook it gingerly. "Yes. Thank you."

Odum nodded to the kids, turned, and started walking back to the coffee cart. The smile slid from his face. It was an evil world, filled with monsters that bite. Kids understood this, but adults always forgot.

Until they were bitten.

He bypassed the coffee cart and crossed the street back to the station. Suddenly the air outside didn't seem so fresh, and thoughts of a double latte sickened him.

After work, Jude pointed his car toward home and let the day evaporate from his mind. That was no problem, as the day had been fairly uneventful in his janitorial guise. Same old Frank-isms from his supervisor, same old schedule, same old everything.

The difficulty was getting *last night* out of his mind. Even today, he half wondered if the vision that battered his thoughts had been a dream, some odd part of his paranoia bubbling to the surface. It looked like a dream, with the odd negative colors and burnt tints painting the faces and photos of people he didn't know (*but did know*) sliding past him. It felt like a dream.

But it wasn't a dream. He knew it.

And, it had been accompanied by that wretched taste of copper. A shiver raced through him as he thought about it. It was, after all, the taste of death—the taste on his lips each time he'd died and returned from the Other Side, a sickening reminder of things he'd tried so desperately to forget.

He turned down Broadway and drove slowly, taking a small detour on his way home. He wanted to drive by the accident site, to see if he could find . . . something. A connection he'd missed, a key part of the picture he hadn't seen the previous night.

Jude pulled over and parallel parked, then opened his door to get out. He walked the whole block, watching, waiting. Nothing happened. No copper in the mouth, no Kodachrome visions. He stopped, looked at the street where the truck had plowed into the hapless pedestrian. The vision played in his mind again: a dark figure, rimmed in light, taking flight and spinning, then landing with a wet thud.

Jude realized now he didn't know the man's name. He had been told, if that was the right word, the names of the wife and daughter—and even the granddaughter—but not the man's. All those thoughts in his mind weren't his thoughts, and that disturbed him. Made him think of something deeper than paranoia. But no, *told* wasn't the right word. He hadn't heard any voices, outside or inside of his head. He just *knew* all those things, as if they were past facts already stored in his memory. Even though all of it, especially that blather about being forgiven, had come from somewhere else.

He looked up the street to the next block. Rachel's jewelry store was there, just a few doors from the Red Lodge Cafe. Maybe he could just . . .

The Red Lodge Cafe. Jude looked up at the neon tipi sign, flickering orange and blue, as a circuit connected inside his mind. A sign. Kristina had told him to look for a sign. Last night, before the accident, the taste of copper had filled his mouth. Yes, it was the taste of death. But maybe it wasn't just the taste of death for him.

Maybe he was tasting the deaths of others.

That would explain, in an odd way, why he'd tasted copper before seeing the accident. But now, as he stared at the bright neon colors of the Red Lodge Cafe, his mind told him what he'd been missing before: *He had tasted copper more than once the previous night.*

Jude walked up the street toward the cafe, knowing he needed to talk to a waitress.

He was leaking. That was the only word he could think of to describe the sensation. Leaking. He had always been so careful to separate the work of the Normal from the work of the Hunter, but now a small fissure had opened between the two, and the only place he felt safe was in his basement root cellar, surrounded by earth and burlap.

Maybe something organic. A brain tumor, perhaps, eating away at his medulla oblongata and clouding his judgment, blurring the line between the two. It had always been so easy to turn on one side and turn off the other, keeping each side an impenetrable dike to the outside world.

But not now.

Earlier that day, for the first time, the Normal had followed a possible Quarry. Hadn't trapped and taken the Quarry; things had stopped long before that. But the Normal had actually tracked a Quarry inside the grocery store, considering what hunting might be like. That easily, the Normal slipped. That easily, the levee was breached.

And if you didn't stop a leak right away, you were just setting yourself up to drown.

He sat down and hooked the electrodes to his temple. He would need a more powerful shock this time, something more sustained to keep him immune from human emotions and depravations. Something to keep the Normal from becoming interested in the work of the Hunter.

Pavlov had trained his dogs to salivate at the sound of a dinner bell; he had gone further and trained his own mind to shear itself into two separate entities by simple will.

Obviously, some remedial work was needed. A bit of negative reinforcement.

His behavior modification system was homemade. One of a kind, his own design. Simple enough to build with some parts from the local hardware store, along with a little knowledge of electricity.

He clenched his teeth, then threw the switch and embraced the current. The machine had been integral to *becoming*. The machine would make sure he would keep *becoming*.

The leak would be plugged.

Jude opened the door to the Red Lodge Cafe, then hurried inside. It was just rolling into dinner hour, and the place had more people in it than he had ever seen. Of course, Jude was usually here when he knew other people wouldn't be.

He scanned the cafe, looking for her. Behind the counter a gray-haired waitress poured a cup of coffee for a grizzled man sitting at the counter. Out of the kitchen bounced a large, middle-aged waitress, bearing a couple specials of the day.

Those were the only two. She wasn't here.

He moved to the counter and flagged down the woman pouring coffee. She shuffled over and looked at him with watery eyes.

"Last night I was in here. And there was a young waitress, about twenty years old or so, with short blond hair."

"Ginny?"

"Yeah, Ginny. Is she here?"

"Wish she was, buddy. She called in sick."

Jude's stomach greeted the news uneasily. "Do you have her address or something? Some way I can reach her?"

"Yes," the woman answered, then stood staring at him.

"Can I have it?"

"You think I'm going to give some pretty young thing's address to any wacko who happens to walk in off the street?"

Jude nodded. "I totally agree. It's just . . ." He leaned closer. "It's just, I think she might be in danger."

"Especially if I tell a freak like you how to find her. Beat it."

"No, no, really." He stopped. "Maybe you could come with me. Or someone else who works here. Someone."

The waitress studied his face a moment. "What makes you think she's in trouble?"

He sighed, shook his head. "It's not a story you'd want to hear right now. Could we just go? If she's fine, no harm done. But if tomorrow rolls around and something's happened to her, you'll think about this moment the rest of your life."

She continued to look at him, considering. Finally, without taking her eyes from his face, she shouted to the other waitress. "Brandy, can you cover for me for about fifteen minutes?"

Brandy stopped in mid-step. "It's rush hour here, Linda!"

"Then rush a little more. I'll be right back."

Brandy banged through the doors into the kitchen with a huff. Linda, the gray-haired waitress, dug under the counter and retrieved a purse, then looked back at Jude again. "I just want you to know," she said as she opened the top of her purse and let him peer inside. Jude saw the glint of a small-caliber revolver and nodded his head. "Don't do anything that's gonna make me open this purse. Understand?" Jude nodded again.

She took off her apron and headed for the door without waiting for Jude.

He caught up with Linda—who was quick on her feet—about halfway down the block. "How far?" he asked.

"Just a couple of blocks," she said. "I swear, if I find out you're some kind of stalker or something, I will personally castrate you with a butter knife."

"Understood."

They rounded the corner and cut through an alley, then came to an old house in the middle of the street. "She's in the basement apartment," Linda said as she went down the small flight of steps to a green door with the paint flaking off it.

She knocked. "Ginny? You in there?" They listened for an answer but didn't hear one. She knocked again, a little louder. Still no answer.

Jude looked at Linda, arched his eyebrows. "Should we?" he asked.

She frowned. "Yeah, I think we should. You've got me a little spooked now."

Jude put his shoulder into the door, trying to bust it open. It didn't move. He backed up as much as he could on the basement stoop and prepared himself for another crack at it.

"Hang on," Linda said. "Did you try the handle?"

He reached for the handle. It turned in his hand, and the door creaked open. He looked at Linda and shrugged, then waved her inside first.

They walked in slowly. "Ginny?" Linda called. "You here, honey?" No answer.

They came to the living room, where Ginny sat at a card table, staring at the wall. In front of her was a pad of paper and a large bottle of pills.

Linda rushed over and put her hand to Ginny's cheek as if to check her temperature. "You okay, dear? I—we—just wanted to check on you." Ginny didn't answer; she simply stared at the wall.

Jude entered the room, and the metallic tang of copper assaulted his tongue. He hesitated as Linda looked at him. "What is it?" she said.

"Nothing. Check the bottle of pills." He motioned to the prescription bottle.

Ginny broke her silence. "I haven't taken any. Yet."

Linda looked at Jude, her eyes asking him what they should do. Jude moved across the room and pulled a folding chair up to the table. "Ginny," he said softly, "I'm—"

"The guy from last night," she finished, looking at him. "Peach pie."

He nodded. "We were worried . . . something was wrong."

"That's right, dear," Linda joined in. "Do you want me to get you water or something?"

"No," Ginny said, her gaze fixed on Jude. "What made you think something was wrong?" she asked.

"You wouldn't believe me, and it's not important anyway." He started to reach across the table to touch her hand, then stopped. "I . . . I know this sounds weird, but I need to touch you for just a minute, I think."

"Oh, good gravy," Linda blurted out. "You *are* a pervert. I knew it." She started to open her purse.

Ginny looked calm, almost expectant. As if, on some level, she had been waiting for them to come crashing through her door. "No, wait, Linda," Ginny said, eyeing Jude. "It's okay." Linda stopped but kept one hand in her purse.

Ginny put both her hands on the table and nodded at Jude.

Another headache was starting to buzz inside his skull. He wasn't used to all this talk. In the past day he'd spoken more than he had in the past year. Even worse was the touching; it made his skin itch to think about it. Still, he needed to touch Ginny, because he needed to *know*.

He put his hand on top of hers. Instantly a new film-negative vision began.

In the vision, Ginny sat at her card table, writing on the pad. He could barely make out her features. The deep oranges and blacks of the vision combined to make her face look like a ghastly skull, the eyes hidden in dark ovals of black. Abruptly, in the vision, Ginny put down her pencil, reached for the bottle, poured an assortment on the table, and began stuffing them in her mouth.

The scene hyper-rewound and came to a stop on Ginny in a doctor's office, sitting on a bench. Tears squeezed from her eyes—still sunken and hidden, even though the tears were obvious—and trickled down her face.

Yet again the scene hyper-rewound, then stopped on Ginny sitting in front of an empty canvas. She studied the canvas before tracing a streak of dark purple across it with a brush.

Suddenly the vision ended, and Jude felt like a door that had suddenly been slammed shut against a wailing storm outside. The world snapped back into focus as he shook his head, looking down at the table.

"You okay?" Ginny asked.

"You grew up in Butte. Your parents are John and Shelly. You loved playing softball in high school. Catcher."

"All right, I'm calling the police," Linda said, moving for the phone. Ginny reached out and grabbed Linda's arm, stopping her.

"Yeah, that's all true," Ginny said.

"You need to know, before you do something drastic," he said, his eyes dropping to the bottle of pills, "that you can tell your parents your secret. That they will love you, no matter what. That someday your painting career will go somewhere. That this—" he waved his hand in the air, indicating the nearly empty apartment—"this isn't *who* you are. It's *where* you are. And that, when you think no one else is listening . . . God is." The word *God* felt unnatural and foreign in his mouth, as if he were trying to chew on something too big. Jude was stunned even to hear himself say it. After God had taken his mother, after he'd ridiculed people for their bumbling attempts to convert him, he was now spouting the same gibberish? It didn't make any sense.

Tears brimmed in Ginny's eyes. "Excuse me," she said, then got up from the table and went toward the bathroom.

Jude stood and caught Linda staring at him, her mouth agape. The look in her eyes was one he knew well from his previous life as everybody's favorite life-after-death boy: part wonder, part fear. "I don't know who you are," she whispered after a few seconds, "but thank you."

He nodded. "Do you think she'll be okay now?"

"I'll make sure of it," she answered.

Jude turned to head for the door again, then stopped and looked back to Linda. "I don't know who I am, either."

15

FREEZING
Eight Years Ago

The third death started uneventfully enough. Jude was twenty-four then, a couple of years out of college, and still at his first job. He had earned his degree in business administration, a generic kind of diploma he knew was a big disappointment for some. His father, for one. William Allman was of the firm belief you didn't need a piece of paper to tell you—or anyone else, for that matter—you were smart enough to do something. *He* didn't have one, and he did fine for himself. He saw Jude's desire to go to college as a sign of weakness, an admission he was somehow deficient and in need of something more.

Jude's mother, on the other hand, nearly did a back handspring when Jude was accepted. She came from a hard family, a very hard family, and Jude would be the first one ever to attend a university. In fact, Jude had already gone further than most in the family—including his mother—just by finishing high school.

In the end, Jude's mother probably wouldn't have cared if he had decided to study underwater basket weaving; she brimmed with pride just to have Jude an actual, living, breathing college student.

Others, of course, had different ideas about what Jude should study. The general consensus among people who slightly knew him, and those who simply knew *of* him, assumed he'd declare pre-med and later head off to medical school. It was an obvious choice. The guy who had come back to life a couple of times, well, who wouldn't want him as a doctor?

Still, he eliminated medicine early on. First, he'd always hated hospitals. Second, it would have vindicated all the people who were experts on his life, even though they'd never met him.

He received letters from some of these people occasionally. Most came from the rural parts of Nebraska, but some filtered in from out of state, as well. The writers wondered if Jude could help them by contacting a dead relative, or by telling them if aliens had mutilated cattle at so-and-so's farm, or by healing someone who was sick and who didn't have long to live.

Jude had never billed himself as a psychic—had, in fact, spoken as little as possible about his two deaths. But that didn't stop other people from talking about it.

The business degree, then, was partly a stand for independence, partly a way to slide into comforting anonymity. Sure, a lot of people had business degrees. That was the point.

After graduating from college, he took his first job in South Dakota, working in the marketing department for a farm equipment manufacturer. They made the giant harvesters that mowed through grain fields across Nebraska and the Midwest each autumn. He liked the work, liked his office mates, liked being out on his own.

As an added bonus he got to leave Nebraska, and no one in South Dakota knew him as The Comeback Kid, a moniker the columnist in Jude's hometown weekly had given him after his second death.

The town where he worked in South Dakota wasn't far from Bingham, and he traveled home once every couple of months to see his family and a few friends. By this time, Kevin had gone to Iowa City or someplace like that to work as an engineer for a company Jude couldn't remember. But there were a few other friends around. A few.

The holidays rolled around, and Jude's company closed its offices between Christmas and New Year's Day. Going home was never a question; Jude wanted to see his mother, have a few bites of her peanut butter fudge, sit in her house, and watch the snow fall softly outside.

He packed his car with a single duffle bag before hitting the interstate for what was typically a three-hour trip.

When he left his apartment in South Dakota, a light snow was falling, puffy swabs of cotton that fluttered in a kind of slow waltz. After an hour on the road, the snow changed to something heavier and wetter.

Jude turned on the radio, flipped through AM stations until he found one talking about the weather. Parts of South Dakota and Nebraska, the radio told him, were under a severe blizzard watch, and people were urged to stay indoors except for emergencies.

He hadn't checked the weather or road conditions before leaving. He never did, mainly because the drive had never given him any problems before. He knew it well.

The blizzard watch proved to be well-founded. Soon Jude's car slowed to a crawl while the storm around him clamped its jaws tight and held on. Still, Jude refused to stop; if he did that, he might not get moving again before the storm's end. Besides, it was a regionalized storm, and he had to come out of the other side of it at some point. One more mile, he kept telling himself, and the storm would let up. Five more miles and he'd be on mostly dry roads again. That was what winter driving was all about; he'd seen it happen countless times before.

Until the car slid beneath him.

For a second it seemed as if he were on a carnival ride, a Tilt-A-Whirl maybe, but then he felt a scrape and heard a muffled *chunk* as the car settled into the ditch. He put the car in reverse and hit the accelerator, knowing before he tried that it was useless. He was stuck. He thought about getting out of the car, trying to dig out the snow from under his tires and give himself some traction, but dropped the idea. Many people in this situation would ruin their tires by spinning the tread off or burning all their fuel. Jude was too smart for that. He was a college graduate, wasn't he? He was here for the duration of the storm, unless a snowplow or someone else happened by.

He hadn't packed lots of clothes for the trip, though enough to put on a few extra layers. But when he checked his fuel gauge, he realized he wasn't sitting in the best place: just above an eighth of a tank. Okay, so much for feeling good about being the smart college kid.

He could start the car and run its heater intermittently, but if he was here for more than a few hours, he'd be sitting with an empty tank. And it wouldn't take long for the frigid winds whipping across South Dakota to find the cracks in his car, slide in their fingers and grab hold.

On the radio, a caller was asking some blowhard about American dependence on oil from the Persian Gulf. Jude sighed, turned off his ignition. If he were going to wait out this storm, it wouldn't do him any good to conserve gasoline and waste his battery.

Jude slid down in his seat and tried to nap. He had no way of knowing the blizzard would be the worst one the Midwest had seen in more than a decade.

Nor did he know it would take three and a half days for his car to be found.

Jude woke up, yet again, in a hospital bed. And yet again, he needed a few moments to get his bearings.

He knew instantly what had happened. The taste in his mouth, the sickly taste of pennies at the back of his throat, told him. He had died again. Ghost images, images of the recent past, whispered in his mind, but he pushed them away. He'd never asked to go to the Other Side once, let alone three times, and he wasn't about to dwell on its lingering aftereffects now. Other people would do plenty of that if they found out. The copper taste told him more than he wanted to know.

A nurse walked into the room, her face calm and composed until she noticed he was awake. She stopped as if hitting an invisible wall, then gave a weak smile and backed out of the room again.

Jude heard hushed whispers outside his door before a middle-aged, white-haired man walked into the room and fixed his gaze on

Jude. He waited a moment, pursed his lips as if struggling to find the right words. "Let me just say," said the doctor, "that I can't explain why you're here."

Jude felt a familiar draining sensation in his extremities—actually *heard* the blood slowing in his own veins. He knew what the doctor was about to say, and he wanted to shut him up, tell him to turn around and forget about it all. It wasn't possible once, let alone three times.

Still, he had other things to consider. Other people to consider. If others found out, it would be mayhem. Perhaps, if he talked to the doctor, convinced him to keep all of this quiet, he might be able to get ahead of it and squash the flare-up before it became a raging fire.

"Does anybody else know?" Jude asked the doctor, trying to seem nonchalant.

"Know what?"

"That I . . . about me."

"You came in yesterday. And when you . . . um . . . revived, and we figured out who you were, well . . ." He paused, filled his lungs with fresh air. "It just snowballed from there. The hospital held a press conference this morning."

There it was. Already he was facing a monster, a monster with giant, sharp teeth ready to grind him to nothingness.

Even worse, the doctor still had something on his mind. "When you came in, you were dead," the white-haired man of medicine began. "And let me be clear here: not just clinically dead, but stone cold dead, if you don't mind my harsh language."

"I've heard it before." He knew the doctor would assume he meant the language, but he really *had* heard it before.

"You were past *liver mortis*, when the blood settles into the lowest parts of the body; your blood was even jelled and coagulated due to the temperature extremes. For that matter, you were past *rigor mortis*, when your muscles stiffen." The doctor stopped, waiting, Jude assumed, for a comment or reaction. Jude simply closed his eyes and waited to ride out the wave; the doctor had to get through his epiphany, and Jude had to listen. He knew that. He didn't like it, but he knew it.

"You have no frostbite on your extremities, no lung or brain function abnormalities. As far as I can tell, you didn't even catch a cold. All I can say is: there must be a very good reason why you're still here, because there are a thousand reasons why you *shouldn't* be."

Jude kept his eyes closed.

"Do you understand what all of this means?" the doctor asked, his voice going shrill and strident. The doctor wanted some meaning, some bit of philosophy from Jude that would put his mind at ease and restore his faith in natural order. But Jude didn't feel like playing the part yet. He needed time to build himself up.

It was like having a broken arm. The first time, it's a learning experience, because it's new. The second time, it's worse, because you remember how long it took to recover. And if you're unlucky enough to break your arm a third time, well, you just want to chop the damn thing off and be rid of it.

Jude rolled his head toward the sound of the doctor's voice and opened his eyes. "I have a pretty good idea, Doc."

The doctor stood in silence for a few moments, then looked down. "Well, if you have any questions, I'll try to answer them," he said, defeated.

"Just one," Jude said. "When do I get out of here?"

Jude half expected the doctor to keep him for a few days, make him his pet project of discovery. It had happened before. But in reality the man had reacted the opposite way: he seemed eager to get rid of Jude, forget all about the incident. So, he only kept Jude for twenty-four more hours of observation before releasing him.

Jude was ready to leave, of course. Now, more than ever, hospitals had come to represent everything that was wrong in his life. And his death.

When the discharge orders came, he dressed quickly, then sat on the bed to tie his shoes. That morning on the phone, his mom had said she wanted to drive to South Dakota and meet him, but he nixed the idea. He just wanted to book a quick flight and get home. His three-hour drive had somehow stretched into a five-day nightmare, and he was ready to wake from it as soon as possible.

As he finished with his shoes, he noticed a few uniformed police officers step inside the doorway. Had he hit someone before sliding off the road? Was he getting slapped with a DUI? No, that couldn't be, he knew.

He nodded at the officer closest to him, and the officer nodded back.

"What's up?" Jude asked.

"Not much."

Jude smiled. "What I mean is, why are you here?"

"We're to escort you to the airport."

Escort? "Any particular reason?" he asked.

The officer smiled. "Haven't you seen?" he said. Jude shook his head. "A few people out there," he said as he glanced at his partner.

Jude didn't like the sound of that, but he stood. "Let's get rolling, then."

Jude walked out the door with the two officers. Six more waited in the hallway. All of them avoided eye contact, but most stared when they thought he couldn't see.

An escort of eight police officers. Not a good sign. He ran a hand across his face as he expelled a wearied sigh. "Well, let's get this over with."

The policemen formed a phalanx around him and began to march down the hallway toward the swinging metal doors. Even from this distance Jude could hear people on the other side of the doors. Already he could tell the police officer's comment about "a few people out there" might win a contest of understatements.

He'd been to the Other Side once again. Now it was time to face the other side of the hospital doors. He gulped in a few deep breaths, smelling and tasting the artificial, antiseptic air of the hospital. He pictured the air of the hospital drying him out like a raisin in the sun; only the fresh air outside would restore him, make him whole again. He closed his eyes for a few steps, imagining himself walking on a forest path covered with pine needles and aspen leaves, the smell of earth and dew thick and fragrant in the air around him.

They came to the doors. The policeman in the front looked through the small windows into the hospital lobby and appeared to exchange some brief communication with people on the other side.

Some sort of signal must have been given, because in a heartbeat they crashed through the doors and into chaos. Popping flashes blinded him, and everywhere he felt the yellow-hot glare of television cameras, all trying to capture the first images of Jude Allman trying to leave the hospital.

A sea of mechanized whirs, shouted questions, and jarring bodies washed over them. Jude thought of British soccer matches he'd seen, when masses of spectators joined and became one mindless beast, swaying out of control like a drunkard.

He didn't realize he'd stopped until he felt the officers behind him pushing, inching him through the crowd toward the other side of the lobby. The policemen all had their clubs drawn now, and some were using plastic shields to clear a pathway. As they moved, individual faces emerged from the mass and somehow managed to reach Jude, even through the small army of uniformed officers surrounding him.

A television reporter with stiff hair thrust a microphone in his face. "Can you tell us what you saw?" he asked before the officers closed the breach and pushed him back into the masses.

A Hispanic woman somehow managed to pace the officers for a few steps. She lifted a young girl into the air. "My daughter is blind," she shouted. "Heal her!"

A sweaty bald man with a paunch crawled into Jude's circle on his hands and knees. "The lottery numbers," he hissed. "Gimme the lottery numbers." He grabbed Jude's pant leg and tried to stand, but people outside the tight circle were clawing and pulling him back even before the officers had their hands on him.

The sea spat another woman into the circle, this one with a look of wild-eyed panic in her eyes. "A lock of hair," she chattered. "I just want a lock of hair." She lunged; one of the policemen caught her and started pushing her away, but not before she had Jude's hair in her hand. A patch came off in her hand, and his eyes immediately watered in pain.

The moving mass of uniformed policemen stopped. It was too much. Their exit still seemed too far away. Jude dimly wondered how all these people had managed to crowd into the lobby area; local fire marshals were probably having brain aneurisms.

For a moment, Jude panicked. When they had stopped, the ring of police officers had closed in, forming a tight ball around him, and he was sure the crowd would continue to push until he was crushed.

But then they started to move again, this time to the right. Jude struggled to see. Someone had opened an emergency exit. The alarms must surely be sounding, he thought, but he couldn't hear them above the melee.

They approached the emergency exit, and Jude spotted the woman who had obviously opened the door. She simply looked at him, a warm smile on her face, as he passed. Jude felt as if all of it must have happened in slow motion, except he knew that of course it couldn't have. She made no effort to join the crush and break through. She simply stared at Jude as he passed, then gave him a slight nod.

Bodies closed the gap around her as groping hands pushed Jude through the doors into the street outside and on toward a waiting police car.

On a crisp autumn morning Jude stood on Rachel's porch. Again. Unsure what to do. Again. Maybe even more so, since Rachel hadn't really invited him over this time. And, because it was morning, she'd probably be getting ready for work.

His legs wanted to back off the porch, then stretch out and run forever. Most of his body agreed with his legs. But his mind, with its newfound sense of both wonder and deep puzzlement, wanted him to ring Rachel's doorbell.

He pressed the button and waited. Muffled sounds inside made their way toward the door. It still wasn't too late to listen to his legs; with just a few steps he could be—

The door swung open. For an instant, the fine line of a pucker crossed Rachel's lips, followed by a forced smile. "Oh, hi," she said and dropped her gaze. "I . . . I guess I didn't know you were coming over today."

"Neither did I. Can I come in?"

"Um, Nathan's not here. Nicole and Bradley already picked him up for school."

"That's okay. I'm actually here to see you." He had obviously caught her in the middle of her morning routine; her hair was still wet, and the makeup on her face was somewhere between just-started and ready-to-go.

She stepped back and let him in, then closed the door and followed him into the living room. "Do you want some coffee?" she asked. "I still have some warm."

"No, thanks," he answered. "I usually stay away from coffee. It makes me nervous."

"Scary thought," she said. He nodded at the joke. Paranoia humor. He was fond of it himself, occasionally.

"Am I making you late?" he asked.

"Not at all. I own the place. What are they gonna do, fire me?" She smiled. "Um, if you could just give me a few minutes to finish up. . . ?"

"Oh, sure, sure. Sorry to just, you know, barge in."

"No big whoop. Actually it's kind of a nice surprise," she said, and he could tell from the look in her eyes that she meant it. He looked down at the floor, uncomfortable to have her eyes on him. After a few moments he heard her move down the hall.

He had been in Rachel's home many times, but he'd never really paid attention to it. This time, as he sat, he discovered plenty of interesting knickknacks and doodads populating her shelves and walls. Rachel was obviously a collector, like his mother had been. His mom had always loved to garage sale (in his mother's world, the term *garage sale* was a verb), always bringing back an armful of junk—or *junque*, depending on your point of view—and a mouthful of stories each time she went.

Jude liked to garage sale with her. Sometimes. He always started the day filled with hope and excitement. What kinds of toys might he find? Books? Comics? Records? But his body could only run on excitement for thirty minutes, and garage-saling was never a thirty-minute activity. His mother spent whole afternoons scanning table after table, watchful for *uh-ohs*.

Uh-ohs. That was what she called them: valuable items sold for a pittance by hapless schleps who didn't know better. His mother could smell amateurs immediately, always using them to her advantage.

His mother's greatest uh-oh had been a vase of some kind—what was it?—Rosewood. Roseville. A Roseville vase worth about $750. She knew the vase and its approximate value instantly, but she didn't pay $750. Instead she got it for two bucks. Two bucks. She'd even haggled with the seller on the price; he wanted three, she offered two, and the guy took it.

When they got to the car and his mom explained how much the vase was worth, Jude asked why she had bargained on the price. If she knew it was worth $750, why couldn't she pay three dollars for it? "Because," she had answered, "that's what garage-saling is all about. You dicker. If you don't dicker, the seller is insulted."

Jude doubted most people would be insulted by such practices, but he didn't argue.

Back in the present, he shook his head.

Funny he should remember that bit about his mom. Recently, long-dormant images of her had begun to flicker again—oddly enough, around the same time the headaches worsened. The memories were there, like echoes left on his pupils by a bright flashbulb. When he tried to look at them, they swam out of his vision; but if he didn't concentrate on them, they popped into his mind, formed, and became solid again. His haunted past.

"Okay, I'm ready." Rachel stood at the living room's doorway, dressed in pastel pink with a scarf around her throat. He hadn't looked at her—really looked—for years, and he caught his breath. She was beautiful. Too beautiful for a paranoid janitor with past lives to hide. He lowered his gaze, staring instead at a dish on the coffee table. Maybe it was even a Roseville dish.

Rachel sat on the sofa and paused. "Soooo . . ." she said, coaxing him to talk.

He smiled. "Yeah, I know. I'm not really sure why I'm here. But something odd has been happening—"

"Odd?"

He saw concern spreading across her face, and she was biting her lip. Of course she would be concerned. She knew he had always been a little . . . unbalanced. And to hear him talking about something odd was probably, well, alarming. He needed to be more specific.

"I was at the Red Lodge Cafe a few days ago, and I felt . . . I don't know, something about the waitress."

She stiffened. "You came to tell me you have the hots for some waitress?"

He laughed, actually laughed, for the first time in what felt like eons. "No, no. Nothing like that. I mean, it was the same kind of thing as the guy getting hit by a car. Which you don't know anything about, but—"

"I heard about it."

He stopped and narrowed his eyes. "You heard? Was someone . . . following me?"

Rachel suppressed a laugh of her own. "Nicole—Bradley's mom— said she saw you doing CPR."

"Well, it wasn't really CPR. It was . . . I don't know. I tasted metal in my mouth, you know? And I knew I was supposed to talk to him, tell him something. Then, afterward, the same thing with the waitress."

He stopped, knowing he was sounding worse than ever.

"You know," he finally said, "maybe I will have that coffee after all. This is gonna take a while."

When he finished talking, his coffee was long gone and his tongue dry. He had started speaking, hesitant and nervous, but then had caught a wave and held onto it, riding it out as he told Rachel all about the events of the last two days. Most of the events, anyway. He left out the parts about Kristina and his previous life. Those stories weren't ready to be told. *Keep it secret, keep it safe.*

Jude had been half afraid she would laugh, roll her eyes, or maybe just lean back into her couch and cross her arms. He had been up close and personal with his good friend paranoia for some time; Rachel might easily see all this as some outgrowth of his delusion and suggest he spend a time in a relaxing "facility" filled with "people who could help." In reversed roles, he guessed that was essentially what he would have done. He himself wasn't fully convinced of it; the visions and blackouts constantly nagged at him, making him feel he was experiencing things that weren't real. Or maybe even forgetting things that were.

But Rachel didn't do any of that. She listened. She asked questions. She stopped him a couple of times and made him back up or fill in some blank spaces he'd left out.

When he finished, she sat in silence for a few minutes before speaking. "So what you're saying is," she began, "you're hearing voices that tell you things about other people."

He felt his face flush. He had read all the signs wrong. She *did* think he'd jumped headfirst into Mentalville. "No," he said. "It's not like I'm crazy or anything." He saw the look on her face and stopped. "Okay, a little crazy. Paranoid. I'll give you that. But I'm not totally nuts. They're not voices or anything; they're like . . ." He cringed. "They're like revelations."

"Calm down, Ron," she said. "I'm not saying you're any more crazy than usual. I just wanted to see how you felt about it."

"What do you mean?"

She shrugged. "I guess I feel like if you can admit that it *sounds* crazy, you probably aren't. I mean, if you were really in serious trouble mentally, I think you'd be totally out of touch with reality."

Jude nodded. "Sounds good to me." Still, he faltered a bit. He remembered, not so long ago, thinking people who became paranoid wouldn't realize it was happening. Yet, he *knew* about his paranoia, felt it brewing within him all the time. What was to stop him from heading on down to that next exit labeled *delusional psychotic?*

"I've been thinking about a few things," she said. She stopped and bit at her lip for a few seconds. "You said you tasted copper."

"Yeah."

"Are you sure it was copper?"

"Well, I'm not saying it was actual copper or anything. Just the taste."

"A lot of people say blood tastes like copper."

He studied her face for a moment. "I'm not sure that makes me feel any better," he said.

"Didn't say it to make you feel better. I said it because I think you may be tasting blood."

"Why blood? What does it mean?"

"I don't know. What does copper mean? Blood just seems more sensible. Maybe you're biting your tongue without knowing about it. Don't take this wrong, but your talking about odd tastes, and odd images . . . sounds a bit like seizures."

"Seizures?"

"Maybe. I'm not saying that's the case at all. I just think, maybe, you should go to a doctor." She paused, and Jude could tell she was considering her next words carefully. "I'll . . . pray for you."

Praying. God. Yes, that had been part of it; he had waxed eloquent about God to the waitress, despite the fact that he and God weren't exactly on speaking terms. In some strange way he could sense it was because the waitress herself was struggling with her belief in a god.

"You believe in God," he said, more a question than a statement.

He saw a new fire dance in her eyes. "Yes," she said.

He nodded, sensing she wanted him to keep going. But he'd already spoken more in one day than he had in years; his nerves felt raw and frayed, overexposed. God was the last thing he wanted to talk about, because his mother was the last thing he wanted to think about.

Instead he turned his focus inside. Was he, as Kristina hinted, something more? Or was he simply something much less? Maybe he *was* having seizures, doing things he couldn't remember. It seemed possible, even probable, considering how the memories of his past were all so neatly buried.

"So what are you gonna do now?" Rachel asked.

"Well, I took the day off. I'm going to . . . see my father."

She paused again before answering. "I didn't know you still had a dad," she said.

"A lot of things you don't know about me." He huffed to himself, then added, "A lot of things *I* don't know about me."

"Where is he?"

"Billings."

She nodded. "How long?"

"Actually, I came to Montana when he moved to the retirement home. Until then he'd spent his whole life in a small town in Nebraska. Place called Bingham. That was right after . . ." He paused, catching the thought he wanted to say: *Right after God killed my mother.* "Right after my mother died," he finished instead.

"So you moved to Montana to be close to your dad, but you've never gone to see him."

She stopped there, obviously wanting to let the thought sink in. Yes, he knew that. Yes, it was true. But so what? She didn't know his dad, what had happened between them. He blinked a few times, realizing *he* couldn't think of a lot of things that had happened between them. Most memories of his father were vague or absent. Over the past few days memories of his young childhood had been sparking in his mind here and there, like stars winking on at nightfall. But other than the kite thing, they were all memories of his mother.

"Why now?" she pressed.

Good question. He hadn't talked to his father in years. Hadn't thought about him in almost as long. They were in separate galaxies, with a wide gulf between them. In his mind's eye his mother's face was a bright, golden-hued, soft focus picture. His father's face, on the other hand, was a blank. There was a feeling of love there, somewhere. But also fear, fueled by a vaporous sense of . . . bad things. He didn't know what or why, and he wasn't sure he wanted to.

So why did he feel he needed to see his dad? His mother was dead, for one. She'd passed away several years ago. But there was more to it than that. He also wanted some answers, some gaps in his memory filled. He could now recall more details about his own deaths, and even mundane facts such as his favorite ice cream—mint chocolate chip—and that Kim Oakley lived on Walnut Street back in Bingham. But other chunks, bigger chunks, were still missing. He'd read once that David Bowie couldn't remember one whole year of his life. Jude felt the same. True, he'd tried his best to forget much of it, but it was coming back in snippets. And with each flash of a memory, a growing part of him was hungry to find out more, remember new things.

Jude realized he hadn't answered Rachel's question. "I don't know why I'm going now," he said. "I just feel like I need to."

She nodded, waited for him to talk more. He looked down at her couch and watched the sunlight streaming in through the window, lighting the dust particles in the air. He put his hand in the midst of the sunbeam, splaying his fingers.

"You ever notice about the air?" Jude asked. "How it has all these particles in it—the dust, you know—but you can't see the dust unless it's in the bright light?"

She nodded. "Reminds me of a song I sang when I was a girl."

"'Dust in the Wind'?"

"'Jesus Wants Me for a Sunbeam.'"

Frank crumpled the newspaper in disgust and pushed it off the table. He'd only been able to complete eight or nine words on today's puzzle, his worst day of the week so far. Number twenty-nine across: capital of South Carolina. Who cares? He'd never been to South Carolina, and he never planned to go. Why did these crossword people feel South Carolina was so special?

Forget it, he told himself as he turned to the *People* magazine on the table. The cover image was of a young actress who had risen to fame doing family-friendly films in her teens but was now raising some eyebrows by playing a prostitute in her latest role. Frank picked up his coffee and sipped it as he stared at the cover. Yeah, there was something comforting, something soothing, about *People* magazine. Especially after a skull-breaker of a puzzle.

He heard a clank outside the break room and paused, the coffee cup halfway to his lips for another drink. He listened, letting the cup sink back to the table. Cocked his head to the side to get a different angle. Nothing else. He shivered a bit, then shook his head and took another drink. Coffee time was a bit quiet without Ron around; guy hadn't missed a day the last two years, and now he'd just decided to take some time off out of the blue. Good for him. Still, Frank hadn't been alone in the break room for quite a while, and it was giving him both the heebies and the jeebies.

He turned his attention back to the cover of *People,* looking at the actress's seductive gaze. How unfortunate she'd decided to sell herself out. She'd been such an adorable little girl, on screen since about age ten, and he'd always liked the innocence he'd seen in her eyes. She'd even kept that virtue through the bad years, the middle school and high school years when kids became uppity and decided they really weren't kids anymore.

When they lost the magic.

Yeah, this actress had kept it longer than most, but it was painfully obvious she'd lost the magic now. He drained the last of his coffee, brushed a few grounds off his tongue, and decided he didn't want to look at *People* after all. The photo of the actress was wrong, and it ruined the experience.

He thought, instead, of the actress's eyes—of her eyes as a young girl. Sparkling, they were. And that, in turn, made him think of his True Work. After all, it was all about capturing the magic of childhood, wasn't it? Of preserving that sparkle he so much liked to see in their eyes?

He looked at the clock on the wall and rolled his tongue around the inside of his mouth, considering. Maybe he could take a little time off himself. Spend a little time in his basement. Matter of fact, he needed to sharpen some of his tools, didn't he? They were dulling, he could tell that just last night when he'd been working with them. They needed honing, a little time on the grinder and the strap.

He licked his lips, excited by the thoughts forming in his head. He rose, a smile spreading across his face as he went to put away all the supplies and lock up.

Certainly it was too late to save the magic in the young actress's eyes. But there were other kids, so many other kids still out there— kids with magical eyes that begged to see. He could show them, couldn't he?

Yes, he could.

Jude pulled his car into the parking lot of the nursing home, turned off the ignition, and stared at the front doors. Somewhere inside the building was his father, William Allman. And somewhere inside William Allman were answers to questions Jude was just beginning to ask.

The front doors of the building slid open, and out walked a woman, holding the hand of a pigtailed young girl. Probably a mom and daughter visiting an aging grandparent. It was good the woman wanted her daughter to see . . .

He realized he didn't recall anything about his own grandparents. No names, no faces, no warm, inviting home. Nothing. The thought scared him.

Jude pulled his keys from the ignition and got out of the car, then walked toward the front doors. He couldn't think about what he was doing now; he needed to do it all in one sustained act. A pause would let him stop and back out.

The doors opened, inviting him to a front desk and a receptionist. He noted a cat wandering the halls and a couple of bird cages out in the lobby area. Pets, of course. The nursing home had pets for the residents whose own families had forgotten about them. In a way, he thought, it made perfect sense. Nursing homes and animal shelters shared a lot in common: they were places where people dropped unwanted family members they never wanted to see again.

The woman at the desk was waiting for him to speak.

"Um, William Allman?" he asked.

"Hold on a sec," she said as she clicked a few keys on her

computer keyboard and stared at the screen. After a few moments she had an answer. "Room 305."

"Thanks." He turned and started to walk, then realized he had no idea where he was going. He turned back around to find the woman smiling at him.

"Take a left here, follow the hallway around the curve, take another left and go in about five or so doorways. His name and picture will be on the door."

He nodded another thanks, then followed her instructions. As he walked to his father's room, he passed a menagerie of forgotten people—some dying, some already dead but not realizing it. Most sat in their rooms with the television blaring; one or two had visitors.

Jude passed a common area filled with people sitting motionless in wheelchairs. Only one of them seemed aware he was there, an old white-haired woman with a brushy mustache on her lip. She motioned to him.

"Weren't you in my class?" she asked.

"No, I don't think so."

"Sure you were. Class of '43, Baker High School. I'm Velda Barnes, remember?"

He started to correct her again but stopped himself and smiled. "Of course I remember you. Velda Barnes. Class of '43."

She smiled, her eyes studying a scene that played in her mind. She patted his hand, then started wheeling her chair down the hallway with one hand. He stood and watched for a moment before continuing on his way.

Before long he was at the door. As the receptionist had promised, his father's name was on a plaque mounted in the hallway. WILLIAM ALLMAN, it proclaimed in bold letters, beneath a photo of his father and mother standing on the porch of a farmhouse. Jude was not in the photo. The farmhouse seemed familiar to him, yet he couldn't quite place it.

Jude felt as if he were standing on Rachel's porch. He wanted to knock on the door, but he also wanted to turn and run. Slowly he reached out and rapped on it, then took a step back and waited. No answer. He started to knock again when a voice came from inside.

"Yeah," the gravelly growl said. He recognized it as his father's voice, of course, although the sound still startled him, and he couldn't quite make himself reach for the handle. On the other side of the door was a very real ghost from his past, and he was now quite sure he didn't want to talk to that ghost.

Again the voice came. "Who is it?"

Jude was now of the mind that coming to see his father was an all-around horrible idea. All he had to do was walk back down that hallway, then go back to the way things were. Maybe he could even keep the whole Kristina thing quiet, continue life as Ron Gress. It would be luxuriously quiet, free from distractions. Sure, he could pull it off.

Jude turned to walk away, almost running into a nurse. "Whoa, sorry," she said, "but it's time for his BP check." She grabbed the door handle. "You can come in, though. It'll only take a minute."

She opened the door and walked inside, leaving it open for him. The curtains were drawn, and the room's stifling darkness prevented Jude from seeing much. "Oh, it's just you," he heard his father's voice say to the nurse. "Why did you knock?"

"I didn't," the nurse said. "You have a visitor."

Jude stepped into the room, waiting for his eyes to adjust. In the corner, the nurse stood over a hunched figure in a lounge chair.

"Well, well," his father said. Jude expected something else to follow, but William stayed silent. Jude walked into the small room and chose a plastic chair opposite his father. The room smelled of detergent and sourness at the same time, as if something rotten had seeped into the walls. It was impossible to totally remove the smell of rot or putrefaction; as a janitor, Jude knew this.

The nurse put a blood pressure cuff on his dad's arm and squeezed the bulb. While the air leaked out of the cuff, Jude's eyes adjusted enough to let him see his father's features. Sure, he was still the same, in most respects. He seemed thinner—a lot thinner, maybe even gaunt. And his hair was more salt than pepper now. But he was still pretty much the same as the last time Jude had seen him. His deep-set eyes were closed as he leaned his head back on the chair; a scowl occupied his face while he waited for the nurse to finish.

The nurse abruptly took the stethoscope out of her ears, pulled off the cuff, and stood up in one fluid motion. The sudden burst of motion startled Jude, much like a flock of pheasants had once startled him by thrumming out of the brush during a hunting trip with William. (*There it was finally: a second memory of his father.*)

The nurse walked by Jude, giving him a forced smile as she moved toward the door. "Next meds in two hours, Mr. Allman," she called out before letting the door slip shut behind her.

William's eyes remained closed, and Jude thought he must have fallen asleep. Just as well. Jude felt like he was on the verge of hyperventilating, and he needed a chance to relax for a few minutes.

"Thought you'd forgotten your old man," his father said, keeping his eyes shut.

Jude cleared his throat, tried to think of something to say. William peeked open one eye.

"No, I didn't forget. I'm just . . . you might say I haven't been myself these past few years."

A humorless smile spread across his father's lips. "I can only imagine," he said as he adjusted himself in the chair. Something caught in William's chest and a bout of coughing gripped him. Jude stood up, but his father's hand waved him back down as he finished the brief outburst.

William opened his eyes again, put his hand on his chest. "Nuts to gettin' old," he said. "Congestive heart failure, they call it. High-falutin name for 'dying,' don't you think?" Jude nodded, unsure what sort of answer his father might be wanting.

"So, where you living?" William asked as he pulled out a handkerchief and dabbed at his mouth. This motion made William look much different than Jude's fractured memories; he was more frail, fragile.

"Red Lodge," Jude answered.

A pause. "Only about sixty miles away."

Jude nodded.

William half snorted, half chuckled. "Wondered where you've been hiding out, and here you are just down the road. Still have one or two folks track me down now and then, trying to find out where you are."

Jude sat up straight. "Looking for me? Like who?"

William shifted in his seat again, a pained look crossing his face. "Dunno. Reporters mostly, I suppose."

Jude nodded, wondering if Kristina had been this way recently. It was possible.

"Brings you all the way from Red Lodge?" his father asked.

Jude looked at the floor as he thought of what he wanted to say. He realized he should have practiced all this, rehearsed a speech of sorts. Anticipated what his father would say. But he hadn't, and now he was left to stumble along. "I'm not sure," he started, hoping other thoughts would come.

"See that," his father said.

"I was just thinking about, you know, me growing up and all. What it was like."

"Don't say." Another memory jolted Jude's system: his dad's annoying habit of talking in shorthand, clipping down sentences to one or two words when he was in a foul mood. Which was, he was now also remembering, most of the time.

"Did we ever . . . I don't remember much about you," Jude blurted. He looked back at the floor, avoiding his father's stare.

He heard another snort. "Odd as ever," William said. "What's it matter, anyway?"

Jude shrugged, finally looked up at his dad. "I guess it doesn't."

He started to stand again, and his dad waved him down a second time.

"Don't be so dramatic about everything," William said. "That always bugged me. Every little thing was like the end of the world to you." William stopped, as if waiting for Jude to fight back. Jude didn't.

Jude tried again. "I do remember a bit. I remember . . ." He swallowed. "I remember flying a big box kite with you." He studied his father's eyes for some sort of emotion or fondness but couldn't detect any.

"Hmmm. Wind *did* howl through there somethin' fierce." William paused, softened for a moment. But only a moment. "Guess you're not such a know-it-all these days, are you?"

Know-it-all? "What does that mean?"

His dad snorted. "What did any of it mean, Jude? How did you *know* all those things?" his dad shouted. He stared into Jude's eyes, fire and rage burning in his own. Jude held the stare, felt he *had* to hold the stare for reasons he didn't fully understand right now. After a few moments his father's face softened again, even seemed to age more. "So . . . you really don't remember," he whispered.

William took his handkerchief out and wiped at his mouth again. He put the handkerchief back, then reached for a pitcher on the TV tray next to his chair. Jude got to the pitcher first, poured two cups full, and handed one to his father. As Jude took a few shaky sips of his own, William said, "Think about the time the barn burned down," he said.

Jude sifted through his memories, doing a specific search for barn fires. No hits. He shook his head. "Don't remember."

"You knew about it before it happened," his dad said, looking him in the eye again. "You told me that morning, so when it *did* happen, I was ready to skin your back-end. I thought you started the fire, see?"

Jude nodded, unsure what else to do.

"And Mrs. Callahan's wreck?"

Jude couldn't recall such a woman, or such a wreck.

"You woke up crying and told me I should call Mrs. Callahan and tell her to stay home. Said she shouldn't go to church and play bingo, because something bad was going to happen. Don't you remember?"

Jude's tongue was thick and hairy, his mind gelatin. His father was talking about things that made no sense to him, scary things that crawled up and down his spine on icy legs.

"What about Elvis?" his dad continued.

Elvis? Did they have a pet named Elvis? A horse? Was one of the neighbors named Elvis?

"Elvis Presley? You don't remember Elvis Presley?" his father said, incredulous.

"Oh," Jude answered. "Yeah, sure."

"You told me he was going to die. I was playing one of his records on your mom's stereo, and you just walked in and said: 'He's going to die next week.' It was just so matter-of-fact. And, you were only like three or four at the time. That's not the way a three-year-old talks." William stopped and took another jittery sip from his cup.

Keep it secret, keep it safe. Jude said it to himself again, even opened his lips and mouthed it without realizing. But it wasn't comforting him anymore, instead only ringing hollow and empty. A new voice crowded into his head. Kristina's voice:

"I think there's something more to you."

"'Course, that was nothing compared to what you said about your mother," his father continued.

Jude, only half listening now, drained the rest of his water. But still his throat burned. He stood and poured more before he realized what his dad had just said. "Mom? What about her?" The fresh cup of water was poised halfway to his mouth.

His father remained silent.

"What about my mother?" Jude pressed, his voice rising in anger.

Jude could see his dad withdrawing, retreating, suddenly becoming very interested in the view out the window. "I'm getting pretty tired now," William finally said in a hushed tone. To prove his point, he put his head back against his easy chair and closed his eyes again, much as he'd done when the nurse checked his blood pressure.

"Look, I really don't remember," Jude said, trying to sound more calm.

William didn't open his eyes. "That's for the best. You mind shutting your door on the way out?"

Jude sat in the room all alone—sure, his dad was there, but he was all alone, to be sure—and fumed. He had come to get answers, and he would be leaving with even more questions. Was there something else about his mother's death he didn't know? He finally stood and stepped toward the door. "I'll come see you again soon," he said to his father.

"Do that," William said.

Jude slipped out the door and quietly closed it behind him.

Jude drove back to Red Lodge holding the steering wheel in a tight, white-knuckled grip. His mind tumbled and jumbled with images, all of them filled with white fury directed at his father.

Jude had never been emotional, even in the days before Ron Gress, and he wasn't prone to crying. But now, as his car moved down the road, he found tears welling in his eyes for the second time in a few days. He had weathered a long dry spell of some six years without any kind of emotion, and now it seemed he would be letting loose a flood fit for the Bible.

Jude started to sob, losing control as it overtook his body. He pulled to the side of the road and shifted the car into park, then put his head on the steering wheel and waited for the sobs to subside.

They didn't.

Jude opened his car door, dimly aware of the odd *ping-ping-ping* from the door alarm, then stumbled around the car to the ditch. A large field loomed before him. He scrambled over the barbed wire fence, dropped into the field, and started walking.

Then jogging.

Then running.

Long, thin reeds of grain, some of it high enough to reach his face, whipped at his skin and clothing. Who was he? What was he? Why was he? The questions pounded in his mind as he followed his feet through the field. He felt like he was waking from a dream, but the reality was much worse than the dream, wasn't it? He wanted to drift back into a long, unconscious sleep, where the world might not be logical, but made sense on a different level. Where the world didn't gouge at you with long claws.

Jude's foot found an uneven dirt clump and he went down, face first. He lay there a few moments, smelling the soil and closing his eyes. Then he rolled over and screamed at the sky above him, his face caked with dirt, sweat and tears.

On a bright autumn afternoon, Jude Allman lay in a broad field, surrounded by reeds of grain, bawling like a newborn.

His latest Quarry had been a surprise. Most lasted a few days, then turned stiff and unresponsive. The brain seemed to send signals, telling the body to shut down and block out surrounding stimuli. When that happened, it signaled the Quarry was no longer terrified. And therefore no longer exciting.

And he would then have to face that unpleasant killing part.

But this particular Quarry was something special. The Quarry still struggled, still screamed, still stayed active after four days—even in the cramped and confined space. Maybe this one would be the magical, transformative event he had dreamed of for years. Maybe this one would stay special forever and wouldn't have to die.

The Hunter smiled. That was the Normal thinking. The Normal didn't like the hunting or killing. Or so the Normal would say if he were asked. The Hunter knew better, knew that at the very moment he was about to pull a Quarry into the car, the Normal was right there alongside, panting with excitement and anticipation.

He had been concerned, of late, that he was a split personality. He'd seen a science program on his television and thought maybe that would explain how he *became.* He did some web surfing, read up on the subject, then quickly discarded the notion. Split personalities, the research said, usually weren't aware of each other. Stress triggered their changes. And, well, split personalities were pathetic. All of them. Some of them whiney, some of them puffed up and full of themselves, some of them even small children. Certainly the Normal loved young children, had a certain affection for them, but he, the Hunter, saw them for what they truly were: Quarry to be stalked.

No, he most certainly was not a split personality. Whereas most people were only one, he was simply two. He had *become*, like a beautiful butterfly. Each of his sides had a role, a purpose. Christians talked of the Holy Trinity, three persons in one being. He was the Holy Duality.

Even so, he knew the Normal wasn't that normal at all. The Normal just liked to pretend—wanted to have all the fun, without sullying his hands in any of the dirty work.

But the Normal's shameful secret was: he was beginning to *like* sullying his hands. That had caused an unpleasant little bit of trouble earlier in the week, when the Normal wanted to cross the line ahead of the Hunter.

He had taken care of that. He pressed a finger to his temple, felt the small scab, smiled to himself again.

Then, he opened the door to the basement where the Quarry was confined, still screaming.

Still special.

An odd new sensation began to trouble Jude as he drove back to Red Lodge: he was scared to go home and be by himself. Right now it seemed too confined, too constricting.

He was alone. Truly alone. He once had a mother who loved him, a father of sorts, but he was still alone, a cosmic orphan.

As Jude guided his car down Broadway Avenue, the bright neon tipi of the Red Lodge Cafe blinked, reflecting on the windshield. He pulled to the curb and parked, then looked at his watch. Just after six in the evening and he hadn't eaten since . . . he couldn't remember. He opened his door, stepped onto the sidewalk, and headed for the cafe.

The cafe door tinkled open with the sound of the familiar cowbell, and comforting smells of gravy, bread, frying hamburger, and other scents greeted him. He was hungry. Starving.

But that wasn't the only reason he was here. He wandered to a booth and sat down, his eyes darting through the place for a familiar face. Then, she came out of the kitchen, carrying a single plate. She slid a plate in front of a man sitting at the counter as she scanned the restaurant for new faces. Her eyes settled on Jude.

She picked up a menu and walked to his booth.

"How ya doin', Ginny?" Jude asked.

She smiled, really smiled, and he had to do the same. "I'm fine, just fine, Ron."

He stopped. "How'd you know my name?" he asked.

"What, you think you can come into my apartment and pull a

stunt like that and I won't check up on you?"

Jude didn't like where this was heading. First Kristina, then Ginny, digging into the life and times of Ron Gress. Kristina had been the first to make the connection, but she probably wouldn't be the last.

Ginny caught the look in his eye. "Sheesh, I didn't run an FBI check on you or anything. Just asked around. Be surprised what a waitress with a smile can find out in a small town."

He relaxed; she was harmless, of course. "Nothing surprises me anymore," he said.

"Famous last words." She put a menu in front of him. As she did, she leaned over and put her hand on his. "I called my parents. I'm going home in a few weeks."

"And the baby?"

She patted her stomach. "Just fine. I feel like it will be kind of a miracle baby after . . . you know."

A miracle. Jude smiled. "Thanks."

She took out her pen. "What do we feel like tonight?"

"Why don't you get me the special?"

"Chicken fried steak?"

"Sounds great."

She took the menu away and retreated into the kitchen. Jude felt drained and tired, his muscles aching from adrenaline overload. Maybe he'd ask Ginny for some coffee when she came back. For now, he'd settle for a few splashes of cold water on his face.

Jude slid out of the booth and walked to the rest room at the back of the cafe. As he stood in one of the stalls, a now-familiar taste came to his mouth.

Copper.

Copper, coating the inside of his mouth with its metallic tang. Copper, hot and molten, sliding down his throat and settling in his stomach. Copper, tasting of death.

He spat in the urinal as he heard the bathroom door open behind him. Jude turned his head to glance at the man who entered, and he saw his face clearly: a snow-white head of hair atop a pudgy, yet chiseled, face.

The pickup driver. The guy who had hit the pedestrian.

Jude walked to the sink, turned on the water, and started washing his hands. He glanced at the reflection of the man's back in the mirror. The metal taste in his mouth began to fade a bit, but Jude cupped his hands, bent over, and drank some of the water to help dilute the bitterness.

Okay. Copper meant death. Until recently, it had always meant his own death—had been the bitter, unwelcome taste on his lips each time he returned from the Other Side—but maybe this new version of it wasn't a signal of his own death.

Maybe he was tasting the deaths of others. And hadn't his father said as much, telling him about the Elvis prediction?

It made sense. He'd tasted copper outside the Red Lodge Cafe, and the pedestrian had died. He'd tasted copper around Ginny, and she'd been considering suicide. And he'd stopped her, so that meant he could help people avoid their deaths. Was this man considering suicide too, perhaps distraught after killing the pedestrian?

Jude continued to wash his hands, taking his time. He watched in the mirror as White Hair finished, then stepped up to the other sink and nodded a greeting.

The man's expression was that hundred-yard stare again. He obviously didn't recognize Jude. Good. If he was right, he needed to touch the guy to complete the vision, the sign, whatever it was.

Jude saw White Hair turn off the water and turn toward the towel dispenser. Now was the time. He turned off his own sink's water and moved toward the dispenser, purposely bumping the man when he reached for towels.

Bright bursts of sepia orange, black, and yellow filled Jude's eyes before dissolving into a clear picture: a kitchen. A bare kitchen much like his own. White Hair sat at a table eating stir-fry, watching *Jeopardy* on a small television. (*Kenneth Sohler, White Hair's name is actually Kenneth Sohler.*)

Thump.

Sohler took another bite of his vegetables, shouted an answer at the television as he chewed. "What is green algae, Alex?" The contestant on the television provided the same answer, and Alex told him to select another category.

Another *thump*, coming from somewhere in the house.

Still, Sohler ignored the thumping sound as he watched the television.

Thump. Thump.

It seemed maybe the pace was increasing now—

Thump. Thump.

On the television, Alex told everyone he'd be right back after this—

Thump.

As a toothpaste commercial flashed on the screen, Sohler took his plate to the sink, dished some stir-fry onto a small plate, and then turned to—

Thump.

—walk toward a door at the far side of the kitchen, where he reached for a knob and opened the door to the basement.

Thump.

Thump.

Jude opened his eyes; the world focused again. Kenneth Sohler dried his hands with a paper towel while staring at him. "You okay, buddy?" Sohler asked.

Jude swallowed, nodded his head quickly. "Just a bit light-headed," he blurted.

"Looked like, I don't know, a seizure or something."

A seizure. Rachel had mentioned seizures. Epilepsy. He pushed the thought from his mind: couldn't think about that right now. "Happens when I don't take my medication."

Sohler shrugged his shoulders, wadded his paper towel, and threw it in the garbage, then grabbed for the door. Jude closed his eyes, listened to the door squeak shut, and forced himself to breathe.

Ken Sohler had a young child locked in his basement. Jude paused a moment. *Or that was just a major league epileptic delusion.*

Jude moved slowly, feeling as if he were underwater. He left the rest room and stumbled back to his booth. Sohler wasn't far away, and Jude had an unobstructed view of him. He studied Sohler's face, looking for clues about his inner character. It seemed he should have some sort of nervous tic or permanent scowl or . . . something.

Jude remembered seeing a photo of Charles Manson, the same photo that was on the cover of *Life* or *Time* or some magazine, and knowing—*knowing*—he was staring into the face of evil. Manson's eyes were dark, deep-set pools of insanity. From that day forward, Jude had thought all evil people must have a similar kind of look. You'd be able to look in their eyes and see that a dark fire burned within. But Sohler didn't look anything like Manson; he looked more like a tire salesman. In other words: normal.

Ginny brought a plate and set it before Jude. She caught his look and glanced across the restaurant.

"Don't know his name," she said. "See him in here quite a bit, though."

"Ever bring anyone with him?"

She thought for a moment. "Hmmm. Not that I can think of."

"Does he seem . . . I don't know . . . okay?"

"In what way?"

"You ever see him explode or get really mad about something?"

"Nope. He pretty much mixes in with everyone else. Doesn't say much, but he tips pretty good."

Jude shook his head, then looked up at her. "Thanks, Ginny. I just . . . had a weird feeling about him. That's all."

She leaned down and whispered to him. "I'll keep an eye on him. If *you* have a weird feeling . . ." She let the sentence trail off without finishing it, then turned and walked toward the kitchen.

Jude ate his food while barely looking at his plate. He watched Sohler instead. This had to be the man who was taking kids. Maybe? No one knew what happened to any of them, because none had yet been found, and there had been several disappearances—half a dozen, at least—in the previous year.

Now that man sat in the same restaurant as Jude, eating the same meal as Jude. And what was he going to do about it? He really wanted to talk to someone. Kristina, more than anyone else, or maybe Rachel. Jude knew inside he should follow the man home and . . . and what? Jump him in the alley?

He really, really needed to talk to Kristina. She would know. That was when his eyes settled on the pay phone near the bathroom. He still had the number for the Stumble Inn in his wallet. She was in Room 305. He remembered it clearly.

Jude stood and walked to the phone. Using his peripheral vision, he tried to see if Sohler noticed. Sohler didn't seem the least bit interested; he had finished his dinner and was now reading the newspaper.

Jude looked up the number, dialed, and asked for Kristina's room. She answered immediately.

"Hey, it's Ju . . . Ron," he said.

"I kind of thought it might be."

"I have quite a bit to tell you, when you get a chance." He shuffled his feet and stared at his scuffed shoes.

"Really? About what?"

"Plenty of things. But I'm kind of calling for something important right now."

"Okay."

"Let's just say there's something to your whole signs thing."

"Like 'Welcome to the New Jersey Turnpike'?"

He winced. "Sorry about that."

"It's okay. It was actually pretty funny."

"What do I do about them? The signs, I mean."

"That'll be pretty obvious, I think."

The Kodachrome visions and the copper taste. Yeah, those were pretty obvious. But his next steps weren't. "What I mean is," he continued, "how do I know what to do?"

"What to do?"

"Like how to solve the problem."

"I don't know."

He stopped, held his breath for a minute.

"You don't know?" He turned to steal another look at Sohler. Still there, still reading the paper. "That's not much help."

"Are you really wondering what you should do? Or do you already know, and you're just scared to actually do it?"

Jude couldn't come up with an answer. After a few seconds of silence, she spoke again. "You there?"

Jude sighed. "Yeah, I'm here," he said. "That's the problem: I don't want to be."

"Look, if you want me to come over," she said.

"No, I'm not at home right now. And somehow, I think I'm not supposed to go home just yet."

"Calling from a cell phone?"

"Do I strike you as the kind of guy who would have a cell phone?"

"Good point. Well, when you're ready to spill your story . . ."

"I'll call you," he said. He noticed Sohler getting up from his table, and panic seeped from his pores. "I'm sorry, Kristina. I'm gonna have to run now. I hope I'm doing the right thing."

"You will," she said.

He didn't have time to respond, so he simply slammed down the receiver and hurried back to his booth. He threw some money down on the table, waved to Ginny, then rushed out the door behind Sohler.

At that exact moment Rachel opened the web browser on her iBook at home. Nathan was playing over at Bradley's for a few hours—she thanked God for Nicole for the thousandth time—giving her a few hours to herself.

Which tonight meant a few hours on the computer. Since Ron's surprise visit that morning, she had spent the entire day spinning him around in her mind, looking for answers. And she hadn't found any. Despite her best efforts, she once again felt herself succumbing to the puppy dog syndrome: feeling sorry for him, wanting to help him, comfort him. Maybe even God was directing those feelings.

And yet.

And yet that knot of jumbled emotions wouldn't leave, and his morning visit had also done much to complicate those feelings of danger. He'd talked about tasting copper; right away that made her think of an epileptic biting his tongue—especially when coupled with his gobbledygook about visions.

She typed *seizures* into her screen's search box, hesitated a moment, then added *hallucinations* and quickly hit the Search button. There, she'd done it; she'd admitted to herself that Ron was having hallucinations. She scrolled through the list of results until she came to a link labeled "Joan of Arc and Temporal Lobe Epilepsy." The resulting page was a scholarly article examining the life of Joan of Arc, concluding that her visions had been the result of epileptic seizures.

Rachel picked up her glass of water and took a long, deep drink. Did Ron suffer from epilepsy? (Or, as the article called it, TLE?) And if so, did that make him a danger to their son? Her maternal instincts were telling her yes.

Okay, if he had a history of mental instability, mental illness, whatever, he may have been a patient at various institutions. Maybe he'd escaped right before coming to Montana.

She backed up and typed *Ron Gress* in the search bar. Several thousand hits; no good. She tried *Ron Gress* and *Red Lodge* and came up with a few dozen results, most of them related to his employment with the local school district. Had he ever said where he'd lived before? Nebraska. He'd mentioned something about his dad living in Nebraska his whole life. She tried *Ron Gress* and *Nebraska*. The first half dozen or so were road race results. She smiled, doubting that Ron had run any marathons recently. The seventh result was an obituary. She winced when she read it: a young baby, only days old, had died in Bingham, Nebraska, thirty-two years ago. Bingham. Yes, she recognized it now; Ron had mentioned that town specifically—had talked about it when he mentioned his father. Creepy, kind of. But certainly no grand conspiracy at work; people, including babies, unfortunately died.

She returned to the Red Lodge results and clicked on the public employment records for Ron again. She was about to close the window when she noticed Ron's birth date: it was the same as the dead baby's from Bingham. She was sure of it. Just to double check, she pulled the birth record out of the browser's recent history.

Yes, the Ron Gress who was the father of her child shared a birthday with a Ron Gress who had died when he was just three days old. And both of them were from the same small town in Nebraska.

She felt a cold sliver of ice starting to wedge its way into her spine. This was beyond coincidence, and her mind raced immediately to one conclusion: Ron had stolen his name from a dead child.

Everything inside told her this was the case. It made such perfect sense. He'd escaped from some mental facility—probably somewhere in Nebraska, if not in this place called Bingham—then changed his identity. Slipped to Montana, a la the Unabomber, and hidden out for several years.

She had no way of proving that, but she thought she'd probably spent enough time searching on Google. She shut her iBook and went to the sink to refill her glass with more water. Outside the window above her sink, orange and yellow leaves cascaded to the ground. She watched them a few moments, trying to appreciate their beauty, but thoughts of Ron refused to leave her mind.

She had no way of confirming her theory, but did that matter? She'd met the chief of police, a nice enough guy with a name like a Nordic god. Odin, but not quite that. What was it? Odum, that was it. If she called and talked to him, let him know what she'd found, it might be worthwhile; if Ron was wanted somewhere else, she'd be doing a good deed. If it was a dead end, well, where was the harm?

As another golden leaf floated lazily to the ground, Rachel turned and went to the phone.

As soon as Jude was outside, he made his feet slow down. He wasn't going to do the kid in the basement any good by piquing Sohler's suspicions; if Sohler smelled anything amiss, he'd most likely try to lead Jude away from his home.

Jude watched the man walk down the block and get into his pickup, its front now dented from the accident. Jude strolled to his car, using what he hoped seemed a casual pace, then opened the door and jumped in. Sohler was pulling out of his spot, so Jude jammed his key into the ignition and cranked it. He wheeled out into the street, following a half block behind.

He tracked the pickup as it headed north of town, toward the more isolated homes hidden in the surrounding forest. Of course that would be the case; a child kidnapper would want plenty of privacy, wouldn't he? Jude thought briefly of phoning for help. Maybe he could call the police officers he'd met at the wreck. He couldn't remember the name of the first one, but he did remember Chief Odum. Yeah, he could call Odum and explain everything.

He took his foot off the gas, letting Sohler get more of a lead. No, Odum was a bad move. Odum would ask how Jude knew about the abducted kid, and he was pretty sure the chief wouldn't buy any story he might come up with, no matter how clever.

Still, he could call anonymously, couldn't he? Call Chief Odum and tell him to check out the address of the home, that he was a neighbor who had heard screams or something. Wouldn't that work?

Maybe. Except another thought lingered in the back of Jude's mind: He didn't know what was going to happen in Sohler's house.

If Sohler killed his victims, he could pick tonight to do it. He could pick the minute he walked through the door, in fact. Maybe he even made it a ritual: he liked to go to the Red Lodge Cafe for the daily special before he killed the kids and dumped them in a ravine behind his house.

No. Jude would have to stop this man himself. He wasn't sure how he was going to do it, but something deep inside told him he was going to try.

Up ahead, the pickup signaled and made a left turn into a sloping driveway, away from the mountains and toward Rock Creek. Jude slowed but drove past. He pulled to the side of the road a few hundred yards away and killed the engine, then got out of the car. Through a grove of aspens he saw the brake lights of Sohler's pickup flashing. That meant the driveway was only an eighth of a mile at the most; he could jog to the house easily.

Jude considered his next move. He had no weapon. Maybe he could rummage around and find . . .

An idea flashed in his brain.

He jumped back in his car, started it, and spun gravel as he turned around and headed toward the gas station about a quarter mile back. He floored the accelerator, worried each passing second might be the last for some child. And wasn't that strange, now that he thought about it? He knew Sohler's name, but he didn't know the name of the child in the basement. He had seen the face in the shadows, but he had never—well, maybe *received* was the best word for it—the name.

Jude careened into the gravel parking lot of the gas station, spraying rocks away from his tires as he braked to a stop by the pay phone. As soon as the car was in park, he was out the door and heading for the booth. He reached for the phone book, cursing as he realized he didn't have to follow Sohler to get his address. He could have looked it up in the phone book, maybe even sneaked out of the Red Lodge Cafe ahead of Sohler and freed the child.

Jude forced the regret out of his mind. He had a job to do right now, and he needed to concentrate on it. He flipped open the phone book and found the 'S' listings, then looked for *Sohler, Kenneth.*

He took a deep breath, then picked up the phone and dialed. A man's voice answered on the second ring. "Hello?"

Jude closed his eyes, then spoke slowly. "Mr. Sohler? Mr. Kenneth Sohler?"

A pause on the line. "Yeah?"

"This is, uh, Chief Mike Odum down at the Red Lodge Police Department. We have a bit of a problem we could use your help with."

"A problem? What is it?"

He took another deep breath. "If you could come down to the station, sir, we can talk about it here."

The line stayed quiet for a few moments before the voice spoke again. "Is this about . . . did you find . . . Janet?"

Who was Janet? A girlfriend? A co-worker? Could it be a child he was holding captive? No, he wouldn't be mentioning her to the chief of the Police Department. Still, it seemed Janet might be the right hook to lure him out of the house.

"Yes, sir, I'm afraid it is about Janet."

He heard a long, drawn-out breath at the other end. "I'll be there in fifteen minutes."

"Thank you, Mr. Sohler. We appreciate your help." He hung up the phone. The phone's handset was slippery with his sweat, and a dull roar rumbled in his ears, but he had done it.

Jude went back to his car and got in—he'd left it running in his rush to dial the phone—then killed the engine. Kenneth should be speeding by in just a few minutes. He hoped.

He waited two or three minutes but saw no pickup. Saw no car of any kind, for that matter. An icy block of dread began to settle in his stomach. What if he'd just hurried Sohler into killing the child?

He hadn't thought of that possibility after forming his plan, and now . . .

Jude looked at his watch, then slammed his car into gear. It wouldn't take him more than a few minutes to get there.

When he passed the home, he saw the pickup still sitting in front of it. He chose a driveway farther down the highway and pulled into it. He killed his lights as he parked alongside the driveway, just inside the aspen grove. He put the keys in his pocket and slid out of the vehicle. It was twilight now; in just a few more minutes the whole valley would be dark.

Jude jogged through the trees toward the house. Warm yellow lights glowed inside the home now, although he couldn't see anybody. At the edge of the trees he paused and considered. He had no choice; he needed to break into the house, because he *knew* something bad was happening.

He crept toward the front door, hoping Sohler didn't have a dog that would start barking and warn of his presence. He bent over, crouching as he moved to the front door, then peeked in the window.

Sohler was coming toward the door.

Panic gripped Jude for a second, but he didn't have much more than a second. It was dark out here, no outside lights on the home.

He jumped off the front steps and pressed himself into the corner between the steps and the home's foundation. Coming from the brightly lit house, Sohler's eyes wouldn't be adjusted to the darkness. And who would look into the shadows by their front stairs as they left? Not Sohler, Jude hoped.

The door squeaked open even before he had totally settled into a crouched position. He made himself go stiff, and he held his breath as he heard the shuffling of Sohler's shoes just inches above his head. After a few terrifying moments of silence, Jude heard an unmistakable metal-on-metal slide he knew very well: the sound of a dead bolt engaging.

Even after Sohler walked down the front steps, Jude continued to hold his breath for a few seconds. Silence returned. Maybe Sohler was standing in front of him, unseen, waiting for Jude to move.

Then, the door of the pickup creaked open and shut again. The engine roared to life, and the lights came on.

The lights. Here was something else he hadn't thought about. If Sohler happened to be looking at his front steps as he backed up and turned around, he'd see a man crouching at the front of his home. And if, like so many other folks in these parts, Sohler happened to be a hunter, he'd certainly have a gun mounted in that pickup.

Jude squeezed his eyes shut, as if closing them would blind Sohler to his presence. He felt the beams of the headlights streak across him, but the truck didn't stop. He opened his eyes again. The truck finished turning and started down the driveway to the main road. Jude watched until the taillights disappeared in the trees and brush. A moment later he heard the truck accelerating in the distance.

He let out a long, deep breath and wiped at his forehead with the back of his hand. The crisp autumn evenings in Red Lodge dipped into the forties regularly, but Jude was sweating as if it were the middle of July. His hand shook as he pulled it away, and his thighs were starting to cramp. Too much adrenaline in his system again.

Jude stood, made his way back up the concrete steps, and peered inside. Lights were on, although he was pretty sure no other threats were in the home. Pretty sure.

He squeaked open the screen door, then tried the main door. Locked. Of course; he'd heard Sohler sliding the dead bolt into place. He surveyed his surroundings again as he took off his jacket and wrapped it around his right elbow, then put the padded elbow quickly through one of the door's glass panes. The glass shattered easily and sprayed to the floor.

He stood still for a few moments, listening for the sound of approaching footsteps. None came, so he unwrapped his arm and put on his coat again, then reached inside and felt for the dead bolt. It turned smoothly, unlocking with a soft click.

After a deep breath he pulled the door open and walked inside, still trying to move slowly and silently, even though he wasn't sure why. He still felt as if he were being watched by a predator of some kind, a predator waiting for the right instant to pounce.

At the end of the hallway, as he thought, Jude came to a living room. A small couch sat in the center, with a TV—dark and silent—against the far wall. He stopped and scanned the room, checking all the places he felt a person could reasonably hide. Though the home looked clean, at least in the hazy darkness, he could smell the dank sweat of decades seeping out of the walls.

A quick click and hum startled him before he realized it was the sound of a refrigerator's compressor. Exhaling slowly, he turned the next corner and recognized the room where he stood. It was the kitchen, exactly as he'd seen it in his vision.

He couldn't let himself stop and think about how all this was so surreal, so . . . impossible. The kitchen was real, and that meant the vision was real, which meant a child was locked behind the door just fifteen feet away.

As he hurried into the kitchen, he tripped on the uneven floor between the hallway's wood flooring and the kitchen's linoleum. He almost fell but righted himself; in his clumsiness, however, he knocked over a metal bucket. Its tinny clang reverberated throughout the house. So much for a career as a cat burglar.

And then, a *thump*.

A thump just like he'd heard in his vision. Behind the basement door.

Followed by another *thump*.

Jude stayed frozen in mid-step a moment longer, then rushed to the basement door and stretched out his hand for the knob.

Thump.

The knob turned easily, letting him pull the door toward him. The door wasn't nearly as silent; its hinges gave a painful squeak as if unwilling to reveal the secrets behind it. The smell of earth and something else—a smell he recognized but couldn't quite place—filtered out of the open door. He put his hand into the inky darkness, feeling for a light switch.

Another *thump*, very near now, just ahead of him in the darkness.

His hand found a switch, and a dull light of mustard yellow gasped to life above his head.

Jude looked down the narrow staircase to the basement, then took a few steps down.

Another *thump*, this one right next to his head.

He recoiled, felt his foot slipping on the next step before he caught himself and avoided a long tumble down the stairs. He turned his head to the left and squinted to see in the darkness.

As his eyes adjusted, he saw the bars of a crudely made cage, sitting in what must have once been a first-floor pantry. Jude scanned the area, noting where the two-by-four framing had been ripped out. Yes, there had once been a wall here, but now it was open, giving access to the space from the basement.

As he peered into the darkness, eyes stared back at him: the eyes of a young boy, hunched inside the cage. The boy struggled to keep his eyes open in the dull light. Dirt caked his hair and face. How old? Five? Six? About Nathan's age, Jude guessed. As he watched, the boy threw his head backward, hitting a bar on the cage and creating a loud metallic *thump* that made the bars of the cage shake almost as much as Jude's innards.

The sound he'd been hearing.

Jude looked into the boy's wide bloodshot eyes and thought again of his own son. Tears filled his own eyes and he said softly, "Hi, I'm Ron." Then: "No, I mean, I'm Jude." Somehow it seemed he needed to whisper.

The boy flinched, as if he'd been bitten. "It's okay," Jude continued. "I'm gonna . . . I'm gonna get you out of here." He knew he was on the verge of sobbing, yet he didn't want to scare the boy.

Blank eyes stared at him a few more seconds, then the boy

slammed his head against the bars again.

Jude found a door in the cage, fastened by a makeshift sliding bar. A dead bolt. Of course. He put his hand on the bolt and tried to slide it, but it was stuck. The boy, meanwhile, moved toward the far end of the cage, apparently trying to get as far away as possible. Jude heard a low whimper coming from the boy, a whimper that pierced his heart more than anything he'd seen.

Jude used both hands to pull at the dead bolt, forcing it to slide by sheer will. The door to the cage swung open slightly before Jude grabbed it and pulled.

He put his hands out toward the boy. "Come on," he coaxed. "I'm not gonna hurt you." The boy cringed, then clanged his head against the cage bar several times in rapid succession: *thump thump thump thump thump.* Jude decided to try a different approach. He left the door to the cage open and backed up the stairs. The boy watched him but didn't move. "It's okay," Jude said. "Come on out."

The boy crawled across the small cage and put his hand out on the closest stair, his eyes never leaving Jude. Jude smiled and nodded, coaxing the boy onto the stairs. When the boy was totally out of the cage, Jude stepped down one stair and stopped. The boy didn't move away, so he quickly descended the next few stairs, holding out his hands, until he had the boy in his arms.

He picked up the boy, amazed at how light he was, turned around, and went to the main floor again. Then he moved across the kitchen to the living room, carrying the boy like a fragile vase.

That was when he heard a young girl's voice calling.

At the Red Lodge Police Station, Chief Mike Odum was confused, annoyed, and going on angry. He had questions mounting up, with no corresponding answers.

One of these questions was standing in front of him—a man named Ken Sohler, claiming Odum himself had called no more than fifteen minutes before. Problem one? Odum hadn't called. He *knew* that answer. Problem two? This Sohler guy seemed . . . not quite right. Something had Sohler on a rampage—he blathered on about a Janet without making much sense—but Odum also detected a wild, vacant look in the man's eyes. Lies hid behind those bloodshot irises, and he guessed Sohler would do whatever he could to keep the lies tucked away.

Odum sighed as he shifted back in his chair. He wasn't even supposed to be here this late, but he'd been catching up on work.

He looked at Sohler across the desk. "So what we *do* know, Mr. Sohler, is this: someone called your home, claiming to be me, and asked you to come right down to the police station."

"You said you had Janet."

Janet. Right. "Okay, Mr. Sohler. It wasn't me. But let's start with this: who is Janet?"

Sohler looked at him, his eyes blank. "My wife."

"Good, that's something to go on. Now, where is your wife?"

"I thought *you* were going to tell *me*."

"You lost me."

"Three years she's been gone. And when you called and said you found her—"

"We've been down this road a couple times, Mr. Sohler. No one from this office called you."

"So you say."

Odum nodded his head as he began to understand why Sohler was on edge. His wife had disappeared, and that simple fact had been poisoning his mind since. Odum had seen this kind of thing before. "Okay, Mr. Sohler. What troubles me is this: someone obviously wanted you out of the house. Do you have any valuables hidden in your home? Anything someone might want to steal?"

A pause. "No."

"Nothing, huh?"

Sohler's eyes looked to the floor. "Nope."

"Live by yourself, Mr. Sohler?"

"No. Uh, I mean, since my wife . . . you know."

"No one else around?"

Sohler stared into space and said nothing. Odum smiled to himself. Love to play poker with this guy; he'd have all the man's money in twenty minutes.

"Maybe we should go check your home, just to make sure."

Sohler's face flushed. "No, that's okay. I'm sure . . . I'm sure everything will be fine." Sohler stood. "Sorry for the whole misunderstanding; seems like maybe someone was just playing a joke on me. I bet it was . . . um, Joe."

Odum smiled again. "Yeah," he said. "Joe."

"Anyway," Sohler continued, "I'll call you if anything seems wrong." He turned and hurried out of Odum's office.

Odum looked after Sohler, breathing in the sick, sweet smell of fear the man had left behind. Something was wrong—very wrong—in Ken Sohler's home. He didn't have evidence of a crime, so there was no way he'd get a search warrant. Still, he'd like to have a look around that home. All he needed was an excuse.

Any excuse at all.

"Hello? Is that you?" the young girl's voice asked. "I'm . . . I'm sorry about the police."

Jude looked at the boy in his arms. The boy had no reaction to the voice, no reaction to any external stimuli, from what Jude could tell. Another child? It made sense, certainly. Something like half a dozen kids had disappeared in the recent past; maybe there were even more hidden inside the home. Jude walked across the living room toward a small hallway at the back of the house. He clicked a switch, and an overhead light illuminated the living room behind him. Down the hall were two closed doors, and light spilled from the crack beneath one.

"I can be a good girl now," the muffled voice said. "I promise."

The words chilled Jude and stopped him for a moment. He was only a few steps from the door now, and he hugged the boy tighter. He took the last two steps to the door and tried it.

It was unlocked.

Inside the room, a blond-haired girl stared back at him. A metal collar around her neck was chained to the bed.

"I did something bad," she said simply. "The police called."

Jude stared at her as he thought about what he wanted to say. "You didn't do anything bad. You'll be okay." He stepped across the room, put the little boy on the bed, and began to work on her restraints.

"Who are you?" she asked.

"I'm . . ." He paused, wondering just what he should say. "I'm a janitor," he finished. The chain padlocked at her neck was linked to the bed's frame, and he didn't have anything to break the chain.

"Do you know . . . are there tools or anything around here?" Jude asked.

"I don't know," she answered.

"It's okay. Just . . . I'll be back in just a minute." He rushed from the room, rummaging through the house, looking for a hammer, anything that might help him break or pry off the chain.

As he was looking through a closet by the bathroom, a thought occurred to him. He went back into the living room, where he found what he was looking for sitting on a table by the couch: a telephone.

He picked up the phone and dialed 9-1-1. A dispatcher's voice answered. "I need, uh . . . an ambulance," he said. "Someone's been shot. 1313 Creekview Drive."

The dispatcher started to ask something, but Jude hung up. He returned to the bedroom with the kids. "It's okay," he said as he walked into the room. "The police are coming."

Both kids stared without saying anything. Jude went back to the young girl and started to pull on the chain, trying to break her free. After a few seconds of struggling, he found tears spilling from his eyes, and he had to stop and put his head on the bed. Soon huge sobs overtook his body, and he poured out all his frustration on the pink bedspread. A big, blubbering fool. That was what he had become in such a very short time, the "something more" he now was.

Jude felt the young girl's hand gently rubbing his back. "It's okay," her voice told him. "You'll be all right." And somehow that made it worse, to think this girl who had been through so much was comforting him. Much like his son had done not so long ago.

Jude needed to pull it together. His crying wouldn't do anything for these kids, and even though the police were on the way, he was still uneasy—as if something sinister were lurking in every dark corner of the house.

He rubbed at his eyes as he stood. With the police on the way, should he just leave the house? It would be cleaner, easier. Although he was Jude Allman, he was still Ron Gress to all the folks in Red Lodge, and he didn't want to answer too many questions about his past. He'd only been Ron Gress for six years, after cribbing the birth records, and police searching through those records would soon figure that out. It would be best if he weren't here when the police showed up.

Except.

Except that feeling he still had, licking at the base of his spine and telling him not to leave the kids.

He turned to the kids. "The police will want to know everything that happened. Understand?"

The girl nodded; the boy continued to stare.

"They'll want to know about me—"

"I'll tell them Ultra Man saved us."

Jude smiled. "Ultra Man. My son likes Ultra Man. I think he wants one for Christmas."

"Are you?" she asked.

"Am I what?"

"Ultra Man."

"No. I'm just a janitor." He ran his hand through her hair but stopped when he heard an engine, ramped up high and approaching fast. "I think the police are here," he said. He hurried to the living room and peeked out the window where he saw the headlight beams of an approaching vehicle.

He went to the door and started to open it. Odd that the police didn't have their sirens or emergency lights going, but maybe they wanted to . . .

Jude's insides seized up when he realized the approaching vehicle wasn't a police cruiser. He slammed the door shut, vaulted back to the window, and peered out.

It was a blue pickup with a dented front-end.

Sohler's pickup.

Fresh terror juiced through Jude's veins as he sprinted back to the room with the kids.

He had to free the girl. Jude had already looked around the house and hadn't been able to find a hammer or anything else that would make a good weapon. He'd have to use his fists, probably, give Sohler a big haymaker when he walked into the house. If he stood behind the door and surprised . . .

No. He couldn't chance that. What if he missed, or screwed it up somehow? What would happen to the kids? He had to stay with the kids, protect them.

Jude closed the bedroom door, trying to appear calm and collected. He didn't want to panic them. His lungs felt as if they were filled with spun fiberglass; each breath, more and more difficult to take, made his whole chest itch and tingle.

He turned the lock on the door, then backed away and cleared his throat. "Let's just stay in here until the police come," he said, hoping his voice sounded calm. Of course Sohler would be knocking at that door soon, but he wasn't sure what else to say to the kids yet.

He heard a squeak, the flap of the screen door, then footsteps on the hardwood floor. Four or five steps later, he lost the sound. But, was that another door squeaking open? The basement door? And of course, Sohler would have seen the broken glass of the front door instantly.

A bellow rang through the house and leaked in beneath the locked bedroom door: "Where is he?" The voice sounded pinched, guttural, panicked. Insane. The boy made a quiet moan, and Jude could barely keep himself from echoing it.

More footsteps, pounding across the living room floor and coming closer. Jude saw the shadow of shoes breaking the light under the door.

"Tiffany?" the voice outside yelled. "Where is he?" The doorknob jiggled wildly but held. "Open this door right now." The door shook as he pounded, then shuddered when he put his shoulder into it. "You don't want to make me come in there. You know that."

Tiffany, her name was Tiffany. Jude turned his head to look at the young girl and saw tears starting to stream down her face. She stared back at him, her eyes asking what she should say. Jude softly shook his head and put a finger to his lips. No need to try and talk with the man; what would it accomplish?

"Okay," Ken's voice outside the door said. "I just want you to remember one thing, Tiffany. When I get in there, I'm gonna have a special surprise for you. A real. Special. Surprise."

Tiffany started to sob. Jude put an arm around her, pulling the boy close with his other arm. And at that moment, as he sat with his arms around two helpless children, something inside him clicked.

He had no idea what else was about to happen, but he knew one thing with cold, bitter certainty: Ken Sohler would not touch either of these kids while he was alive. If Sohler managed to get the door open, he'd be in for a "real special surprise" himself.

Boots slid on the wooden floor of the hallway, receding down the hall. A few seconds later the screen door on the front of the house slammed. Sohler had gone outside. Probably to get something, and all the somethings Jude could think of went from bad to worse very quickly.

He scanned the room, his gaze stopping on a sliding window above the bed. If he could just get Tiffany unchained from the bed, he might be able to boost the kids through the window. As he again studied the chain wrapped around the bedpost, it came to him: *take the bedpost.* It was a metal bed frame, but the wooden posts themselves didn't seem too sturdy.

Jude pulled the bed away from the wall. He tested the post, pushing a bit, and it wiggled.

The screen door slammed once again. Footsteps, hurried. The bedroom door shuddered, and a few splinters fell to the floor. Outside, Ken's voice, more shrill, filtered through. "Oh, little pig, little pig."

Another blow, and more splinters. The chipped edge of an ax blade jutted through a small crack. Tiffany screamed, while the boy fixed his gaze on the door.

Jude stepped back, then kicked at the bedpost. It loosened. He kicked again, bending it out. Another kick snapped it away from the frame.

The ax bit once more, and now a large chunk of the door toppled to the floor. Jude jumped onto the mattress and looked outside. Bare ground below the window, covered by a thin layer of larch needles. Good. He motioned for the kids to join him as he tried to slide open the window, but it was stuck. Painted shut, most likely.

He hesitated a moment, then put the wooden bedpost through the glass. Carefully he punched out all the jagged edges with the post before he boosted the kids up and out: first the boy, and then Tiffany.

The ax hit again, and more wood broke loose. Jude had been scared the sound of shattering glass would bring Sohler around the back of the house, but it seemed Sohler was making too much noise to hear. Or maybe Sohler just didn't care.

Jude snaked both of his legs out the window and sat on the sill, then turned around to look behind him. An arm squeezed through the hole in the door, searching for the doorknob. They wouldn't have much of a lead. Thirty seconds, maybe. Fifteen seconds, more likely. Jude pushed himself out the window, then rushed the kids several yards away. Tiffany was dragging the loose bedpost now, still attached to her chain, and that gave him an idea. He stopped her and slid the chain off the end of the detached post. He pointed the kids toward a nearby stand of aspens, and they started running again.

The kids weren't going to outrun a maniac with an ax. That left him only one choice. Jude hefted the bedpost from hand to hand and took a deep breath. Then he turned back toward the house.

Warm, buttery light spilled from the broken window and illuminated a small patch of the dark lawn. Sohler's head appeared in the window frame, popping up like some twisted jack-in-the-box. He pulled himself up into the window, and Jude immediately saw he had missed his best chance: if he had been back by the window, waiting, he could have hit Sohler with the bedpost as the man struggled out of the opening.

But now it was too late. Sohler, heavy ax glinting at his side, was coming toward him.

Jude wanted to run, but he stopped his feet. (*The kids, keep him away from the kids.*) And then Sohler was in front of him, swinging his ax in a wide arc like a baseball bat.

Jude hit the ground, feeling the air whoosh by as the weight of the heavy axhead forced Sohler to finish his swing. Sohler's rage was boiling over, his face constricting into a deathly grimace.

Jude rolled to his right and came to his feet again. Sohler had regrouped and was raising the ax above his head. No more home run swings to throw him off-balance.

The ax started to swing forward, and Jude knew the momentum would commit Sohler to another full arc. He stepped to the left this time. Sohler buried the axhead in the ground, and its thick oversized head stuck there. Sohler dropped his shoulders, trying to work the ax free, wanting to prepare another swing.

But it wasn't a swing Jude would let him take. Jude raised the broken, splintered bedpost and swung it as hard as he could. Still trying to free his ax, Sohler took the blow across the crown of his head. The wood cracked with a hollow, sickening peal; a stray splinter sliced down Sohler's forehead and right cheek, creating a red gouge on his face.

Sohler stood and looked at Jude, blood streaming down his forehead and into his eyes. *This wasn't supposed to happen,* the eyes seemed to say as he took a stumbling step forward. He let the ax slide from his fingers and brought up his arms in a lunge, reaching for Jude's neck.

But Jude was ready. He shuffled back, planted his right foot, then swung his right fist toward Sohler's temple in a vicious hook. The punch connected, and Sohler went down.

Jude stood panting for a few seconds. He wiped the sleeve of his shirt across his forehead, watching for any movement from the unconscious form at his feet.

There wasn't any.

Something caught Jude's eye. Two beams of light, streaking across the aspen grove where the kids were hiding. Headlights.

Jude turned and sprinted for the trees. In a few moments he found the kids hiding behind a fallen log. Crouching beside them in the brush, he turned to look at the home. He saw the back of the house where they had escaped, but he couldn't see the front from this angle. Did he imagine the headlights? Was his mind playing another trick on him, making him think the police were here?

A commotion erupted from inside the home: a slamming door, the sounds of muted voices. A silhouette appeared in the light of the broken window, then a flashlight clicked on and found the dazed body of Ken Sohler in the grass, now regaining consciousness.

Jude tapped both of the kids, and they worked their way around the side of the house, staying safely hidden in the aspens. Soon after they moved, Jude saw the flashlight's beam combing the trees, searching the area where they'd just been.

As they paralleled the house, the front of the home came into view. A police cruiser was parked behind Ken's blue pickup. Its lights weren't flashing, but Jude saw the cherries on top of it. Next to the car stood an officer, his face partially obscured by the two-way radio he was speaking into.

Jude looked down to the two kids. "See that policeman?" he whispered to Tiffany. She nodded. "I want you two to walk over to him right now. He'll take care of you."

Tiffany nodded, then abruptly put her arms around him and hugged. She grabbed the hand of the boy and stepped out into the yard, dragging the chain behind her. Jude moved farther back into the brush and trees but didn't move out of sight until he saw the kids talking to the officer. The officer opened the back door of his car and was starting to put in the kids when Jude finally turned and ran.

In a few minutes he was back at his car. He slid into the front seat and turned the key, then slowly drove out of the driveway and turned back toward Red Lodge.

While passing the driveway to Sohler's house, he again saw the parked police cruiser. This time its lights were flashing, alternately painting the trees blue and red.

Chief Odum glided down the hall of the local Carbon County Hospital, running his hand across the textured wallpaper. Odum was a tactile person: he liked to touch, to feel, to get a physical sense of everything around him.

It was dark outside, and visiting hours were long over, but not for him. He turned a corner at the end of the hall and walked into the room registered to Ken Sohler. Docs wanted to keep the guy overnight; the next morning they'd release him into Odum's custody.

But Odum wasn't in the mood to wait until morning.

"Good evening, Mr. Sohler," he said as he sat down next to Sohler's bed. Sohler looked as if he'd been through a meat grinder. His bandaged head was obviously swelling—somebody coldcocked him good—and a deep gash was puffing his right eye closed. "Guess things weren't all that tidy around your house, were they?"

Sohler looked at the floor, didn't answer.

"What say you and I have a little chat about that?"

Sohler didn't move.

"Tell me about Janet," he said.

Sohler's eyes lit up. "She's . . . beautiful," Sohler croaked. "I—" Sohler caught himself and stopped talking.

"How long's she been gone?"

Sohler shrugged.

"Three years, I think you said," Odum prompted.

"Maybe."

"What happened when you went home?" Odum motioned to

Sohler's head. "Somebody cheap-shot you? You know him?"

"Never seen him before."

Odum leaned back in his chair. "What about Tiffany and—what's the little boy's name?—Joey."

Sohler looked away, then shrugged again.

Odum felt a rage welling inside him but only let it creep through as a mean grin. "Well, now, I guess we'll find that out soon enough, won't we? But if I remember correctly, you said you were the only one in that house, and that doesn't seem to be the case." He stopped, watched Sohler squirm a bit in his hospital bed. "So you don't exactly have a good track record with me."

Odum stood up. "Get a good night's sleep, Mr. Sohler. And think good and long about any other secrets you have hidden. Because by tomorrow morning, I'm gonna know all of them."

Odum turned and walked from the room. He stopped outside the door to chat with Jeff Barber, the officer who would be guarding the room overnight. Odum had kept the whole thing quiet so far; no press had caught wind of this night's developments. But he was only a few hours into this ordeal, and he knew soon—probably as early as the morning—he'd have all kinds of reporters and photographers infesting his town like termites.

By then, of course, Sohler would be in his custody, and Odum could control access. Until the doctors released the man, he felt a bit twitchy about leaving Sohler here. Too many variables. No way he could keep the termites out for long. So, here was Officer Barber, a bit too big for his uniform, sitting in an ancient orange chair and guarding the entrance to the room. Not the ideal situation, to be sure, but it would have to work. He patted Barber on the shoulder, then turned and went down the hall.

Odum wanted to head back to the office and work some more, yet he really needed to get home, have a bit of time to himself. He needed to rest, because tomorrow was shaping up to be a big day indeed.

First, he'd probably have to deal with the Feds. This whole incident would have them sniffing around his town, tripping over their own feet while they tied Sohler to all the surrounding disappearances. Odum didn't like the thought of that happening, only he couldn't stop it now.

He was more interested in talking to the young girl named Tiffany. He had been able to reconstruct most of what had happened that evening. Even so, too many questions bounced around the corridors of his mind. Who made the call to Sohler? Probably the same person who broke into the house, freed the kids, and then played a tune on Sohler's head. But how did he know Sohler? What was the connection?

Odum had wanted answers to some of his questions this evening, but the kids fell asleep on the drive to town. When he pulled into the station and opened the back door, there they were: curled up in the back seat together, both fast asleep. Probably the best sleep they'd had in months.

The kids, and the questions, could wait.

Chief Odum sat down with Tiffany the next morning, offering her doughnuts from the City Bakery. He usually didn't go for doughnuts that much—he'd rather savor a latte sans sugar—but he figured they'd win over the girl. What kid didn't like doughnuts?

Odum sat down next to the girl and pushed the box her way. "Hungry?" he asked.

She nodded.

"Go ahead and take one. You like maple bars?"

"Have any chocolate?"

He smiled. "Chocolate. Good choice." He picked out a chocolate bismarck with sprinkles, put it on a napkin, and pushed it toward her. "I got some milk for you, too," he said, pointing toward the carton of two percent sitting on the table. She looked up at him, then reached for the milk.

He waited for her to have a drink and a few bites of the doughnut. "I'd like to talk to you, if that's okay," he said.

She picked up a napkin, wiped chocolate from her mouth, nodded.

"Good, good. Let's start with names. I'm Chief Odum."

"My name is Tiffany."

"And the little boy? Do you know him?"

"Joey. He's my brother."

"Okay, Tiffany. Do you mind if we talk about last night?"

"Nope."

"Joey was in the cage, right?"

She nodded, licking frosting off her fingers.

"Did you let him out?"

This time she shook her head.

"So who did?"

She stopped chewing and thought for a few seconds. "I'm not sure. Must have been Ultra Man."

Odum smiled. Ultra Man. The hot kid toy of the year; stores expected to sell out of them during the fast-approaching Christmas season.

"Ultra Man? Do you sometimes pretend he helps you?"

She shook her head. "Just last night."

"What did he look like?"

"Well, he said he wasn't really Ultra Man. He said he was just a janitor."

"You ever see him before?"

"No."

Odum frowned for a moment, then smiled as all the dots connected. He'd met a school janitor recently. He'd even taken a call from that gal at the jewelry store, claiming she thought he might be hiding under a false identity. And hadn't the janitor met Ken Sohler at that pedestrian accident last week? Yes, he had. Everything was connecting very nicely.

It was time to draw the line to the last dot.

A few minutes after four in the morning, Rachel awoke to the sound of the phone ringing beside her bed. Who would be calling this early, waking her up to . . .

She jolted upright. Maybe it was Ron. Something wrong with him.

She answered the phone: "Hello?" She heard wind blowing across the mouthpiece on the other end, and what a sounded like a truck engine upshifting somewhere in the background. Whoever was on the line was outside. Pay phone, probably. Had to be Ron, the only person in the world who didn't have a cell. "Ron? Is that you? Are you okay?"

A voice spoke up—thick, guttural, somehow slurred. "This is the gal has his kid?"

She froze. It wasn't Ron at all. And whoever it was, there was no way she was going to let Nathan be brought into the conversation. "I don't know what you're talking about. I'm expecting a call from my brother Ron Iverson, who's stationed in Germany." She hoped the lie sounded believable; she'd made it up on the spot. She wanted to hang up, disconnect this evil voice from even being in the same house as her son. At the same time she felt she needed to stay on the line, find out who—or what—this was.

"I'm talkin' 'bout Ron Gress. You know him. Might wish you didn't, soon." The phone clicked, then went silent, and bounced to a dial tone after a few seconds.

Quickly she rose from bed and padded to Nathan's room. He was facedown on the bed, pillow next to him—his favorite sleeping position. While it looked uncomfortable to her, she noticed her son sleeping that way often.

She went to the bed, brushed her hand on his cheek, and felt its reassuring warmth. Yes, he was fine. After walking to the other side of the room and checking the window—locked—she slid out into the hallway and closed the door gently behind her again.

She made a quick trip around the house, checking locks and windows. For once, she wished she had a big security system like Ron's.

When she reached the kitchen, Rachel flipped the switch to the overhead light and pulled out a coffee filter. Might as well make a few cups, because she wasn't going to be sleeping again this morning.

Jude awoke, stiff and sore, in his recliner. His muscles felt overstretched as if he'd been pulled on some kind of medieval torture device.

At the same time he felt oddly refreshed. A current of energy coursed through him, an uncontrollable excitement waiting to be let out.

He looked at the clock. It read 5:30, which shocked him for two reasons. First, it wasn't within five minutes of 6:30. Over the years, his mind and body had become so accustomed to waking at 6:30 that he felt odd, out of place, waking at a different time. Second, he was surprised to find he'd actually awakened an hour *earlier* than usual. No wonder his body still felt sore; he was running on just a few hours' sleep.

Jude disarmed his alarm system, then shuffled through the rest of the house. He embraced his usual routine, checking all the cupboards, closets, doors, and other hiding spots. It comforted him, calmed him—something that felt important since his body had robbed him of much-needed sleep. He noticed three messages blinking on his answering machine and pressed the button to listen.

"Message one: 3:57 A.M.," the answering machine's mechanical voice told him. It was just background noise. Wind, and maybe traffic. He thought he heard the Jake Brake of a large diesel in the background. The message ended abruptly. The mechanical voice came back. "Message two: 6:07 A.M."

"Ron, it's, uh, Rachel. Pick up if you're there." A few seconds of silence. "Okay, maybe you can't hear me, or maybe you're out. I just . . . I just want to make sure you're okay. I got a strange call a few hours ago, and . . . like I said, I just want to make sure you're okay."

"Message three: 9:47 A.M."

"Ron, I guess I got a little buggerboo on your time off." Frank, from school. Frank was always full of colorful colloquialisms Jude never quite understood. "I thought you were just gonna be gone yesterday. Anyway, no whoop-de-doo. You have a boatload of vacation time, so use it. Just let me know when you wanna polish the old pine again."

Jude scratched his head. The times didn't add up; maybe the answering machine's internal clock was off. It was one of those digital things he mistrusted; he spent as little time as possible with it, so its time probably *was* off.

He went to the kitchen, rummaged through a drawer, and found a watch. Its digital readout also said it was 5:45. Still puzzled, he shuffled to the front door, unlocked the dead bolts, and peeked outside. Low light, just as he would expect at about six in the morning this time of year.

Or six in the evening.

He shut and dead-bolted the door again, then moved to his television. He pressed the power button and flipped to a local channel as he backed up to sit in his living room chair. A commercial for a local dry cleaner was playing, and Jude waited impatiently for the main program to come back on. Just before six in the evening, the local news should be . . .

The local weatherman came on, the squinty one who annoyed Jude. "Let's take a look at your current conditions for this evening," he began before Jude stopped listening and forced the voice into the background.

Jude hadn't slept five hours. He'd slept *seventeen* hours.

As the weatherman droned, another memory flash of his father came—just for a few milliseconds. In the flash, Jude was young, maybe eight or so. He lay in bed, looking at his father sitting beside him. The flash didn't last long, but Jude somehow felt his father was upset. Mad, maybe.

The thirty-two-year-old Jude pushed the eight-year-old Jude from his mind as his innards rumbled in hunger. Perhaps his brain had skipped twelve hours, but his stomach wasn't about to do the same. He walked over to the refrigerator and dug for something to eat. He found a couple packages of lunch meat and ripped them open, then grabbed a Diet Pepsi and returned to the living room. Another commercial break.

Jude stared at the phone for a while, then picked it up and dialed Frank's office. It was the machine, of course; Frank would have gone home by now. At the beep he left a message. "Hi, Frank, it's Ron. Sorry about the confusion on the time off. I wasn't really planning on today either, but I'm feeling a little under the weather. I think I'll take your advice and maybe just take off the rest of this week."

He hung up the phone and punched the volume on the TV. The main anchor filled the screen. "As promised," the anchor said, "we have a live update on our top story. Kim Reardon is at the Red Lodge Police Department with the latest."

Jude recognized the reporter standing outside the police department. She was a striking woman with short-cropped hair and an earnest voice. He liked her; he guessed she wouldn't stay in Billings too long before moving up to a larger television market. "Thanks, Lynn," the reporter said. "As we told you earlier, a 9-1-1 phone call last night started an incredible turn of events at a local Red Lodge home. I spoke with Police Chief Michael Odum about ten minutes ago, and this is what he had to say."

The tape rolled footage of Chief Odum, who looked even more imposing when standing next to the diminutive reporter. "Chief," the reporter asked, "can you tell us what happened last night?"

"We received an emergency call from a local residence. When officers arrived on the scene, they found two children held captive inside the house. At present, we're attempting to locate the owner of that house for questioning."

The reporter nodded. "We've seen a number of regional child abductions recently. Are you making connections to any other cases?"

"We're investigating leads, but I can't comment at this time."

The television went back to Kim Reardon, live outside police headquarters. "Lynn, the police department did release the name of the home owner." A photo flashed on the screen. "He is Kenneth Sohler of Red Lodge, and that's about all we know about him right now. Sohler is—"

Jude flipped off the TV. Odum's words spun in his mind: *"We're attempting to locate the owner of that house . . ."* That wasn't right—he saw the police at Sohler's house last night, and Sohler had been knocked cold in the backyard. Had he recovered that quickly, crept into the woods surrounding his house, and escaped? Didn't seem likely. Did someone else own the house, and Sohler was renting it? No, the reporter had said Sohler's name specifically.

Most likely, he decided, Odum was hiding something from the press. Child disappearances had become big news in the past months—good for ratings and all—and Sohler was the cause. Odum hadn't said anything like that during his television news interview, but Jude knew. Everyone watching that broadcast knew. If a man had two kids locked up in his house, and if other kids had been disappearing regularly, well, you didn't need to be a math major to add those two things together. Satellite trucks from all three Billings television stations were probably parked outside of the Red Lodge Police Station even now.

Jude sat, still exhausted despite sleeping through until evening. It was a rare occurrence—first ever, from what he could remember—but probably understandable. What his body, his mind, had been through the night before was too much, way too much for someone who had spent six years insulating himself from outside stimulus. No wonder he had shut down for so long.

He thought of the television report, and of Sohler, once again. What created a monster like Sohler? Was he abused as a child? Did something warp his mind, making him think children were a danger?

And what was up with the police? Shouldn't they have Sohler in custody?

He sighed heavily. These weren't things for him to worry about. It was time to go back to just being Ron Gress, mild-mannered janitor. He'd done his part, and now it was time for the police to do theirs. That was what they were for.

At that moment he heard a knock on his door. Had to be Kristina, speak of the devil and all that. And, despite himself, he was eager to see her. He climbed from his chair and headed to the door, opening it without hesitation.

It wasn't Kristina.

Instead, he found himself face-to-face with the police officer he'd first seen at the accident scene the other night. Jude couldn't quite remember his name.

"Mr. Gress, I don't know if you remember me, but we spoke a few nights ago. I'm Officer Jim Grant, with the Red Lodge Police Department."

That was it. Officer Grant. "Sure," Jude said.

"Could you come with me, please? We'd like to ask you a few questions at the station."

Jude felt his heart lurch for a long moment, staggering out of its normal rhythm. This was danger territory. Jude knew himself, knew his capabilities. No way he was going to stand up to ten minutes of intense questioning, let alone a couple of hours. And if the police wanted to bring him to the station, that probably meant they'd been digging. He hadn't covered his tracks carefully, and it would be easy to discover Ron Gress was an apparition, a nonperson without any real past.

Jude pushed these jumbled thoughts aside and forced his mouth to move. "Can I ask why?"

"Let's just talk at the station, Mr. Gress."

Okay, he knew he couldn't handle it. But he would have to anyway. And maybe, just maybe, this wasn't about him. Maybe it was about Sohler. Maybe the little girl at the kidnapper's house—Tiffany—had told the police something about his being there. He'd expected that, on some level. He'd told the girl he was a janitor; if she remembered, she'd say something about it to the police. That wouldn't add up, of course. *Why would a janitor be there?* the police would ask themselves. Next they would say, *Beats the snot out of us, but didn't we talk to a janitor last week who was part of that accident with Sohler? Why, yes we did, and isn't it funny to think these two have met before? Why don't we find that janitor and get him down here to tell us about it?*

Sure, that could be it. Probably was it, now that he thought about it. With any luck they'd be digging for information about Sohler rather than digging for information about himself. That, he could handle.

That was the way it would be, then. He'd go with Officer Grant to answer a few questions. "Okay," Jude said to Grant. "Let's go." He waited for Grant to step away from the door, then went out himself, pulled his keychain from his pocket and locked it, dead bolts and all. Now wasn't the time to get sloppy about home security.

Officer Grant's car was a basic Crown Victoria. Jude wasn't sure if he was supposed to sit up front or in back, but Grant motioned him to the front, started the car, and headed toward the downtown police station. Jude didn't live far away; they would be there in five minutes or so.

At the first turn Jude turned to look at Officer Grant, who kept his eyes on the road. Grant wasn't much of a conversationalist, obviously. Not that he himself was, but Jude somehow expected police officers would always try a bit of chatter when they were bringing in people for questioning. Loosen 'em up a bit, get 'em to let down their guard, oil the jaw joints so they'd feel warm and fuzzy and trusting enough to spill their secrets.

Grant pulled into the parking lot, and a few minutes later they stood inside the building.

At the desk they took a left turn and walked down a hallway lined with offices. Except, Jude found out, one of the doors on that hallway wasn't an office at all. It was something he recognized from cop shows he'd watched as a kid: the interrogation room. Grant escorted him into the room, then retreated.

The room put no effort into breaking from the mold of your standard interrogation chamber. Its walls, floor, and ceiling were stark and plain. A heavy metal table loomed in the middle of the room with chairs on both sides.

Jude sat down and tried to clear his head. He took a few deep breaths, willed his heart to stop sledgehammering the cavity of his chest, and did his best to appear calm and relaxed. Looking nervous in here would do him no good; he knew full well someone, maybe even a few someones, would be staring at him from behind that large mirrored wall in front of him right now.

Jude thought he'd been handling it all pretty well, keeping up that veneer of serenity, until Chief Odum opened the door of the room and walked in.

Instantly Jude felt his internal circuit breaker trip. This wasn't the way it was supposed to happen. The chief was supposed to stay on the other side of the mirror while one of his officers questioned him. Jude's gaze fell to the table as Chief Odum sat down across from him, and he could not bear to look up.

Jude continued looking at the smooth surface of the table, but in his peripheral vision he could see Odum smiling. Probably noting Jude's all-too-obvious reactions and feeling as if he had a nice fish on the line.

"Mr. Gress," Odum said, "thanks for coming down. We have a few things we were hoping you could clear up for us."

Standard boiler plate cop talk. Nothing too dangerous. "Okay," Jude answered.

"All right, then. You have any idea what this is about?" Odum asked.

Jude shrugged. Of course he had an idea what this was all about, a very good idea. But he wasn't about to admit that. Least of all to Odum.

Odum held up a photo of Tiffany, the girl who had been locked in Sohler's home. "Have you seen her before?"

"Yes. Tiffany." Jude decided he would only talk in short sentences, give only the information asked. That was the way it was done. Of course he had already offered more information than was asked by giving Odum the girl's name, but he was new at this thing. Gotta expect a few stumbles just out of the gate.

"And this boy?" Odum held a photo of the boy in the cage.

"Yes." This time he didn't offer a name, partly because he didn't know the boy's name.

"How about this man?" A photo of Ken Sohler.

"Yes."

"Of course you know this man," Odum said. "We all met just a few days ago at that vehicular accident, didn't we? You were there." Odum waved Sohler's photo. "He was there." He paused. "I was there."

Odum paused. Jude decided he wouldn't speak; Odum hadn't asked him a direct question. After a few moments Odum smiled again and lined up the photos of Sohler and the two kids. "We've got three pictures here, Mr. Gress. But we don't have the whole picture, if you can see what I mean."

Jude shrugged.

Odum continued. "The whole picture includes you, now, doesn't it? You showed up at that accident with Sohler last week. Then last night, you were at Sohler's house."

It was a statement, not a question. Okay, maybe if he talked a bit about last night, that would give Odum the information he needed to follow a new trail—a trail that led away from his own background. He closed his eyes for a moment. Time to step off the cliff. "What do you want to know?"

Odum smiled again. "Oh, how you know them, for starters. What you were doing in Sohler's house."

"How'd you know I was there?" Jude asked, although he had a pretty good idea.

"Let's call it a professional secret."

Jude sighed. He was pretty sure he knew, anyway. "The boy, I'd never seen before I got into the house. And the man—Ken Sohler— well, I had a bad feeling about him when I first saw him."

"A bad feeling?"

Jude nodded. He knew he was starting weak, very weak. But leading with "I had some psychic visions" didn't seem like the best opening line.

"When you first saw him, you say," Odum said. "That was at the accident?"

"Well, no. I mean yes. The first time I saw him was at the accident. But then I saw him last night at the Red Lodge Cafe. That's when I got the bad feeling."

Odum offered the knowing nod of a man who's had a few meals at the Red Lodge Cafe. "So what happened?"

"I saw him, and I just felt like something was wrong. Really wrong. So I . . . kind of followed him to his home."

"And?"

"Well, you probably know. I needed to get him out of the house, so I called and said I was . . . you." He expected Odum to be quite mad about this, but he wasn't. Or, more likely, he'd already boiled about it and had now cooled down.

"So you got Sohler out of the house. Then what?"

"Well, I went into the house—"

"He left the door unlocked?"

"No, the door was locked. I, uh, busted out a window in the door." Surely Odum already knew that. He just wanted to make Jude uncomfortable. "Anyway, once I got inside, I heard a thumping noise. Like metal, you know? And I discovered the boy—I still don't know his name."

"Joey."

"Joey. I found Joey locked in a cage just behind the basement door." Jude felt tears starting to form in his eyes, but he forced them to open wider, dry a bit. He wasn't about to cry in front of Chief Odum. That would be a bad move, akin to flopping on his back and showing a weak underbelly.

"The basement? Did you go into the basement?"

Jude was a bit surprised by the question. "No. Why? Was there something important in the basement?" A thought crossed his mind—a particularly nasty thought he wished had never come. "Were there . . . other kids?"

Odum leaned back in his chair, ignoring Jude's question. "So tell me about the girl," he said.

"After I got the boy, um, Joey, out of the cage, we found her in the bedroom. She was chained to the bedpost, so I kind of knocked the bedpost loose. Then we slipped out of the back window when Sohler was chasing us with an ax. I . . . well, I hit him with the bedpost." Again, he was pretty sure Odum knew this already.

Odum stared into Jude's eyes. "Mr. Gress, that sounds like a pretty good story. But why do I get the feeling you're not telling me everything that happened."

Jude winced. "I don't know—."

"See, that's just it," Odum interrupted. "There's so much of this big picture *I* still don't know. Like your real name."

Uh-oh. This was headed into dangerous territory. Jude swallowed, and he knew Odum wouldn't speak again until he gave an answer. He backpedaled, mostly so he could avoid answering the question about his identity. "If you talk to the kids, Tiffany and Joey, they can tell you they haven't seen me before. They can tell you—"

"Oh, they've told me everything I need, Mr. *Gress*," he said, leaning on the name. He sat a few moments, saying nothing, then: "Would you be willing to submit to a polygraph test?"

Jude blinked, stared down at the table. He wouldn't have a prayer of passing a lie detector test, even telling the truth; he was a jumble of paranoid tendencies and nervous tics.

Jude's mouth was dry, and he wasn't sure what to say, so he muttered a quiet "Maybe I'd better call an attorney."

"Maybe you should. If you'd like to do that, I'll be more than happy to provide your lodging for the evening right here. Your attorney can come talk to you in the morning, and I'll let you out in twenty-four hours. We can play the game that way." Odum licked his lips. "Or, we can just make a gentleman's agreement right now that you'll be down here bright and early tomorrow, and I'll let you go home and snuggle into your own bed for the evening. Your choice, of course."

Jude noticed he'd been unconsciously itching at the inside of his forearm; he stopped, glancing at the red mark he'd left. Odum had pried open his mind already, figured out there was no way he'd choose a jail cell over the safety of his home. At home he could lock out *them*, keep the bad out. Maybe Odum was even one of *them*, and if he stayed here, he'd be locked in with . . .

Jude shook his head. This was no time to let his paranoia rise to the surface and take over. But he was trapped. Odum knew it. He knew it.

"I'll . . . I'll be here tomorrow morning."

"Good, good. Officer Grant will escort you back, keep an eye on your home for the night—" Odum flashed another grin—"for your safety, of course, Mr. *Gress*."

Jude closed the door behind him, went through the familiar locking ritual. A cold skewer of steel rode inside his intestines, and his head felt sweaty, itchy. It wasn't supposed to happen this way.

He walked into the kitchen, opened his refrigerator, and looked for something to drink. Orange juice. He shook it and drank it as he stood in the kitchen. The juice helped, calming his roiling stomach. He sat in the single chair at the kitchen table, running the recent events through his mind.

He hadn't counted on anything like this being part of the deal. Talk to a few people, tell them to straighten out their lives. Sure, fine. Rescue kids in danger, also fine. But now it seemed the carefully constructed cocoon he'd built for himself was going to be burned away, charring him in the process. He didn't want to help others if it meant exposing himself in the process.

If he took that lie detector test in the morning, Chief Odum would be well on his way to figuring out that Ron Gress wasn't really Ron Gress. He'd already said as much. And it wouldn't take a whole lot of digging for Chief Odum to find out who he really was.

He closed his eyes, sighed, forced thoughts of being discovered out of his mind.

The worst part was, this was a giant leap backward just after he'd taken a few small steps forward. He'd been paranoid for a long, long time, and in these last few days he'd felt himself coming out of that cloud cover. He didn't hear footsteps walking down the street behind him. He didn't feel eyes watching him while he worked. Last night he hadn't even armed his alarm system. That was all good, and in his mind he knew it had something to do with . . . well, Nathan. And his father in some odd way. And yes, Rachel. For the first time in a long time, he was thinking about other people, and their happiness. And that was part of what had let him go along with this "looking for signs" stuff from Kristina. There was something nice about rising above the self-centeredness.

He took another drink of the orange juice. But here was the other question: *had* he been getting better, or were all these events of the last few days mere delusions themselves? He tried to be soberly analytical, examining the evidence. Paranoia, repressed memories, blackouts. Rachel had suggested epileptic seizures, a real possibility. Mix it all together, and he wasn't exactly a poster child for mental fitness. Wouldn't delusions fit that pattern? Couldn't his mind have imagined all of it?

He shook his head, another unconscious effort to clear it. No matter. He would just ignore it. This incident, he decided, would bring the Kristina experiments to a dead end. He didn't fit her superhero image, and she'd just have to die without doing her own good deed.

The whole vision thing, the signs . . . those *had* to be delusional. (*No, they're not. Coincidence can't explain it all.*)

He slammed down his fist. Yes, it was delusional. He would allow no other explanation. This was all his mind playing tricks on him, pulling the taste of copper from his past and putting it in his mouth at moments of high stress. Yes, and the visions were part of Rachel's epileptic seizure scenario. After all, they were filled with odd colors and sequences, and he really had no way of knowing the visions were correct. (*Yes you do. Ginny, the waitress*—) He cut off the thought, gulped down the rest of the orange juice. Case closed.

He was about to be discovered, which would destroy all he'd been building. Along with any sliver of normalcy he might share with Nathan. (*And Rachel? Maybe.*)

He needed to clear his mind, reset his thoughts. And he immediately thought of one way to do it.

When Rachel opened the door and saw Ron standing there, she felt the familiar knot clench in her chest instantly. He was all right. Almost without thinking, she pulled him in and hugged him, then caught herself as she felt his body stiffen in the embrace. She let go, turned, and walked across the room. "Where have you been?" she asked. She felt as if she needed to do something with her arms, so she crossed them. "I . . . tried to call you this morning, and I've been worried. I got a strange call last night, and—" She stopped, unsure what to say next, because her mind was unsure what to think.

He stared for a moment, then slowly blinked. "I, uh . . . know. I got your message. I wanted to call you back, I meant to, but I was just at—" He took a deep breath, closed his eyes, opened them again. "I'm sorry, I've been through a lot the last few days, and I'm just fried. Could we maybe talk about it all tomorrow?"

She nodded. Now, more than ever, she was conflicted. On the one hand, he was still the pathetic puppy; he was a sick man, possibly, who needed her help and prayer. She should show him kindness and understanding. She knew this. On the other hand, the nickname she and Nicole had given him—Boo Radley—fit more than ever. She'd discovered buried secrets in this man's past, and she'd done the right thing (she was sure it was the right thing, because she'd prayed about it and felt at peace) by calling the police and telling them what she'd found. The man standing in front of her probably wasn't Ron Gress. So who was he? And who had called her home looking for him?

He stared at the floor. "I'm sorry," he said, "to be so pathetic. Just have a lot going on."

Yes, you certainly do, she thought to herself. *A lot you probably don't want other people to know about.* Then she remembered their last conversation. "Saw your dad?" she asked.

Ron, or whatever his real name was, gave a weak smile. "Yeah, I saw my dad. For starters. We need to talk about some things. Soon. But tonight, can we just . . ." He trailed off, seeming like he was searching for a particular word. "Can we just be with Nathan?" he finished.

He wanted to talk, which was good. She could talk, maybe let him get a little bit off his chest, perhaps that "I ran away from a mental health facility years ago" confession. That she could handle.

Having this man, this Boo Radley, in the same room as Nathan, however—how could she dance around that? "Um . . . you know, why don't we talk now?" she said, going over to the couch and sitting down.

And then Nathan came bounding into the living room. "DADDY!" he squealed at a level somewhere above a hundred decibels, and sprinted across the room to vault into Ron's arms. Ron, she noticed, actually opened his arms, actually welcomed the hug from his son.

"I'm making a robot with Magnetix," Nathan said to Ron. "Wanna see?" He started pulling Ron down the hallway toward his bedroom.

Her radar was maxing out now. "Nathan," she said. "It's almost your bedtime, and Ron's—" But they were already down the hall, Nathan chattering about his creation.

She followed, she *had* to follow. She couldn't just leave her son alone with this man. What would happen if he went into another seizure or something? She walked into Nathan's room. "Here," she said, "let's get your pajamas on." She went to Nathan's dresser, fumbled through the doors before finding some Ultra Man pajamas, then went back and grabbed Nathan's hand. "Come on. We'll, uh . . . change in the bathroom."

"Mom! I can change here. It's just Daddy!"

She bit her lip. "I know, dear, but it's not—"

"Your mom's right," Ron interrupted. "It would be more polite to change in the bathroom." Ron looked at her, and in his look she didn't see the sad emptiness she'd seen before. She saw something warmer. More human.

"Okay," she half whispered, still looking at Ron. "Let's go." She pulled away her gaze and took Nathan into the bathroom to change, barely registering her son's chatter.

"You okay, Mommy?" Nathan said as he popped his head through the neck opening of his pajama top.

She mussed his hair. "Never better," she lied.

"Can Daddy tuck me in?"

She felt panic in her veins. She'd guessed this question would come. It was only natural. She closed her eyes, said another quick prayer, opened them again. "Yes," she said, surprising herself as she said it. Okay, she could do this. Let Ron tuck him in, and just keep an eye on things. That would be fine, wouldn't it? She bit her lip again.

Nathan rushed back into his room. She followed him and stood awkwardly in the doorway for a few moments. "I'll, uh . . . just be out here," she said numbly. Ron looked back at her, that warm, *human* glow still in his eyes. A look that made her uncomfortable because it was so trusting.

"We'll be okay," he said, and hugged Nathan.

She backed out of the door, closing it most of the way behind her, then peeked through the crack. She was only willing to let faith go so far where her son was concerned.

In the room, Nathan jumped on his bed as if it were a trampoline, even executing a leg tuck and roll. Ron laughed. "Don't let your mom see you doing that. She'll be scared you're going to break the bed. Or your neck."

"Nah, she don't mind," Nathan said.

"Oh, really? Well, why don't we just call her in and ask her?" Ron turned and looked her direction. She jumped back a step and immediately tried to think of a good excuse why she was eavesdropping. Ron cupped his hands to his mouth and acted as if he was about to call out. Nathan squealed, then leaped to his feet and covered Ron's mouth.

Ron laughed, a good long laugh that came from deep inside, and Nathan joined in. He hadn't seen her at all, it seemed.

Nathan fell back on his pillow, letting his head bounce a few times in comic exaggeration. "You gonna read me a story, Dad?"

"Sure, we'll read a story. You pick." Nathan scooted to the bookcase at the end of his bed, picked out a book, then rolled over and handed it to Ron. Ron opened the book but paused. "But before the story in this book, I want to tell you a story about me," Ron said.

This was it; Rachel knew this was it. Ron was going to tell Nathan something about his past. She didn't feel comfortable watching, but she didn't move, either. She could listen, couldn't she? God would give her something.

"Okay, Daddy."

"I wanted to tell you about the best present I ever got in my whole life."

Nathan's eyes saucered; talk of presents was always a good thing. "The best present ever?" he asked breathlessly. "What was it?"

"It was this great picture of a hand." Ron held out his hand, tracing around the fingers with the index finger of his other hand. "It had all these colors on it, and it was the most beautiful thing I've ever seen."

Nathan smiled. "My hand, Daddy?"

Ron nodded as he bent to kiss him. "Your hand."

Rachel realized at once she had been wrong, and her radar went to zero. Ron hadn't told a story and made himself cry. He had told a story and made her cry. She swiped a few tears from her cheek and backed down the hallway as quietly as she could. God had indeed given her something in that scene: a reassurance Ron wasn't a monster, but a man.

Trouble was, she wasn't sure that was the answer she'd wanted. It was the far more difficult answer.

In the kitchen she poured another cup of coffee and brought it into the living room. Ron would be out any minute, and she wanted to say something to him. What, she didn't know. But she knew she wanted to say something.

As she sat down, she abruptly thought of a scene from the movie *Alien*. Why she'd thought of it, she had no idea, but there it was. When she'd seen it as a kid, the opening scenes had bothered her—more, in fact, than anything in the rest of the movie. In those scenes, the ship's crew started waking from a deep sleep. In their little rocket-shaped pods, the astronauts looked dead; the pod doors blocked out air, keeping them preserved. When the pod doors opened and the crew slowly began waking, Rachel had started getting a headache from the tension. She hadn't paid attention to the rest of the movie, because she'd simply sat immobile, breathing deeply. The thought of those closed doors had cramped her lungs, and she'd needed *air*.

The thoughts came together. Ron was one of those crew members. He'd been in deep sleep for a long time, and he was waking up. And just like in the movie, it was painful to watch.

Ron walked into the living room, interrupting her reverie. She stood, felt awkward. Sat again. She picked up her coffee, took a sip, gave him a weak smile.

"Won't be long 'til he's out," Ron offered.

"Lots of excitement. Your coming over was a special treat for him."

"Well," he said, "I've had my share of excitement lately, too."

"You'll have to tell me about it sometime," she said.

"I promise."

He walked to the door and opened it. "Don't take this wrong or anything," Rachel found herself blurting before he could leave, "but you seem different."

He stopped, his hand on the door handle. "Different how?"

"I don't know. Like a different person."

He smiled. "Maybe I am," he said. After the door clicked shut behind him, she closed her eyes and listened. His car door creaked open and shut; then the car started and moved out of the driveway. A few seconds later the sound of the car receded into the distance.

Her prayers had worked: God was helping her see Ron as an actual, honest-to-goodness person.

She just hoped there wasn't an alien inside him.

The guy who ran the polygraph machine (*What would he be called? Polygraph Technician? Lie Detector Administrator?*) sat at the end of the table. He looked something like Mr. Clean to Jude, mostly because of the bald head. Jude was about to take a lie detector test from Mr. Clean. There was a joke in that somewhere, but Jude couldn't think of one; he was getting too nervous.

Jude tried not to concentrate on the wires and paraphernalia. Electrodes sprouted from various parts of his body, including his temples. A blood pressure cuff gripped his right arm. And the actual polygraph machine itself was enormous: when Mr. Clean sat down behind it, Jude could see just eyes and the top of a bald, shiny pate.

Maybe this was a mistake. Jude hadn't done anything wrong, sure, but that didn't mean he'd come through the test unscathed. Just sitting here was nerve wracking enough, and the electrodes were beginning to itch. With his left hand he reached up to scratch. Wires popped off and hung limply.

Jude gave a weak apology. Mr. Clean said nothing. Instead he stopped jotting notes on his clipboard, stood, and reattached the wires, this time to Jude's arm. When he sat down again, he checked a few readouts on his Frankenstein machine, marked something with a black marker, and finally looked at Jude. Jude, the Laboratory Rat.

"Okay, Mr. Gress. I'll ask a series of questions, and you'll just answer yes or no."

Jude tried a smile, but he was sure it came across as more of a grimace.

"Let's start with the date, then. Is today September twenty-eighth?"

First question, and he didn't know the answer. Jude Allman, once upon a time, had been good with dates. Ron Gress, on the other hand, never had much use for them. When you didn't keep a busy social calendar filled with charity events and social soirees, you had no need to worry about such things.

"Um, I don't know," Jude said truthfully. "Is today September twenty-eighth?"

"Yes," Mr. Clean assured him.

"Then yes," Jude said. Mr. Clean made another mark on the readout. "Did I get that one right?" Jude asked. He needed a little humor, a bit of levity.

Mr. Clean didn't chuckle. He looked at Jude, his mouth unyielding and straight as a razor.

Okay, so much for humor. It wasn't working for Jude, either; he felt more like throwing up than smiling.

"Are you thirty-two years old?"

Jude took a breath. "Yes."

"Is your name Ron Gress?"

He answered automatically. "Yes," he said, then realized that wasn't the total truth. "Um, no," he added quickly.

The technician arched an eyebrow at him, then looked down at his readouts again. "Do you have a son named Nathan Sanders?"

"Yes."

"Do you know a man named Kenneth Sohler?"

"Yes."

"And have you had any contact with Kenneth Sohler in the last twenty-four hours?"

Jude paused. Where was this going? "The last time I had *contact* with Mr. Sohler, it was a bedpost making *contact* with his head." This test was beginning to make him a bit angry.

"Yes or no, Mr. Gress."

"No."

"And do you know where Mr. Sohler is now?"

"No, I don't. Do you?"

"Have you and Mr. Sohler been kidnapping children, Mr. Gress?"

Jude blinked a few times, felt as though he'd just stepped out of a nice warm shower only to have a bucket of ice poured on him. Did Mr. Clean ask if he'd been kidnapping kids? The kidnapper—Sohler—wait, wait. Jude recalled the television interview, and Odum saying they were looking for the owner of the house. Maybe Sohler really *was* missing, and maybe the police really *did* think he had something to do with the abductions.

Crazy, yes. But not over-the-top crazy, not beyond the realm of possibility. The kids would say he'd rescued them, wouldn't they? And the police would confirm what the kids said with Sohler's story and injuries. If Sohler were missing, he'd be the key link to exonerating Jude.

He tried to swallow the dry medicinal taste in his mouth. It wasn't copper, but it worried him just the same. He felt his body collapsing in on itself, as if his bones were gone and he was just a balloon of skin filled with leaking helium. (*Dad sitting over my bed.*) An image of his father flashed into his mind for a brief moment, (*over my bed*) but it was gone in a white-hot instant. Other flashes danced before his eyes like a disastrous fireworks show—not flashes of memories but flashes of his mind misfiring. It was the brain's equivalent of Does Not Compute, and Jude struggled to reboot. He couldn't grasp how things had taken such a wrong turn. *Tell me if you've been kidnapping kids, Mr. Gress—or whatever your real name is. Child abductors like to change their names and use aliases, you know. What are you really hiding?*

Then his eyesight cleared, and what he saw wasn't a black cloud of pity for himself. His mind turned red, red as rage, red as blood. Jude bolted from the table, popping electrodes away from his body as he stood. This evidently wasn't what Mr. Clean had expected; he recoiled.

Jude turned to the one-way mirror behind him. One of the electrodes—or maybe it was the blood pressure cuff—valiantly fought to stay connected. He heard the sound of the giant machine sliding across the table, trying to follow him. It fell to the floor, a final fitting sound for the world crashing down around him.

"Hey, what the—" Mr. Clean began, but Jude wasn't looking at the technician anymore. He was looking at his own reflection in the one-way mirror, picturing Chief Odum on the other side.

"I think you and I need to talk, Chief Odum," Jude said. "Now."

Same setup, different room. Jude sat across from Odum again, only instead of a white table, it was now Odum's desk—a large steel desk that looked like a leftover from the' 1950s.

Jude simmered. He was a suspect, and it made him mad to think anyone would accuse him of mistreating kids, locking them up the way Sohler . . . He shuddered, pushing the thought from his mind. In the meantime, he was sitting here, about to play some more cat-and-mouse with Chief Odum. If he was right, Sohler was missing; so why wasn't Odum out there looking for the guy? He had to be the kidnapper everyone was talking about in the news.

Jude cleared his throat. "Based on your tester's questions, I'm guessing Sohler's gone."

Odum sat quietly, rocked back in his chair. After a few moments of silence, he spoke. "You're guessing right."

"You lost him." A jab, trying to make Odum wince a bit.

Instead, Odum smiled bitterly. "I did at that, Mr. *Gress*. Had him under twenty-four-hour watch, waiting for the discharge orders." Odum leaned back in his chair, seemed to consider his next words carefully. "Somebody else, though, had other ideas. Early morning hours, night before last—say about three in the morning—someone got the drop on Officer Barber, knocked him out, I'm guessing. Barber never got a look at the guy, or if he did, he can't remember. A concussion has a way of scrambling the brain for a while. Anyway, I thought that person might be you, in to spring your friend from the hospital." Odum smacked his lips, looked at the ceiling. "Of course, you understand."

"He's not my friend, I told you that."

Odum shrugged.

"So he's been loose for—what?—a whole day?" Jude said.

"Little more than that."

"And you didn't bring me in for questioning until last night."

Odum nodded. "We were keeping an eye on you. Thought you might be making a move, going to meet him somewhere."

Jude shuddered. For a few years he'd had the growing feeling he was being watched, monitored, followed. He'd been healing recently, realizing it was paranoia. Ironically, now that he'd shaken that feeling, he really was being followed.

"Why haven't I heard anything about it? Seems like it would have been all over the news by now."

"Seems like it, doesn't it?" Odum flashed another bitter grin. "One benefit to having a small police force, a *close-knit* police force."

Jude felt his anger rising. "But shouldn't you be looking for him?"

Odum closed his eyes. "I'm working on it, Mr. Gress. The entire Red Lodge police force is working on it. And then some. Feds have punched their dance card, too."

Jude felt the exhaustion radiating off Odum and backed off, letting his anger subside. He shook his head, trying to loosen the jumbled thoughts fastening themselves to his skull. No way he was going to figure it all out right now. Oddly, he found himself wishing Kristina were here. She would have some ideas, say something to help.

"Sorry about your equipment," Jude said, a mild peace offering extended to Odum.

Odum shrugged. "Polygraph results make good toilet paper, and that's about it. Machine wasn't even downloading data. Just an old trick to get people sweating."

"Well, it worked."

"Partly. I still don't have a lot of answers I'm looking for. Some of them from you."

"Do we really have to go into this right now?"

Odum wiped at a line of sweat trickling down his forehead. "Sitting here trying to go toe-to-toe with me isn't going to do much. One, you'll lose the match—I've got the gun, I've got the badge. Two, we'll waste a lot of time."

"Okay, okay." Jude sighed.

"So who are you, really, Mr. Gress?"

Time to trot out the lie he'd been rehearsing since last night. "My real name is Kevin Burkhart," he said, pulling out the name of his childhood friend from Bingham, Nebraska.

Odum scratched down the name. "And why are you using an assumed name, Mr., uh, Burkhart?"

"I made a few bad business decisions, ended up going broke. Bankrupt, actually. So it made sense for me to just start over. New life, new place, all that."

"And you decided to start over as a janitor?"

"Something about good, honest work, Chief Odum. Cleans the soul."

Odum smiled. "That it does. And where was it you made these bad business decisions?"

"I worked in Iowa for a while, but things went bad when I went back home to Nebraska. Little town named Bingham."

Odum's eyes narrowed for a few seconds, and Jude could tell he was sifting through his memory banks. After a few seconds, a smile. "Bingham . . . that resurrection fella was from there, right?"

Jude nodded. "Jude Allman. Yeah, I used to hear that all the time."

"So did you know him, that Jude Allman guy?"

Jude returned Odum's smile. "Doesn't everybody?"

Frank was all smiles when Jude showed up at work. "Ron, me boy," he said through crooked yellow teeth when Jude walked into his office, "thought you were gonna be gone for a while. But it's nice to have you back."

Jude glanced at the clock. Just after noon—the polygraph test and conversation with Odum had taken his whole morning. "Yeah," he said. "Felt better than expected, so I thought I might as well come in for a bit this afternoon. Give you a hand."

He looked at Frank and tried a smile. It was a good thing Frank was a janitor, because he wouldn't be able to fall back on modeling. Frank never combed his hair (or if he did, the hair ignored the comb entirely), his complexion was pockmarked, and he was about seventy pounds on the high side of husky. But the worst part was the teeth. Frank could easily have inspired the Billy Bob novelty teeth so popular in gag stores.

Still, even though Frank looked a lot like a beast, Jude thought of him as mostly harmless. Frank thought he was a comedian and always spewed odd little phrases—sticking in a "me boy" after everyone's name when he hailed them being one of the more curious ones—but he was all right.

Jude started to dig into the closet for a dust broom. "Thought I'd clean the gym. That okay?"

"You want to clean the gym, I'm not gonna melt your ice cream about it." Frank looked at the clock on the wall. "You takin' some time off got me to thinking, anyway. I'll cut out this afternoon, take off tomorrow, too. I—" He paused, and Jude stopped to look at him. He could tell Frank was thinking hard about something; best to encourage him a bit so he didn't blow a gasket.

"You what, Frank?"

"Well, I got some special things going on. You maybe ought to see my basement sometime. You and your boy. Love to show him sometime." Frank licked his lips, his eyes glossing over.

Jude thought for a moment. He was pretty sure Frank was harmless, but he was also pretty sure he didn't want to head over to Frank's for tea and crumpets anytime soon. Some things were better left unknown. "Um . . . okay, Frank. I'd like that." A lie, but what harm could it do?

The glassy pallor disappeared from Frank's eyes, and Jude saw the slow gears of Frank's brain engage again as he pushed aside a partly finished crossword puzzle and stood. "Well now, Ron, me boy," he said. "You'd best get to that gym. And I'd best get home and get started."

Jude smiled. He'd never had any big run-ins with Frank, and he was sure he had the obligatory smile or chuckle to thank for that.

Jude grabbed the dust mop and stepped out into the hall; the hallways stood empty now that all the kids were in class. He walked down the hallway, dragging the mop behind him. He'd made it through the lie detector test okay, he thought. Had even given Chief Odum a plausible lie that would hold up under a bit of light fact checking; he felt confident that Odum was more occupied with thoughts of the escaped Kenneth Sohler and would probably abandon tracing him when he ran a check on the name *Kevin Burkhart*, finding such a person had once lived in Bingham, Nebraska.

With that bit out of the way, he could concentrate on becoming normal again. On forgetting all about visions and signs and other garbage, and just concentrate on being a dad. As he walked, he began to pack away thoughts of the last several days and put them away on a forgotten shelf—a high, out-of-the-way shelf.

He turned left at the end of the hall, heading for the gym. He liked to work in the gym, because it was usually quiet when PE classes weren't in session. The gym was separated from the rest of the school, so you had to travel out of your way to get there. Jude reached the double doors and stepped inside. His footsteps echoed in the silence.

Dust-mopping the gym was usually good for fifteen or twenty minutes' blissful quiet. Routine, it was all about routine. That was what he needed. (*The boy—Joey—he locked him in a cage.*) Jude shook his head and packed that thought away, banished it to a high shelf.

He placed the dust broom on the floor's varnished surface and started a wide swath right in front of the bleachers, falling quickly into a comforting pattern. Down the floor, then back up. Down, up. (*She was chained to the bed.*) He folded the thought neatly and put it in the pile with its cousins.

He brought to mind the lie detector session with—

"Hey, Mr. Gress." Jude stopped, looked up. At the other end of the floor was a young boy, about Nathan's age. The boy had to know him personally; the others mostly called him "Mr. Janitor."

Jude pushed the mop back toward the boy until he could get a look at the face. Yes, he did know this one. It was Bradley, Nathan's friend. Rachel was friendly with Bradley's mother. What was her name? Anna or something? He started digging through his memory files, and the image of the bedpost connecting with Kenneth Sohler's head flashed before him. He shifted back into mental neutral, decided Bradley's mom could remain known as "what's-her-name" for now.

"Hey, Bradley," Jude said. "What are you doing down here?" (*Nicole, that is her name.*)

Bradley held up a backpack. "I left it here yesterday," he said. "My teacher gave me a hall pass!" Bradley displayed the white plastic card as if it were a trophy, and his grin doubled in size.

At that moment Jude detected an odd taste in his mouth, a familiar tinge. And then it hit him full force: the coppery taste, as if all his teeth had suddenly turned to phone wire. He covered his mouth and coughed, wished he could spit.

Bradley's grin faltered. "You okay, Mr. Gress?"

"Yeah, Bradley. Fine, just fine." This was it. He could give in to the delusions, touch the kid, and get himself into more trouble convincing himself that something was about to happen to this kid. Or he could do the perfectly rational thing: ignore it all, realize it was just his mind playing tricks, and wait a few days. When nothing happened to Bradley, he'd have all the proof he needed to write it off as pure bunk. Psychobabble.

Then another thought occurred to him. If he was having seizures, and if the coppery taste of death was what brought them on, he shouldn't be around Bradley when it happened. He could hurt the kid without realizing it.

"You better get to class, don't you think, Bradley?" His voice was shaky, jittery, but Bradley didn't seem to notice.

Clouds brewed in Bradley's eyes as he looked at Jude. It was as if the boy sensed he was in the wrong place, but also the right place.

"Come on," Jude said, unthinkingly reaching toward the boy. His hand came within a few inches until he recoiled, realizing what he was about to do. No touching. It was a rule he'd lived by quite well, until recently. And he was more than ready to reinstate that rule now.

Bradley looked at him a few more seconds. "Guess I'll go now," the boy said, then turned and crashed through the double doors behind him. Jude followed, watching as Bradley walked the lonely hallway, then turned a corner and disappeared.

That evening Jude returned to his home, feeling the need to lock the door and arm the security system. This hadn't seemed as important in the last few days, but in light of his trip to the police station that morning, he felt safer knowing the system was armed.

He hadn't seen any unmarked cars parked outside his home, yet that didn't mean they weren't around somewhere. You never knew when—or how—*they* were watching.

Jude shook his head, banishing the paranoid thoughts. He moved through the house and noticed a red light blinking on his phone's message machine. Kristina? Frank? Rachel? He felt his heart tug, hoping it was Rachel. He went to the machine and pressed the button. On the recording, he heard the Jake Brake of a diesel truck, and under it a raspy voice: "Well now, cowboy. That's an awfully small thing to do, hit a man in the head like that. Hit him when he's down, even."

Jude's blood chilled. It was Kenneth Sohler, leaving a message on his machine. Had to have been Sohler the night before, too. Must be holed up at a truck stop or something.

"You best be looking over your shoulder."

Click.

The rest of that night Jude felt jittery, full of nervous energy. Part of it was fueled by Sohler's phone call; obviously the man was intent on finding him. And really, he should call Chief Odum, play the message for him.

Tomorrow. He'd do that tomorrow. The message would help clear his name.

But that decision still didn't relieve the unexplainable sense of dread he felt. Something bad was going to happen. Something very bad, indeed.

He just wished he knew what it was.

Maybe he should leave, avoid it all. He'd done that before, moved on and disappeared. It was probably the best idea, all things considered: just pack up a few clothes, grab a bit of cash, and hit the road. Start over again somewhere else.

But there had been no Nathan, no Rachel, before.

He heard a car pull up and cut its engine. Who was it? For once, he regretted sheetrocking the windows. He went to the door and paused, his hand resting lightly on the knob. Maybe it was *them*, putting him under surveillance again and . . .

"No!" He spat the word, surprising himself. No, it wasn't *them.* There never had been any *them.* He knew that now, and he wasn't going to let himself slide back into that way of thinking. Not when he was so close, so close to having a normal life.

He opened the door a crack and peeked outside. A black and white police cruiser sat on the street. The car's dome light came on, and Jude recognized the face of Officer Grant, the man who had escorted him to the station the previous evening. Officer Grant nodded, then turned off the dome light.

Jude closed the door. Okay. Message received, Chief Odum. He wasn't going anywhere.

He sat in the lone chair at his dining table and watched his hands tremble; his whole body was shaking, threatening to come apart, and he couldn't control it. What had he done? What in God's name had he done? His mind, his oh-so-logical mind, told him he'd done nothing wrong. But his soul, his heart, whatever you wanted to call it, told him the opposite.

Jude scratched at his forehead. The thoughts inside felt like tiny insects, crawling and burrowing. He couldn't stop the infestation, and they were multiplying. Multiplying.

A knock came at the door.

What? *Who?* His shaking stopped for a moment.

"Jude? Hello?" Another knock. Kristina. Somehow he knew it would be her. Part of it was a process of elimination: how many people came knocking on Ron Gress's door, especially late at night? Only one. Part of it was . . . something else. He didn't know what.

He considered whether or not he should answer. Of course she would know he was inside—

"Jude, I know you're in there."

—but after all, what was she going to do? Break in?

He looked down at his hands, willed them to stop shaking. "Hold on just a second," he yelled. He couldn't let Kristina see this. Any of it. He took a few deep breaths and stood.

"I'm coming," he said, forcing his legs to move. He wanted to see, to make sure it was really Kristina. Just to be sure.

Jude first disarmed the security system before heading to the door. He slid back the dead bolts but kept the chain secured, and opened the door a crack to peek out. Kristina stood waiting.

"Open the door, Jude."

Jude closed the door again, slid the chain out of its channel, and opened the door wide for her. He blinked a few times. Across the street he saw the dome light inside Officer Grant's car come on again, a puzzled look on Officer Grant's face. Jude waved to him as Kristina walked in, then shut and dead-bolted the door behind her.

"I hope I'm not too late," she said.

Jude froze. She *knew*. She knew he had made a mistake—a mistake that would end in disaster. He cleared his throat. "What do you mean?" he asked.

"You know," she said. "Too late. Too late at night."

He relaxed. A little. Still, he had the impression that *wasn't* what she'd meant. "Actually . . . I have a few things I should tell you."

After they sat down in his living room, he poured it all out, like a mountain stream swollen with spring runoff poured itself into a larger river headed for the coast. He let go of everything, and when he finished, he felt empty. It was a good feeling.

Kristina sat looking at him for a few moments before speaking. "Rough couple of days," she said.

"I've had better."

"You wanna know what I think?"

"I'd like that."

"You're worried about what you did today. Or, more appropriately, didn't do. To be blunt, you should be. One, it's never a good idea to ignore the signs as they're given to you. Two, you need to keep in mind every decision in the universe has ripples, echoes that spread out from it."

"So I've also doomed the universe," he said with a touch of acid in his voice.

"I'm not saying that. I'm saying there will be repercussions, and there's nothing you can do now except wait and deal with them when they come."

"Thanks for the pep talk."

"A pep talk we wouldn't be having if you were doing what you're supposed to."

"And what, exactly, is that? I've never been real clear on this. You're the big expert."

She stared at him, said nothing.

Okay, it was time to cool down. Kristina was here to talk things through with him, not be his punching bag for guilt. "I'm sorry," he said. "I just . . . I'm scared."

"That's good," she said. "Fear can make you do the impossible. The miraculous."

"Is that what you think? I'm some kind of miracle worker?"

She pulled out a manila envelope and handed it to him. He looked at it blankly, then at her again. She nodded, so he opened it. Without looking, he knew what he'd find inside: his book. *Into the Light*.

"I've bookmarked some pages," she said. "Open it up to the first one."

Jude opened the book to a page marked by a yellow sticky note. *First death—age eight*, it read.

"Okay," she said. "Now check out the second and third notes." He flipped to the second yellow sticky: *Second death—age sixteen*. And the third: *Third death—age twenty-four. See a pattern?*

He looked at her again. "Eight," he whispered. "It happened every eight years."

She nodded. "So, is that a coincidence? You tell me."

He sat, listening to the hard tick of the analog clock in his bedroom down the hall—the only noise in the house. "Don't take this wrong, but so what? What's so special about eight?"

She shrugged this time. "Nothing. Everything. We always want everything to mean something, unless it really *does* mean something. Then we want to ignore it. But if you read the Bible, if you study the significance of numbers in it, you'll see the number eight always represents a new beginning, a starting over." She paused, her eyes flickering. "A resurrection."

Jude caught himself starting to roll his eyes. This was getting a little too out there. And yet, he noticed, the trembling in his body had stopped.

"Look," Kristina said, "I think we can say you've come to the point where you know there's something different about you. Something special."

"Different. I'll give you that."

"But you've never explored *why*, have you?"

"You're assuming there's some reason."

"You're assuming there isn't. You want to assign everything to coincidence, but I don't think it's coincidence at work here. I don't think Jude Allman has anything to do with coincidence."

"So?"

"So you're only partway there. You found out you can see things about other people, help them avoid death. And, you have this power over death yourself, as the man who keeps returning to life. So what are you doing with it?"

He sat motionless. "Nothing."

"That's right. Nothing."

He shook his head. "No, that's all wrong. I've had, I've had these bad memories, you know? I've ... um ... had these blackouts and things." He felt the trembling beginning again and tried to quell it. "And look, everyone's going to die. You—you're going to die. Why haven't I had any kind of vision about you?"

Kristina grabbed his hand, and her skin was cold—almost icy. "You have all the evidence you need, but you're trying to disbelieve anyway. That's human. Why do you think having visions about *anyone* means you'll have visions about *everyone?* Miracles are a suspension of natural law, so forget about what you think should be happening, and concentrate on what *is.*"

For a few moments the only sound was Kristina trying to catch her breath.

Jude looked at her, nodded slowly, smiled. "As if you see miracles every day."

"Hey, I'm just one of the weirdos who follows you around, remember? What do I know?"

"You're never gonna let go of that, are you?"

Now it was her turn to smile. "Not a chance."

Jude realized she was still holding on to his hand, but her skin was warm now. In a way, it was pleasant, enjoyable. If only Kristina weren't dying, maybe . . .

He sat back, pulled away his hand, and cleared his throat. "You're very convincing, but there's still the matter of these seizures, or whatever. The blackouts. I mean, the mind is a very powerful thing, and I could be imagining a lot of things. I could be imagining you."

She smiled. "Maybe you're just a brain in a jar, and you're imagining everything."

"It would be more helpful if you said, 'No, I'm not a figment of your imagination. I'm real.'"

"Well, of course I know *I'm* real. It's you I'm not so sure about yet."

After Kristina left, Jude armed his alarm system, went to his room, and sat on the easy chair, thinking about Kristina's words. It made enough sense, in some ways. But he didn't really want it to. Okay, so there was something . . . different . . . about him. Fair enough; that certainly fit, whether he was becoming psychic or psychotic. Different.

Jude took a deep breath. What he needed right now was to be

plain vanilla. He needed to return to work, to get a bit of normalcy in his life. To see Nathan and Rachel after work, chase a rare and unfamiliar feeling. To be the kind of father he never had.

Being different from everyone else could wait. For now, until his head cleared, he needed to be the same. Tomorrow would come and go, Bradley would be perfectly fine, and he'd look back on this conversation with Kristina and laugh.

32

The Hunter and the Normal sat with electrodes taped to their (his) temples. He (they) had administered an extra long session of treatments, but inside, this didn't really matter. The shocks didn't hurt anymore. They were low buzzes, humming in the ears like nasty wasps, yet without any real sting. Maybe it was time for more extreme measures. That was what the broken shard of glass was: extreme measures.

It was time to accept. He (they) had *become*, but the next step of *becoming* was *accepting*.

They had been careful, tentative of recent. Lying low, as the saying used to go. As the Normal—dressed in the Normal's clothes, walking with the Normal's gait, smiling with the Normal's teeth, and speaking with the Normal's voice—they had gone beyond tracking a Quarry. Even enticed a Quarry and started driving to the house. Started.

Downtown, the disciplined side took over, and the Quarry was set free. It was a simple thing, and the Quarry wouldn't say anything. Probably hadn't even known it was a Quarry, and that was the exciting thing about hunting as the Normal. Maybe, more Extreme Measures . . .

Then, the maybes disappeared. It was time to *accept*, the next stage of *becoming*.

But it was also time for Extreme Measures, because Extreme Measures would help them *accept*.

The Hunter and the Normal picked up the large shard of the

glass, then ran the sharp edge of it across the exposed skin of their stomach. The jagged edge traced a trail of crimson, but the glass, too, was just a nasty wasp, without any real sting.

He. They. Extreme measures. Becoming. Accepting.

33

Jude felt perfect the next morning, really perfect for the first time in . . . maybe ever. Alive. He smiled as the word crossed his mind. Yeah, alive. Jude Allman was alive. Imagine that.

Yesterday's worries, yesterday's trembling fear, had dissolved like a bad dream. He held up his hand and looked at it. Steady as always. And that conversation with Kristina last night, well, maybe that *had* been a dream.

He sat in the break room for coffee kickoff. He always called the first fifteen minutes of the day coffee kickoff because Frank called it coffee kickoff. And far be it from Ron Gress, Compliant Janitor, to rock the boat. Coffee kickoff it was, even though he usually stayed away from the stuff. Today would be even more enjoyable, because Frank was gone. He'd said yesterday he was going to take some time off, something about working in the basement.

He even decided to try a bit of coffee today; counting the cups he'd had at Rachel's and the cafe, it was his fourth in about five years. He didn't do it because he craved coffee but because he craved something normal. He raised the cup to no one in particular and did a quick toast to Frank and his most important work in the basement.

Yes, normal. That was what he was now. None of the life-after-death nonsense, no imaginary visions or imaginary people. Just normalcy.

Jude took another sip of the coffee—decided to cut it with a healthy amount of creamer, straight black was just too harsh—and opened that morning's local *Carbon County News*. The big story was about the search for Kenneth Sohler. *Authorities refuse to speculate about Sohler,* the article said, *but sources have said Sohler had connections to at least two of the missing children.* Chief Odum had kept the story quiet for a few days, but evidently it was breaking news now.

The image of Sohler's bloody face appeared and swam in his vision again. He quickly put down the paper and picked up Frank's *People* magazine instead. He smiled to himself. Frank reading *People* always struck him as such an odd match—like Martha Stewart becoming a wrestling fan, it just didn't match. One-on-one, Frank was pretty chatty, full of odd turns of phrase. And the young kids seemed to like him; he was always talking to them in the halls. But all in all, Frank, he of the Billy Bob teeth and the Michelin Man physique, just didn't fit the typical image of a people person. Or a *People* person.

Jude started thumbing through the pages, trying to find one that caught his eye, when something in his peripheral vision moved. He looked up and saw Kristina in the doorway.

"Sorry," she said, obviously noticing he'd been startled.

"'Sokay," he said. "Guess I jump kind of easy."

"Guess so," she said.

Silence.

"How'd you get in here, anyway?" he asked.

She smiled. "It's a school, not a maximum security prison."

Okay, he hadn't really meant *how*, it was more of a *why* question, but he wasn't going to argue semantics at the moment. She'd probably get to the why soon enough. Jude was kind of glad to see Kristina, anyway. He'd been thinking of her, and he really needed to get some things straight. She clearly had the wrong ideas about him. The superhero thing, for sure. But he also felt like there was something more, like maybe she wanted him to be a last fling in a macabre way.

But he couldn't. He couldn't, because of Rachel. Not that there was anything there, either. But he'd been thinking a lot about her recently, and he wasn't about to spend time with Kristina while thinking of someone else. Plus, Kristina scared him, in a lot of ways. Made him uncomfortable. And—let's be honest here—there wasn't much of a future with Kristina. She was dying.

Kristina didn't speak, so he tried to prime the pump. "What brings you here?"

"I just wondered if you'd maybe want to have dinner tonight. Good old Red Lodge Cafe."

Well, there it was. No choice now but to spill it all. "Look, I'm not . . ." Not what? "I just don't think I should."

"Why not?"

"I need to tell you something. Something kind of important." He motioned for her to sit down at the break table with him. Should he offer her a cup of coffee? No, best not to get too comfortable.

"Okay," she said as she sat.

"It's all . . . nothing."

"You'll have to be just a bit more specific."

"The whole story: the *Into the Light* book you loved so much, the TV movie, the talk shows—all lies."

He looked for a reaction, but she didn't move. "I see," she said.

That made him mad. "I see" was something people usually said when they really meant "I don't believe a thing you're saying."

"No, I don't think you do see," he said. "What I'm saying is: all three times I died, I *remembered nothing*. There was something there, yes, but I couldn't ever remember it. The only thing I ever brought back from the Other Side was this horrible taste of copper, this taste of death. But is that what a dying person wants to hear?"

She stared a moment, then shook her head softly. "No."

"No. So I went along with the white light, and the warm voice, and the comforting presence. All of it. They got their book. They got their movie. And I got out. But here's the important thing: I lied about all of it. All of it. So where does that put your theories?"

He stopped. His brief anger at the "I see" comment had passed, and maybe he'd been a bit harsh. She was, after all, dying. She just wanted answers, and he was blowing apart her ideas about him. Jude

Allman wasn't anyone special, and he could tell her nothing about what waited for her on the Other Side. Already he regretted spilling this; she'd find out soon enough, and there would have been no harm letting her have hope.

He mentally kicked himself but continued. The cut had already been made; best to just take the whole tumor. "After all that, I just wasn't . . . right. I couldn't let anyone touch me. I even . . . do you know I can't lie down?"

"What do you mean?"

"Scares me, so I sleep in a recliner. If I try to lie down, I feel like I'm gonna choke. Maybe even . . . die." He knew how laughable that sounded coming from Jude Allman, the Incredible Resurrection Man, and he half expected her to chuckle. She didn't. "Crazy, huh? But now I'm feeling . . . I dunno . . . something's changed. Something maybe with my son, and I need that. But I also need to come clean with you: I'm not who you think. Or what you think. I'm pretty sure I have a chance of getting better, but all your talk about signs and being special and all that other cryptic stuff . . . well, I think that's making me sicker."

Kristina stood. "I'm sorry you feel that way," she said, looking at the floor. Then she turned and left the break room.

Great. She had probably come here this morning, scared to open her heart and talk about how she really felt, and he hadn't even waited. No sir. He'd torn open the locked door and stomped all over her heart with jackboots.

He went to the broom closet and found the dust mop. Coffee kickoff was officially over, and he needed to get to the gym, be alone. Maybe the gym didn't need another cleaning.

But Jude did.

Rachel heard the knock on her door, the knock she knew was coming all morning long. She looked out the peephole and then opened the door to let in Nicole.

"Hi," Rachel said. "I'm running a little late. Sorry. Just need to wash Nathan's face and put on his shoes."

"No problem," Nicole said. She turned to look back at her car; Bradley was in his booster seat, and he waved to her through the glass. Nicole turned back around and smiled. "We're a little early."

That was the great thing about Nicole: she would do anything to make you feel better. Even tell little fibs like "I'm early" when she was right on time. Rachel stepped back from the door and invited Nicole inside.

Nicole hesitated. "Um, I think I'll just stay out here. You know . . . I mean, with everything that's happened around here . . ." She let the sentence trail off, but she didn't need to. Rachel was a mother; she knew. Rachel immediately thought of the threatening phone call, then pushed it from her mind. Whoever had called her, it had nothing to do with Nicole or Bradley.

"If you need a few minutes," Nicole continued, "maybe I could just bring Bradley in."

"Oh, no, no. Just a face scrub and the shoes. Back in two shakes."

Nathan sat at the table, watching cartoons on the small television. She wasn't a huge fan of television, save one time of day: mornings, when she was getting ready for work. The television kept Nathan occupied and let her map out her battle plans for the day. Sometimes she would even sit down with the paper and a cup of coffee while Nathan watched his cartoons. But not usually. Not often. The guilt precluded her from sitting and enjoying herself while her child must surely be rotting his mind in front of the boob tube. So most days it was just an hour of television while she showered and dressed. An hour wasn't so bad.

Rachel looked at the breakfast in front of Nathan. At least he'd eaten most of his cereal. "Take one more bite of banana while I put on your shoes," she said. He didn't take his eyes off the television as she put on his shoes, but he did what she asked: he stuffed the rest of his banana into his mouth.

"I said a *bite* of your banana, not the whole thing. That's too big."

He shrugged his shoulders and finally looked at her. He smiled a big banana grin at her, and she brushed at his hair. "Okay," she said, "just one more thing."

"Waa my fay?" he said through a mouthful of banana.

"Yes, wash your face." She pulled his washcloth off the counter and ran it across his cheeks. She kept a washcloth for him in the kitchen, just for such occasions. He suffered the daily face washing ritual with more dignity and grace than usual, and she finally finished by giving him a kiss on the nose. "Okay, bucko. Bradley and his mommy are here to pick you up."

"Awright!" he said, the TV now entirely forgotten. He ran toward the front door, and she followed.

When Nathan opened the front door, Nicole wasn't on the front steps. Rachel peeked outside and saw Nicole was back at the car, making faces at Bradley through the window. She couldn't hear Bradley, but she could see he was squealing with laughter inside the car.

"All ready to go," Rachel called to Nicole as Nathan negotiated the steps and ran over to the car.

Nicole turned around. "Okay, Rachel. We'll see you this afternoon." Nicole grabbed Nathan's hand and walked with him to the other side of the car.

Rachel waved and closed her front door. She was late, way late if she wanted to open the shop by nine o'clock.

Accepting and *becoming*. It had been so much easier than expected. They were two, and they were one. Always had been, probably. But they had been so careful to separate the two before, afraid *not* to separate the two. The Normal needed to mix in, the Hunter needed to be invisible. And that was a quite satisfactory arrangement for some time. The two coexisted peacefully, and their rigid intolerance for blurring the line between them—well, that was what the treatments had been all about.

Still, these past few weeks the Normal was hungry to be there when the Hunter was working. And the Hunter had enjoyed wearing the Normal's skin. It was new, fresh, different. Exciting. Really, did they need to be so careful about making the Hunter appear different? They had tracked Quarry for years, and no one had ever been able to put them together. They were too smart, too careful for anyone to catch them; that much was patently obvious. So why not hunt as the Normal? Did they not deserve to do so, as a reward for all their careful work over the years?

They had been working on it for the last few days now, toggling the switch in their mind. When they had *become*, the switch turned one of them off, while activating the other. But with the *accepting*, it was much more subtle: one merely came to the forefront, while the other stayed in the background. Both still there, participating.

They called the image of the light switch into their mind again, concentrated on the black lever. It clicked down, and the Hunter was in the driver's seat while the Normal rode shotgun. They concentrated on the image again and the lever flipped up. *Switch*. The Normal took over.

They had decided they really didn't need to travel to do their hunting. Nor did they need to rub dirt on their body to mask their scent. They probably never had; both had merely been precautions. But such precautions were indeed frivolous now that they had *accepted*. All those years of *becoming* perfected the technique. With the technique now honed to a hard, steel edge, precaution was unnecessary.

So this morning, when they had driven down the same neighborhood street they had driven hundreds of times, they saw everything with new eyes. They saw a car in the driveway of a home they hadn't paid attention to before.

But they paid attention today.

Inside the car was a young boy, probably no more than six or seven. And just getting into the car, with some help from a woman, was another boy of about the same age.

They smiled as they drove by, then looked into the rearview mirror. That was the most delicious part of *accepting*: the world around them opened up in new possibilities. Hunting grounds heretofore off-limits—too close to home, mustn't hunt there as a precaution—became rich and vivid with possibility. Where once there had only been landscape, buildings, and homes, there was now Quarry. Lots of Quarry.

Switch.

Five minutes, tops. That was how quickly they had bagged two Quarry. Three Quarry, if they wanted to be technical about it; the woman certainly could be counted.

They breathed deep as they sat in the front seat of the car. Their supercharged senses let them smell the chloroform in the air, just the slightest tinge. Pavlov's dogs salivated whenever they heard a bell; the

Hunter and the Normal began to salivate whenever they smelled the chloroform.

In front of the house they turned off the car's engine, then sat listening. Most would hear only silence, but the Hunter and the Normal enjoyed sounds unheard by human ears. They listened to the pines and aspens growing. They listened to the earth breathing. They listened to the clouds gliding overhead.

Beside them, the woman began to stir. She was larger, so she would naturally metabolize the chloroform faster. But no worry. They pulled out the soaked rag and put it over her face. A few breaths, and she faded into the Land of Nod again.

They turned to see the Quarry in the back seat. Both were still, their bodies limp and lifeless. Not for long, of course. In another fifteen minutes or so, they would be in storage, wrapped in burlap bags and safely tucked away in the basement root cellar.

The top of their head tingled in anticipation as they opened the car's rear door and dragged out the bodies. They thought of the smell of burlap, earth, and faint chloroform, mixing together in a delectable combination. They paused, snaked a key into the front door, pushed it open.

The latest dose of fumes would keep the woman unconscious for another thirty minutes, so the Hunter and the Normal carried both Quarry down the stairs to the basement, individually this time because the staircase was narrow. They put both Quarry on their worktable, pulled burlap bags from beneath the table, and enjoyed the burlap aroma for a few seconds, actually closing their eyes and inhaling.

First, they shoved one Quarry into the burlap, a specially made casing stitched together from a few old potato sacks. Then, a length of knotted rope to secure the top of the bag. Finally, the bagged package went on one of the ceiling hooks. Soon the Quarry would wake. It would struggle, cry, maybe scream a little as it tried to work its way free. But, hanging in the air and surrounded by darkness, the Quarry would be deliciously disoriented. That was the appetizer: listening to the begging and pleading, the crying. The Hunter and the Normal desperately wanted to be around for that, but they would have to return to the Normal's life for the rest of the day. That appetizer would remain untasted until tonight when they returned home.

Satisfied, they turned to the second Quarry and began bagging it. Now they realized for the first time they were whistling. No tune in particular, but whistling. *Whistle while you work.* Yes, indeed. They concentrated on the burlap, noticing the intricate pattern of its weave.

Then their world exploded in a bright flash of red, followed by a hot, stinging clamp of pain at the back of their head. Suddenly, somehow, they were on their knees—maybe they had even hit the table as they fell—and confusion spilled through their mind.

The world came into focus again.

The woman they had kidnapped with the Quarry—the wretched, unwanted woman—stood above them with a shovel in her hand.

They scrambled to their feet quickly. She raised the shovel for another blow, but they sidestepped, then grabbed the shovel's handle to stop her. She was strong, certainly stronger than the Quarry they were used to capturing, but they were far, far stronger. They wrested the shovel away, letting it fall to the floor with a hollow, empty clang. Her smell changed then, from the soapy smell of rage to the familiar, acrid smell of fear. A smell they knew and loved.

She turned to run, actually making it up a few steps before they caught the leg of her jeans. She worked her leg free and kicked hard; her foot hit them in the forehead, then began scrambling up the stairs again.

Calm. They were calm now. They had shown a lapse in judgment, but they would soon have the situation under control again. They mounted the stairs after the woman. Ahead, the sound of the front door slamming came back to them.

They went out the front door and saw her getting into the car. She squirmed inside, then looked out through the window; fresh jolts of terror contorted her face. She was on the edge of hysteria now, they could tell. And they rather enjoyed it. Perhaps they would have to consider stalking larger Quarry in the future. But not this one. This one would not be a plaything; she would have to learn a lesson for trying to ruin their quiet time with the new Quarry.

They reached the door of the car, bending to peer in the window. The door handle didn't work, of course; she had locked the doors and was trying to start the car, her jittery hands flailing at the steering column. She thought she would be safe if she could just get the car started.

Slowly, methodically, they pulled the key fob from their pocket and held it up for the woman to see. Her reaction was delicious, much more so when they pressed the button that unlocked the doors. Her punch-drunk mind hadn't processed that extra bit—the shock of seeing the keys had frozen her in place, not allowing her to consider they would be able to gain access to the car.

They opened the door in a flash, before her idling brain could put her body into motion again. They grabbed her by the hair, pulled her out of the car and onto the ground outside. Her preservation instinct kicked in again, and she struggled, trying to break free. But they already had the gun from beneath the front seat. She hadn't known a gun was there, of course; if she had, it may have changed the complexion of this whole game.

They put the barrel at the back of her head, pulled the trigger, enjoyed the flash-bang-smoke smorgasbord for the senses. Her body went limp, and the game was over.

Sad, in a way. They would have enjoyed more squeezing.

They should have picked up the sound of her—the *smell* of her— coming down the basement steps, but those senses had been focused, so focused, on the Quarry. An understandable mistake, of course. They weren't used to having other guests around while they worked in the basement, so they had made a mistake. Must fix that. A good session with the machine that evening. Maybe even more Extreme Measures.

They would take care of the woman's body in a bit. For now, they had more work to do in the basement.

Jude left work a bit early that day—it was easy enough to hand off things to Frank, who had finally rolled in around three o'clock, just in time for his beloved afternoon coffee break—and started to think about what to do next. He was feeling bad about being a jerk to Kristina that morning, and on his way home, a terrifying thought occurred to him:

She will tell.

Why hadn't he thought of that? He had probably made her mad; he'd certainly upset her enough to chase her away. To strike back, she could simply let the world know where she had found the infamous Jude Allman: masquerading as a janitor in Red Lodge, Montana. Nathan would know. Rachel would know. Everyone would know. He would never again be Ron Gress; he would never again be normal in this town. Just a few weeks ago he would have easily solved the problem by packing up and heading on down the road. Every town needed janitors. But now he wanted to be a father to Nathan. And Rachel . . . well, best not think anything of the sort now, not when she was probably a few hours from finding out he had lied to her for the last six years.

So really, putting in a full day at work hadn't been an option for him. And as Frank himself had said, he had a lot of vacation built up—hadn't really taken any vacation before, that he could remember.

What to do about Kristina? Maybe he could apologize.

He locked the door to his home behind him, and he thought of setting the alarm system, more out of force of habit than any feeling that he was in danger.

He was still thinking about Kristina, wondering if he should maybe go over to the Stumble Inn, find her and apologize, when a knock came at the door. Well, she had saved him a trip. He sighed, got up from his chair, and walked to the front door. Yeah, he would apologize. That would be the best thing.

But when he opened the door, it wasn't Kristina at all. It was Officer Grant from the Red Lodge Police Department, a pained look on his face. "Mr. Gress, I'm sorry to bother you," he said. "But I think you'd better come down to the station with me again."

Fifteen minutes later, Jude sat in Odum's office. The chief stared at him across the desk for a few moments before speaking. "I'm gonna give this to you straight, Mr. Gress. Mr. Burkhart. Whatever. Let's just call you Gress."

Jude nodded.

"Your son is missing."

A circuit breaker on Jude's nervous system tripped, shutting down all power. "What?" he whispered, his voice a guttural croak.

"Your boy's missing, Mr. Gress." Chief Odum let out a sigh and sat back in his chair. "Actually, it's two of them: your boy and a friend. A Bradley Whittaker."

Jude sat, unable to move, unable to speak. Bradley, whom he had refused to touch and give a message to. Bradley, whom he had condemned. And now the ripple effect Kristina had spoken of was crashing down on him with the roar of a tidal wave: he had refused to act and had sacrificed two children—including his own son—because of it.

"Now," Odum continued, "I know you're not part of it, Mr. Gress. I've had folks following you. And after our little letdown with Kenneth Sohler at the hospital, believe me, you haven't been out of sight since."

Jude continued to sit, unable to move, unable to speak, unable to breathe.

"A lot of cops like to tell the family to go home, get some rest, let us do our jobs. I say: you wanna try to help find your son, you go right ahead. So I'm gonna give you a rundown on the details."

The police chief didn't seem to be as fidgety now; he was leaning forward over his desk, his eyes bright and clear.

"Here's what we know: Eight o'clock this morning Nicole Whittaker—that's Bradley's mom—gets in the car with Bradley to go pick up your son. At 8:10, she shows up at your home—I mean, your son's home. By 8:20 they're back on the road. At 8:40, both boys are gone at the school's second bell. Meanwhile, a guy over on Fourth Street notices a running car parked out in his alley. He goes out to check, but there's no one in it."

Jude finally found his voice. "Nicole's car?" he asked in a low whisper.

Odum nodded, then continued. "Then, about eleven this morning, a bum at the city dump is searching the Dumpsters for cans, and he finds Ms. Whittaker."

"Dead?"

"Not quite. Had a bullet in her head. She's alive, up at St. Vincent's in Billings."

"Has she been able to say anything?"

"We doubt she'll be able to speak with anyone soon. There's concern she may not make it through the night, to tell you the truth."

"Rachel?" Jude wondered if Rachel already knew about Nathan. Of course she knew, she would be the first to know.

Odum stood and walked to the door behind Jude. He opened the door, then motioned to someone in the hall. A few moments later Rachel stood in the doorway, her eyes puffy and swollen, her hair wild, her face drawn and vacant.

He rushed across the room to her, pulled her in tight as he felt her starting to sob. He looked at Odum, who simply nodded and walked down the hallway. And now, yes, Jude liked Odum, felt himself actually liking the man.

Jude returned his attention to Rachel, let her crying subside a bit before gently pulling her face away from his shoulder. "We're gonna find them," he said, surprised at the authoritative tone in his own voice.

Rachel wiped away her tears, and he saw her expression changing. The game face, pithy football coaches liked to call it. She was putting on her game face. No more crying. "So," she said, "any ideas?"

Yes, he did, in fact, have a few ideas. "We need to get to Billings. See Nicole at the hospital." More specifically, he himself needed this. If Nicole really was dying, he felt there might be a Kodachrome vision waiting for him—one that might show him something about Sohler, or where he was hiding the kids.

He turned to walk out of the police station but noticed Rachel holding back. "What? What is it?"

"My son's been kidnapped," she said. "Our son. And you want to just trot off to Billings? We need to find that guy—that Sohler guy, or whatever his name is, they've been talking about on TV."

"We will," he said. "If I can just reach . . . um . . . *touch* Nicole."

Her eyes became hard flint.

"Sounds weird, I know," he continued. "But remember? I talked about the visions before?"

"Yes," she said. "I also remember we agreed it might be some kind of schizophrenia, or seizures."

"But it's not. It's *real.*"

She shook her head. "I'm staying. I can't just leave, not when I can feel Nathan's out—"

"I'm Jude Allman," he interrupted. There. He'd said it. He'd told her.

She was stunned into silence for a few moments, then a disbelieving snort rose from her throat. "The dead guy?"

"Yes."

She stared at him, and he could see the thoughts piecing together in her mind. "You . . . you said you were from that little town in Nebraska."

"Bingham."

"Yeah, I knew I recognized the name of the town for some reason. I . . ." She shook her head.

"Rachel, please. This is something I have to do. If I'm right, we'll know where Nathan is, and Bradley, too. It'll only take us a couple hours, and you think you're going to get anything out of the police here in that time?" He paused. It was time to let it all out, let her know everything. "And I need to tell you a lot of stuff along the way."

"About Nicole and the kids?"

"About everything."

After a few seconds he saw the decision flash in her eyes. "Okay, Ron. I'll drive." She reached into her coat pocket to retrieve her keys. He watched as she did this and realized he'd never really looked at her before, actually concentrated on her features. She was suddenly the most beautiful woman in the world, and he was about to reveal things that would make her hate him forever.

He sighed. "Not Ron. Jude." She stopped and looked at him, then turned and headed for the door.

Odum noticed for the first time how golden the world around him had become. Autumn tended to sneak up slowly, making only slight changes to your surroundings each day, changes you wouldn't notice. But after a month of those slight changes, the whole landscape was something entirely different: weeks of slight changes added up to one big change. And this was the day it all hit Odum. The aspens along Rock Creek had burnished into a deep, rich amber. Here and there in the stands of pine, larch trees offered spots of ochre. The sunlight, lower on the horizon now that the season had shifted, bathed everything in a warm, metallic glow. Gold. Odum was surrounded by the color of gold.

Odum sighed as he sat down for a briefing with the FBI and his officers in the field. He knew the Feds would descend on him after Sohler did his Texas Two-step out of the hospital. And now, two kids had disappeared this morning. But he'd been prepared, laying the groundwork. He knew this meeting was bound to happen at some point.

He had given a couple of press conferences, done some interviews with television stations, been an all-around cooperative good boy today. Yet he hated it. The cameras, the lights, the noise, the . . . self-importance . . . it all drained him.

Now he'd have to prepare for another round of draining. But he also knew he'd be able to find Sohler sooner or later, and that would tie all the seams together.

Soon the press corps would grow, claiming the side street beside the station as their own stomping grounds. Of course this was a big story: a new kidnapping. Hello *Hard Copy* and *National Enquirer*.

This recent kidnapping would raise so many questions.

Odum sat and half listened as the Feds briefed him on the investigation's progress over the past several hours. They had done interviews, combed the Dumpster scene, and impounded Nicole Whittaker's car for analysis. Yes, they were covering all the bases, but Odum knew they hadn't turned up anything interesting. Nor would they.

He leaned back and looked out the window at the golden autumn landscape. Even though his department hadn't made any big breaks, he also sensed this whole thing was about to detonate. It had reached his town.

Odum sighed again. The end of it all seemed near, very near. He could feel it in his bones.

And his bones hurt.

Behind the steering wheel of her Ford Explorer, Rachel piloted them toward Billings. Ron sat, finally mute, staring out the window. He had spilled everything; like a dam opening its floodgates he had hit her with a rushing torrent of past lives and lies. That familiar knot in her chest tried to tighten again, to take her breath away. After all, she had been standing directly below the dam when Ron decided to open up those floodgates, and getting hit with a million gallons of water from a cold, deep reservoir would take anyone's breath away. How the Egyptian soldiers must have felt when Moses closed the Red Sea on them.

Still. Something about what he said made an odd sort of sense, put things in perspective. She could see the clarity of it, and in a way that made her see him more clearly as well. She breathed. The knot loosened.

As important as all this was, it wasn't that important right *now*. Nathan was. And Bradley. And Nicole, of course, dear Nicole, who was probably her only true friend in the world.

As much as she loved Nicole, though, and as much as she wanted to visit her in the hospital, this drive to Billings was a struggle. Like climbing Everest without oxygen. Every mile traveled was a mile farther from Nathan, and each one became exponentially more difficult. She felt as if she were attached to a giant bungee cord, and she was now stretching it to its fullest extent. The cord wanted to whip her back to Red Lodge, but she refused to let go. If she went all the way to Billings, the cord might snap, and she might just snap herself. She'd lose that . . . *connection* with Nathan, who she felt was still in Red Lodge somewhere. Her maternal instinct told her this was so, and she knew better than to dismiss that instinct.

But Ron said they needed to go to Billings, and something told her that was right also. She had been forming silent prayers in her mind all morning, trying to push aside the never-ending screams of terror filling her consciousness.

A new voice had awakened inside her while she prayed.

The voice instantly quieted the screams of horror, and she knew it was a gift from God. Maybe it was even the voice of God himself. *Go with him*, the voice said.

And so she had. She felt the bungee cord tightening as she drove, but she also felt the voice (and that was the way it had happened: she *felt* the voice, rather than heard it) telling her she was doing the right thing.

Rachel finally turned to look at Ron. No, it wasn't Ron, was it? He had just told her that. It was Jude. Jude Allman. *The* Jude Allman. "So," she said, "you think going to see Nicole will help you find out something?" The voice inside her answered *yes*, but she waited for Jude.

"Yeah. I think so. I hope so."

"Jude Allman. You know, I halfway thought you never really existed. I thought he was just someone the media made up—"

"In lots of ways, he is."

"—And then I end up having a child with him. You. Whatever."

She looked out her window, noticed the giant fields of grain stretching away from the road. It was late this year for the grain harvest. Usually it was gone in late August or early September. Here it was the end of September and the stalks of grain still swayed in the autumn breeze. They were close to the hospital now, passing through the farm fields just outside of Billings.

Rachel hoped she wasn't heading to a bitter harvest of her own.

She moved her lips, softly saying another prayer, and Jude turned to watch. She kept going, ignoring his stare.

He spoke when she had finished. "Remember that news story about seven years ago—the gunman at a little church in Nebraska? That was Bingham."

She *did* remember it. She hadn't been a Christ follower then, hadn't even met Jude yet. But the story had still disturbed her. "I remember," she said. "The guy busted into the middle of the service and killed five or six people. But you can't—"

"Eight people. My mother was one of them."

Rachel felt her lungs stop. Where was the voice of God inside her now? What could she say? "I . . . I'm sorry," she stammered.

"Your God killed my mother after she decided to start going back to church." He turned and looked out the window again.

She sat in silence for a few moments, hoping for another prompting from the voice inside. None came. She didn't want to talk about this now, not at all. She only wanted to find Nathan, wrap her arms around him, never let him go.

And yet she couldn't do that, not on the road to Billings. And Jude had just opened a door for her to walk through. How could she just ignore it?

She sighed. "In the Bible, there's a story about Joseph. His brothers, out of jealousy, sold him to merchants as a slave. But Joseph eventually became the governor of Egypt. When Joseph saw his brothers again, he said to them: 'You meant evil against me, but God meant it for good.' It might not make sense now, but I pray someday you'll see that God can—and does—use evil to accomplish good."

After a few minutes of silence, Jude spoke again. The anger seemed to have melted away, because his voice was softer. "That doesn't make me feel any better," he said simply.

"I didn't say it to make you feel better," she said. "I said it because you needed to hear it."

She expected a rebuke, or a complaint, but none came. Instead, he said, "You sounded a lot like Kristina just there."

"Who's Kristina?"

"Later," he said. He pointed to a sign ahead of them.

The large directional sign told them the entrance to St. Vincent Hospital was two blocks away.

As they hurried down the hallway toward Nicole's room, Jude felt the itchy dread of hospitals once again working its way into his stomach.

Part of what bothered him was the way hospitals were built, like large serpents intertwined on themselves: you always lost your sense of direction. Jude had hiked into many wilderness areas and forests, and he could always tell where he was. He'd never been lost, in fact, in the backcountry. Put him in a hospital of any size, though, make him turn a couple of corners, and he'd barely be able to tell up from down, much less north from south. Something about being closed in, surrounded by endless hallways like a rat in a giant maze, made him ill, uncomfortable.

They had stopped and asked for directions at the front desk, if *front desk* was a term that fit. It was somewhat near the main entrance, although hidden around a corner and not immediately visible. They had taken the elevator to the third floor, and now they were walking across the sky bridge to the south wing where they would take another right turn, then a left. Yeah, hospitals were a lot of fun.

(*Dad sitting over my bed.*)

The micro-memory was there again, flashing in the front of his mind. His dad, bent over his bed. He thought, at first, his dad had been talking, telling him something. But that wasn't right; his dad was listening. He was listening to something the younger version of Jude was saying.

He tried to cull more from the image, but nothing came. It was already gone.

They made the first left after the sky bridge, and Jude could tell they were now passing patient rooms in the ICU. Names of patients zoomed by on the doors as they walked. Scott Franklin. Janine Harrell. David Elkers. They made a right, then continued down the hallway, past more names. Debra Branson. Mike Lambert. William Allman.

William Allman.

Jude stopped and stared at the name on the closed door. Rachel noticed he had stopped, and turned back. "No, no," she said, pointing to the room next door. "This is Nicole's room right here."

He nodded, then started to move toward her as she reached out for the room door's handle.

A nurse in green scrubs busted out of the door to Nicole's room. "What?" the nurse said, seeming momentarily flustered. "Oh, I— you'll have to wait a few minutes," she said. Another nurse was moving down the hallway toward them now. "We're having to re-intubate." Together the two nurses went back into Nicole's room, pulling the door shut behind them.

Jude was stopped midway between Nicole's room and his dad's room. Rachel turned to look at him, and he read the frustration, the panic, in her eyes.

William Allman. His dad. In the room right next to Nicole. He nodded toward the door just behind him now. "It's, uh . . ." He swallowed. "It's my dad."

Her eyes narrowed for a moment before she walked back to look at the name on the door. "William Allman?" she said. "That's your dad? Here, in this room?"

"I think so," he said.

"What are the chances?"

He let out a deep breath. "Chance has a habit of following me around lately."

Rachel looked at him, and he couldn't tell whether the feeling behind those eyes was pity, or confusion, or sadness. "I suppose it does," she said simply.

They stood at the door for a moment. He noticed Rachel was biting her lower lip, probably without realizing it. Jude secretly hoped Rachel would forbid him from going into his father's room, that she would tell him they couldn't mess around with unburied ghosts from his past because they needed to save Nathan, the whole reason they were here. He suspected all those thoughts went through her mind, but she didn't voice any of them.

Instead, she said something that frightened him: "Go on in."

He wanted to. He didn't want to. And so his feet stayed frozen in place, doing nothing, caught between the gulf of yes and no. And it wasn't until he looked at Rachel that he thawed.

She drew in a breath, exhaled, closed her eyes for a second before opening them again. "No, really," she said. "We can't get into Nicole's room right now, anyway."

"Do you wanna meet him?" he asked. She considered for a moment, then glanced down the hall toward Nicole's room. Jude understood what she was thinking. She wanted to hurry, to return to Red Lodge, to find Nathan as soon as possible. Of course she wanted all that; he felt the same pressure. Except it somehow seemed too coincidental to have his dad here. He was sure, somehow, he was supposed to talk to his dad before seeing Nicole.

Jude tried to communicate all this to Rachel with his eyes, and he must have succeeded on some level, because while standing there nervously and biting her lip, she slowly nodded her head.

Jude returned the nod, grabbed the handle to his father's room, and pushed open the door.

Darkness blanketed the room as drawn shades blocked the late afternoon light. Jude heard something filtering softly from the TV, but he couldn't quite make out what it was. ESPN maybe. He moved slowly and quietly—why he didn't know—and as he did, a thought popped into his head: what if this was a different William Allman? It wasn't all that uncommon a name. Maybe there was another one—

"Well, I'll be dipped." It was his father, speaking from the darkness. Jude blinked his eyes rapidly a few times, willing them to adjust to the low light, but his father's figure remained mostly silhouetted in the shadow.

"How ya doin'?" Jude asked.

As if in answer, a deep, rattling cough came from the darkness of the bed.

"Don't think I'll be jumping up to box a few rounds anytime soon, but whatever. This?"

His father was obviously referring to Rachel. "Oh," he said, "I'm sorry. Dad, this is . . ." What was Rachel? The mother of my child? The woman who's put up with my paranoid ramblings for six years? He cleared his throat and started again. "This is my friend, Rachel Sanders. Rachel, this is my father, William." Friend, he had called her a friend. She didn't wince as he said it, but he did. He'd never really been a friend to her. Never been anything.

She walked to the side of the bed and held out her hand. William took her hand and shook it. "Nice to meet you, Mr. Gress," she said.

"Allman," William corrected.

"Right, Allman," she said. "I just found that out about an hour ago."

Jude still couldn't see his father's features, but he could tell William was looking across the room at him. He pictured the "What is this person talking about?" look on his father's face. "Long story," Jude said.

Rachel walked back over to Jude. "I'll just pop next door and see if I can get into Nicole's room," she said. "Please don't be long," she said before turning for the door. Then she stopped and turned back around. "I'm sorry. Just . . . come as soon as—" Jude grabbed her hand, nodded, and gave it a tight squeeze.

Rachel left the room, leaving the two Allman men alone. Jude breathed in the antiseptic smell, another thing he'd always hated about hospitals. They smelled like death, pungent and rancid, but the smell was somehow masked behind an astringent. Hospitals presented themselves as places where lives were saved, but Jude knew better. Hospitals were places for dying.

His father turned off the TV. "Pretty," he said to Jude.

"Yeah."

"Reminds me of your mother."

"Really?" Actually, now that his dad had said it, it was so obvious. Yes, Rachel Sanders did evoke something of his mother. Not a spitting image, but they shared similar features, similar characteristics.

Jude walked to the bed and stood beside his father, where he could start to make out the features. He'd seen his dad only a few days previously, and yet William had aged more in those few days than he had in the previous six years.

"So what happened?" Jude asked.

"That congestive heart failure thing." William smiled. "Which is just doctor-speak for 'you're an idiot for not taking care of yourself.'"

"So are you gonna . . . be okay?" Jude was filtering through his recent thoughts, thoughts of rage and anger directed at his father. Had those thoughts put his father here? No, probably not; his father talked about a heart problem at their last visit, before most of those thoughts came spilling out. Still.

"Doctors won't say. But then, doctors today are scared of their own shadows. Don't want to tell you anything, because they think you'll sue them. So, they're not really saying I'm gonna get better, but they're not really saying I'm gonna kick the bucket. Me, I'm leaning more toward the bucket scenario."

Jude nodded, feeling he should stay quiet.

"Funny thing you're here," William said to him. "I've been thinking a lot about you since they brought me in last night. Been feeling like I need to tell you something."

"What's that?"

"All these years, I thought you knew all about it. I thought you remembered it."

"Remembered what?"

William rolled his head the other way, grimaced. "I suppose it won't hurt to tell you now. Your mom's dead. Maybe even Carol too."

(*Mommy's gonna find out about Carol Steadman.*)

More of the memory flashed in his mind. His dad, leaning over his bed, listening to Jude talk about Carol Steadman.

Jude cleared his throat again. "Carol Steadman, you mean? Mrs. Steadman?" Jude hadn't thought about her since he was a child. Had totally forgotten about her until this instant, in fact. She had worked at the Thrifty Value store in Bingham, Nebraska.

"I had an affair with her, Jude."

Silence. Not a sound, except the hum of the hospital's machinery and a few clicking footsteps going down the linoleum hallway outside.

"I . . . didn't know that," Jude finally offered. He knew it was weak, but his brain was too muddled to come up with anything better.

"That's the thing, though. I don't know what I was thinking then; I still can't make sense of it now. But it happened, and there was no way you could know, but you did anyway." His father paused, licking his lips. "I was putting you to bed one night, and you just started crying. I remember this so clearly—you said: 'Mommy's gonna find out about Mrs. Steadman, and—'"

—It came to Jude, swiftly and suddenly. In his newly unearthed memory Jude saw a young version of himself, lying in bed with the covers pulled up to his nose. *Snug as a bug in a rug,* his mom would say, only it wasn't Mom sitting on the bed next to him. It was Dad. His mind creaked, trying to grasp something it had to say but unable to do so. And he was scared, so scared of what he had to say to Dad that tears spilled from his eyes and wet the pillow beneath him.

Still, even if he didn't understand it, he could tell his dad about it. He was *supposed* to tell his dad, that was part of it. But the other part was, the eight-year-old Jude Allman had been taught you can trust anything you want to say, anything at all, to an adult. So even if he didn't really know what it all meant, Dad certainly would. And Dad would probably be happy to hear it, and he'd scoop Jude out of the bed and take him to the kitchen for a couple of scoops of mint chocolate chip ice cream, and maybe in the morning they'd go fly that box kite. Jude liked the box kite.

He could tell his dad was thinking about something else; his eyes were staring at him, but they were also looking at something far away. "Dad?" he asked, hope starting to dry his tears. When he spoke, something shifted inside his dad.

A cloud of concern crossed William's face. "What is it?" his dad asked. "You know you can tell me anything."

And his dad was right, sure he was right. Jude knew it was okay to share anything with good old Dad (Mom was better, he wished it was Mom, but this particular thing was *about* Mom). So Jude opened his mouth and continued. "Mommy's gonna find out about Mrs. Steadman, and she's gonna kill herself."

He saw immediately that he'd been terribly wrong, that there were in fact some things you shouldn't tell Mom or Dad or any adult. He had just now found such a thing, and his dad had a look in his eyes that made Jude afraid.

Very afraid.

He wished his mom was tucking him in, that he wasn't alone with his father. He had said the thing he was supposed to; he hadn't under-stood all of it, and he had been sure it was something that wasn't good or right (the part about Mommy killing herself Jude understood well enough, and it scared him), but he had told his father all the same.

He had been sure Dad would understand it all and fix it. That was what Dad did. But as he looked at his father, he saw he had been very wrong. His father understood, that much was clear. Dad was supposed to fix something, but even at that tender young age Jude realized something much bigger, much more important, had just been broken. And it would never be fixed.

Jude shook off the memory of his childhood and interrupted his father. "You were having an affair with Mrs. Steadman," he said, his voice thin and flat. He still saw the scene playing in his mind. The fractured pieces of the memory had been put together again, and now the scene kept playing, rewinding in front of his mind's eye. This was one of those memories he'd kept tucked into the deepest part of the closet (*keep it secret, keep it safe*), hidden under the nice soft blanket that cloaked so much of his mind.

Now he knew. He understood how a young boy with a gift he couldn't understand could create fear in his father—fear he *could* understand. Fear he had always understood.

"I didn't remember that. Not until just now." Jude looked down at his dad's face. The roles were reversed: his father in bed, afraid of the secret he'd just told, the son looking down at him.

"You were scared of me," Jude said softly. It all made so much sense now, with the one memory he'd buried deep inside exposed and melting in the bright light of his mind.

Jude thought he could see tears in his father's eyes. "I suppose I was," William answered. "I knew of your . . . your *gift*, I suppose; your mother and I had seen that lots of times. For years I just waited for your mom to . . . you know. Every day, I lived in this secret fear she would find out. So finally *I* told her because I couldn't live with it. And you know what she said? 'I know.' She had figured it out at some point, but she had already forgiven me—before I ever asked." He paused.

"After she was killed, I let it drive me mad. For a while I made all these crazy plans to attend the trial, to kill the guy myself if he got off. But then I remembered what your mother had done with something that hurt so much: she forgave, because forgiving *me* healed *her*. And, in an odd way, I think that's what stopped your vision, your prediction, whatever you want to call it. Forgiveness."

Jude nodded. He took his father's hand, and spoke softly. "I understand, Dad," he said.

Now his father did start crying, an image that until a few minutes ago would have been discomfiting for Jude. He accessed the memory banks—new memories were coming online all the time, and he'd been taking them out to examine them as they popped into focus—and searched for anything that had his dad crying. Nothing. His dad had never cried that he could remember. Maybe even that his dad could remember.

"That's why," his dad choked, "I need to tell you something else. About the day you almost drowned."

Almost drowned. He'd been dead more than an hour that day, no almost about it. But it was obvious his father had a difficult time accepting Jude's gift. He waited for his dad to get through a few quick sobs.

"After you fell through the ice," William whispered, "for a second, just a second, I . . ."

Jude knew this one, and he finished his father's thought again. "You thought about leaving me."

William broke down in a fresh sob, squeezing Jude's hand as he did. "God forgive me," William said. Any other time in his father's life, Jude would have been convinced these were empty words, an expression that just happened to fit the situation, a colorful way of saying "I'm sorry." But in this instance Jude was sure his dad meant everything the phrase said. He was asking for God's forgiveness. In a strange way Jude knew how to answer this as well.

"He does. And so do I." Jude paused a moment, processing all the multicolored memories flooding back into his consciousness. Only they weren't just a jumble now; they were starting to lock together in a way that made sense. "And I need to ask your forgiveness as well," he said.

His father's eyes widened, and he nodded for Jude to continue.

"For wishing you were dead." He shook his head. "No, not quite that. After Mom died, and I just didn't realize it until now, but I was mad at God for taking her first."

His father didn't seem shocked at this news.

You meant it for evil, but God meant it for good. Rachel had said that just a few minutes ago. "If you had died first, this conversation never would have happened. So in an odd way we're here right now because of Mom." He shook his head again. "Does that make sense?"

His father nodded weakly. "Perfect sense." He closed his eyes, took a few deep breaths. Jude waited patiently; the pain of buried memories was a giant wave, he knew that too well, and he would wait until his dad had made it past this swell.

Finally William opened his eyes and looked at Jude again. "I remembered flying that kite with you—just the other day I remembered. And now that I think about it, the wind wasn't all that bad."

Rachel looked at the giant octopus that was her best friend. Nicole, who constantly took care of Nathan when Rachel needed a break, or dropped by the shop with a latte to surprise her, or made the lemon bars Rachel loved so much, was now an octopus of metal and plastic. Tubes and wires intertwined, connecting her body to machines and outlets. Worst of all, her head had swollen, her features ballooning into an oversized mask.

The ICU was for family only—they had passed a sign that told them as much on the way in—and Rachel realized Nicole *was* her only family here, in a way. The sister she'd never had. But Rachel herself felt more like a wicked stepsister. She thought a moment, trying to recall how many times she'd dropped by Nicole's home, or just called to say hi. Not many. Not many at all.

She bit her lip and listened, hoping for God's voice inside to proclaim something warm and comforting. A baritone *You are forgiven, my child*, perhaps. But the voice remained quiet.

She tasted something salty and only now realized she was crying. Tears traced a thin line down her cheeks and found their way to her mouth, right where she always bit her lip. She wiped at her cheeks with the heel of her hand as she moved next to Nicole. She took Nicole's hand, squeezed, hoping for a squeeze in return. Nothing.

Rachel felt something brush her shoulder, and she jumped, catching her breath in her throat.

"Sorry," Jude mumbled.

At first, she thought he looked pale, as if the blood in his veins had been replaced with a few quarts of milk. But his eyes, ah, his eyes seemed to be overfilled with color, maybe even a different color than normal. She tried to recall if she'd ever noticed their color. Blue? Green? Hazel? Even now, she couldn't say for sure—it was almost as if the color were subtly shifting, like one of those mood rings from the 1970s.

"How's your dad?" she asked.

He shrugged, locked eyes with her. "Hard to say. But I'm better."

Yes, she had to agree, something about him seemed more . . . alive. So much, he had hidden so much. It was amazing he hadn't become more paranoid, amazing he hadn't actually just folded in on himself at some point, hiding a secret like that. And she wondered— for the first time since she'd become a believer, she realized—what it was like to die. What really was on the other side? Was the white light everyone talked about really there?

She cleared her mind, swept all those thoughts away. Her son was missing, and she didn't want to think about dying. She didn't want to think about anything else but finding him. She could feel sorry for herself later, feel sorry for Nicole, feel sorry for Jude and anyone else who might come to mind. But now, right *now*, she had to close off feelings of self-pity. She had to be cold, hard, iron.

"So do you—" Rachel started before a nurse bolted through the door and stopped her in mid-sentence. It was the same nurse who had closed Nicole's door in her face a few minutes ago. The look on the nurse's face said she was annoyed to see Nicole the Octopus had visitors.

The nurse's eyes narrowed. "You family? ICU's for—"

"She's my sister," Rachel said firmly, staring at the nurse.

The nurse nodded and set to work. "Seems to be more stable now. I just need to check some vitals," she said. She waded into the tangle of tubes and wires, leaving Rachel and Jude to stand by awkwardly.

Rachel looked at Nicole's eyes, noted how puffy they were. Even if she were conscious and awake, she probably couldn't open them.

Rachel felt her own eyes starting to blur again.

"Has she . . . been able to say anything?" Rachel asked. She was sure Nicole hadn't, but she wanted to ask *something*. She had to break the awkward human silence in the room; various machines buzzed, pumped and beeped, but those sounds were somehow more sinister than dead silence. Rachel also needed to speak to remove the emotion from her eyes. If she had to speak, she wouldn't cry.

The nurse looked up from her work, shook her head softly. "Still in her own world."

Rachel thought about what Nicole must have been through. Had she seen the kidnapper? Maybe. Was she shot trying to save them? Probably. Most definitely; Nicole would have fought the kidnapper, whoever he is.

"I wouldn't want to wake up," Rachel said. At first she was sure she had simply thought this, but when she noticed both the nurse and Jude staring, she realized she'd spoken the thought aloud. Still, neither of them made a comment. Maybe they agreed with her.

The nurse finished her work, looked back and forth between Jude and Rachel, then left the room quietly.

For a moment neither of them said anything. Then—

"So do I what?" Jude asked.

"Hmmm?"

"You were asking me a question when the nurse walked in. You said 'So do you—' and the nurse walked in."

Right. Rachel couldn't find her thought. What had she been asking? It had to be about Nathan. And Bradley, of course. Nathan and Bradley. They had wasted so many hours coming to the hospital in Billings. The bungee cord wrapped around her waist was overstretched, and beginning to fray. Something had to give, because she needed to get back to Red Lodge and find her son. He was there, she could feel it. But to do that, they needed some answers from Nicole.

"So what happens now?" Rachel asked Jude.

He moved next to the bed, and she could tell something was wrong.

"What is it?" she asked, feeling breathless. *The voice of God, I need the voice of God.*

"Well, it's nothing. That's just it. Nothing. I . . . remember when I told you about the guy who got hit in the street? The copper thing?"

She nodded.

"I've had . . ." He paused, and she could see he was uncomfortable, maybe a bit embarrassed. "Whenever I've had a vision, I've always had the coppermouth first. But right now, nothing. Nothing at all."

"We have to try," she said.

He nodded, already putting his hands on Nicole's arm. Rachel watched as he closed his eyes, closed them tight as if getting ready to dive into deep water. Soon, he opened them again and moved his hands. He touched Nicole on the forehead. Rachel noticed his hands trembling—*he's not used to touching people*, she thought—and then he closed his eyes once more. After a few moments his eyes opened again, and now Rachel saw a glint of desperation igniting and glowing steadily in them.

Suddenly a single word came to her. Obvious and penetrating. Comforting. At a time when she wasn't expecting to hear that voice—indeed, when her mind had been totally preoccupied with other thoughts—God reached to her through one simple word:

Pray.

Of course. That was what she had to do, what she should have been doing the whole time. She should have been on her knees the moment they entered the room, praying for Nathan, Bradley, Nicole. Jude. Herself.

She bowed her head, closed her eyes (not as tightly as Jude seemed to close his eyes, to be sure, but tight nonetheless). It was a simple prayer, really, a plea to God to make things right. In the growing darkness that spread across Nicole Whittaker's hospital room, Rachel asked God to work a miracle.

She opened her eyes and was a bit shocked to see Jude staring at her. She hadn't said the prayer aloud, but he seemed to know she'd been praying. Just as he'd done at the dinner table (a night that seemed to have happened five centuries ago), he once again uttered a word she'd never pictured coming from his lips: *amen.*

He smiled, a faint smile that said thanks, before his face contorted into a grimace. He wiped at his mouth with the back of a hand. An unconscious move, but one a person might make when tasting something unpleasant.

Jude touched Nicole's arm one more time. Immediately Rachel felt an electrical shock course through her own body, a shock that jolted . . .

No, no, she hadn't felt the shock herself. Jude had. But it seemed so *real,* and it was so surprising and unexpected that she felt she had shared the sensation.

She watched as the various muscles on Jude's body tensed and released, as his eyes raced behind closed lids, as a bit of spittle formed at the corner of his mouth and started to wind its way down his chin. It was like those electric paddles hospitals use to kick someone's heart back into the right rhythm: the body stayed tense and taut until the shock had finished. Only it didn't relent. The muscles in his neck and jaw quivered.

Then, just as Rachel started to worry Jude *was* being shocked, perhaps by a loose wire from those cables connected to Nicole, his eyes opened and the quakes in his body calmed. He removed his hand from Nicole's arm, and Rachel looked at the spot where they had been touching. She half expected to see blistered burn marks on Jude's hands or Nicole's arm, but nothing was there. Nothing.

"I saw it," Jude rasped. His throat sounded strained, which wasn't much of a surprise after the trauma she'd just seen his body go through. He seemed scared, very scared, and Rachel did something without thinking about it: she took his hand between her own hands and held it, as if he had frostbite and she needed to warm the fingers.

If she had thought about it, she would have been scared to touch him—scared of being shocked the way she'd just seen him shocked—but something inside her told her to simply hold his hand.

"You saw . . ." A rotten, putrid lump stuck in her throat suddenly, and she had to clear it out. "You saw Nathan and Bradley?" She was at once hopeful and terrified of the answer.

He nodded. "They're okay, Rachel. But . . . we need to get to them. Soon."

"Okay."

"They're still in Red Lodge."

She knew this, she knew it only too well when they left Red Lodge. She did not need to drive all the way to a hospital in Billings to confirm this. As a mother, she knew.

Jude turned to the door and started to leave. Of course they should get back to Red Lodge as soon as possible; she could still feel the bungee cord trying to pull her back. Except.

Except the same authority, the same assurance she'd heard before now urged her to say something to Nicole. Rachel needed to pull Nicole from her puffy dreamland for Bradley. And yes, for herself.

She took Nicole's hand, cradling it between both of her hands as she had done with Jude's.

"Nicole, he's okay. And we'll bring him back. Just hang on to that." She let go of Nicole's hand and gently placed it back on the bed, then looked to Nicole's face one more time.

Nicole's eyes opened. The eyes were vacant and glossy, and Rachel thought she could almost see clouds of gray swirling inside the pupils.

But they were open.

Jude asked if he could drive, and Rachel let him. He didn't think she would; it wasn't as if he borrowed her car all the time, or as if they drove together a lot. They hadn't . . . ever, really.

He wanted to drive because it gave his body something to do. He was juiced on adrenaline-charged energy, and he had hoped driving would calm him. It *was* calming him, in a way. But he probably wasn't in the best shape to be driving, either. Already fifteen or twenty miles had passed, and Jude couldn't remember a single one of them. How could he think of the road, with all the new images cluttering his mind? Jude feared they were images he would never be able to let go. Like rust getting into a car's body, he knew these thoughts would stay lodged in his brain and slowly grow, taking over every other thought slowly and painfully.

Rachel hadn't asked questions yet. She had asked if Nathan was okay, of course (he was, at least for now), but she hadn't pressed him for details. That time was coming, though. He could tell. She was shifting in her seat frequently, staring his direction. She was searching for the right words to break the silence.

Another mile marker ticked by, and Jude recognized this stretch of highway: the section flanked by grain fields. He smelled the pungent aroma of grain, stronger than it had been before. He looked out his window and saw a harvester moving through the field, its giant mouth sucking in stalks of grain and spitting the heads into a waiting truck. A cloud of dust swirled around the harvester in the evening twilight.

Time to reap what you've sown. The thought floated naturally into his head. Yes, it was that time. He had been given a chance to save Nathan—along with Bradley and Nicole—before any of this happened. In fact, now that he looked back on the last few weeks, it was quite obvious everything had been leading up to that: he was *meant* to save his own son, but he had refused. *Time to reap what you've sown.* Indeed.

"Are you . . . okay?" Rachel asked. Obviously she'd given up on waiting for details. He couldn't blame her; in fact, she had been remarkably calm.

"Scared."

"Me too."

Jude knew she was waiting for him now. Waiting for him to tell her, but the images seemed too cluttered. He couldn't get his mind around the violent, shrieking images of the vision. He just wanted to concentrate on something else. It was almost too terrifying to talk about just yet.

Still, he needed to tell Rachel. He owed her that much.

She spoke suddenly, as if reading his mind. "We've been to Billings. You did your . . . whatever. And I'm trying to be patient. But I have to tell you: I'm starting to fall apart here." He saw small wells of tears forming at the corners of her eyes. There it was: her Ace of Spades, face up on the table at last. He'd have to return to those rust-tinged thoughts. He should have done it before; she *had* waited a long time, stepped out in faith with him, as it were.

"The important question is," he said, "are you ready to hear it?"

She was.

The moonless sky of early twilight was a smear of violet above as Jude parked Rachel's car at Wild Bill Lake. Wild Bill was a small man-made lake—no more than a couple of acres, if that. It sat at the very edge of the Absaroka-Beartooth Wilderness. Five miles east sat Red Lodge; five miles west, nothing but rugged backcountry dotted by pines and boulders.

Jude turned off the ignition, and they sat listening to the darkness creep in for a few seconds. Even though it was autumn, crickets and cicadas still rattled in the breeze around them.

"You're sure about this? You're absolutely sure?" Rachel asked. Her voice had a new smokiness to it, as if she'd aged years during the drive from Billings. And perhaps she had; Jude felt a pang of guilt tweak his stomach, knowing he'd brought all of this on her.

"Yeah, I'm sure," he answered.

She was nervous, edgy. She wanted to finish all this before—Jude stopped his thoughts there; he didn't want to think about what would come for Nathan and Bradley if his plan didn't work.

"You sure he's still there, this time of night and all?" Rachel asked.

"With this case? No way he'd be knocking off early tonight. He'll still be there."

"Ready to make that call?" she said.

"Don't think I'll ever be ready. But let's do it."

Rachel rummaged through her purse, then brought out a cell phone and handed it to Jude. Jude remembered the number to the Red Lodge Police Department and dialed it. A man's voice answered.

"Chief Odum, please."

"Who's calling?"

"Jude—er, Ron Gress." Jude gave a quick glance at Rachel, who returned a slight smile. These days it seemed more and more difficult to be two people. He listened to silence while he waited on hold.

Eventually Odum's voice came on the line. "Mr. Gress?"

"Yeah, it's me."

"Calling in for the latest?"

"Yeah. Well, not really. Actually, I suppose I'm calling to update you."

"Update me?"

"I . . . well, I know where the boys are."

Odum held on to a long pause.

"Are you trying to offer a confession here, Mr. Gress?"

Jude rolled his eyes. "I'm trying to tell you I know where the boys are. I know who took them, and it wasn't Sohler."

Silence on the other end. "And how might you know such a thing?"

Jude looked at Rachel, who had her eyes closed. Maybe she was praying again. "I can take you there, if you meet me."

"Where, Mr. Gress?"

"Wild Bill Lake."

"And where did you get this information, if I may ask?"

"You can ask, but I don't think you'll believe me."

"Probably not, but humor me."

"Well, it was kind of a vision."

Jude could hear Odum's smile on the other end of the line. "Ah, so now you're one of those psychics who wants to work with the local police department. Is that it, Mr. Gress?"

"No, that's not it, Chief Odum. But now's probably not the time to debate it."

Odum sighed. "I suppose not. But I have to tell you, I don't buy into any of this psychic mumbo jumbo, Mr. Gress. I'm not gonna waste the time of my people until I know you have something."

"Understood."

"Care to tell me who we're talking about here?"

"His name's Frank Moran. He's a janitor I work with."

Jude heard another smile creep into Chief Odum's voice. "Okay, then, Mr. Gress. I'm in."

When Odum hung up the phone, he had a solid mass of doubt tumbling in the depths of his stomach. Something about this whole situation wasn't right. Wasn't right at all. And the biggest thing that wasn't right was Ron Gress himself. Or Kevin Burkhart. He'd checked that name, found a few records, but hadn't chased that lead any farther. More pressing things at hand.

Now that more kids had disappeared . . . Gress knew something more about them, Odum could tell. And whatever Gress knew, he needed to know as well.

He sighed, got up from his desk. He walked down the hall, then went to the side door. He opened it a crack and looked out, but none of the journalists were around. Most of them would be in their hotel rooms by now, and any action remaining would be out front. Most of them probably assumed Chief Odum had slipped out some time ago; few of them would have even noticed this battered door on the side of the building. It was past dusk and starting to get dark.

Chief Odum wanted to go home. It had been a long day, and he deserved some time at home. But he knew that wasn't about to happen; he'd resigned himself to a long night. Two boys missing, and now he was about to go on a psychic wild goose chase. Odum wasn't sure what Ron Gress was up to, but he was sure it was more than the man let on over the phone.

He opened the door of his cruiser, got in, keyed the engine to life, and wheeled onto Broadway. If what Mr. Gress said was true, there was one more stop he needed to make before heading to Wild Bill Lake. And the stop happened to be right on the way.

He parked on the corridor in front of the Stumble Inn and Renton's Hardware. All of his training, all of his memorized facts about this case and the people involved, had given Chief Odum a gut feeling. Ron Gress had said enough on the phone to confirm that gut feeling, and Odum was ready to act on it. If Ron Gress really knew where the kids were and who had them, he would have to be prepared.

"Okay, just one more phone call," Jude said after Odum hung up. Jude dialed information, asked for the number of the Stumble Inn, then waited for the connection.

"Stumble Inn," a voice on the other end of the line said.

"Room 305, please."

"Hold while I try that extension," the voice said.

This time there was inane elevator music while he held, and Jude decided he had to agree with the Red Lodge Police Department after all: silence was better.

The voice came back. "I'm getting no answer at that extension, sir. Would you like to leave a message?"

"No, no thanks."

He hit the End button on the phone, then handed it back to Rachel. No matter. He knew where the boys were. He didn't need Kristina for that.

"We're all set, then?" Rachel said.

He nodded. "So you know where to go?"

"Yeah."

"You okay doing this?"

"Of course. He's our son."

"I know, but that's not really what I meant."

"Yeah, but that's the answer. That's gotta be the answer, Ron—I mean Jude."

He smiled. "I answer to both."

Jude unbuckled his seat belt, opened the door, and climbed out.

Rachel did the same and came around the car to the driver's side. For a moment they stood looking at each other. Jude had to say something.

"Just in case something happens," he said, "I'm sorry for . . . I don't know . . . sorry for not being me."

"Not being Jude, or not being Ron?" she asked.

"Not being anybody."

Rachel took him in her arms and hugged him. He closed his eyes and fell into her embrace, wanting that to be the end.

But it wasn't.

He felt Rachel pulling her head away from his shoulder, and he opened his eyes to look at her. It was time to get to work. Rachel returned his gaze for a few seconds.

She kissed him.

Then she whispered, "Let's get our son," and broke the embrace. She grabbed the car handle, opened the door, and got in. After one last look, Rachel backed the car out of the parking lot and onto the road.

Jude watched the taillights of her car fade. Twilight was gone now, and darkness had settled in for the evening. Surrounded by the gathering dusk, he listened to the thrum of her car's engine fading into the distance. Soon even that was gone.

He was alone.

Crickets played their late season symphony around him. Not far away, across the roadway, a small creek gurgled. It would be a while before Odum reached him—ten or fifteen minutes, anyway. He might as well sit down and wait. Wild Bill Lake didn't have any overnight camping—a couple of campgrounds farther down the road provided that—but it did have a day-use picnic area. He walked across the pine needles and gravel that covered the parking lot, then found the closest picnic table.

Jude sat at the picnic table and thought about the events of the past few weeks. Dark and frightening, but somehow freeing at the same time. He thought about the events that would surely unfold in the next few hours and shivered, only partly from the chill in the air. There was no upside to what he had seen in his vision, nothing freeing or uplifting. Jude had seen the kind of big, overpowering monster that frequented his childhood nightmares (so many more memories of his childhood kept pouring into his mind now, filling it like an empty pitcher). The monsters of his childhood had kept him hidden under the sheets many nights; he had been too terrified to look toward the closet because, as every child knows, that was where the monsters lived.

Except now it seemed at least one monster lived in Red Lodge, Montana. And Jude knew that monster.

He thought about his recent visit to the hospital with Rachel. He hadn't been able to see anything, and then Rachel had prayed. And when she prayed, he had seen. The taste of copper had flooded his mouth, and the odious vision had flooded his mind.

In so many ways he wished he hadn't seen the vision. It was too real, and too unreal, at the same time. But one uncomfortable thought kept returning to his mind: the vision hadn't appeared until Rachel had prayed.

Maybe.

He closed his eyes, opened his mind, and talked to God. It was the only thing he could think of to take his thoughts off the last vision.

Some time later—Jude wasn't quite sure how long because he'd lost track of the world around him as he prayed—a sound began to eat away at the edge of his consciousness.

It was the engine of an approaching vehicle.

Jude listened for a few minutes, and when he saw the beams of the headlights appear around a corner down the road, he stood and went back to the parking lot. Odum would pick him up, and then it would be time to confront the monster.

Odum's cruiser pulled into the parking lot, bathing Jude's body in a white halogen glare. Jude slitted his eyes against the headlights and tried to see Odum in the front seat but couldn't.

The headlights darkened, while the car stayed running. Jude heard the car door click open, followed by the *ding ding ding* of the door-ajar signal. The interior lights of the vehicle winked on, revealing Chief Odum swinging his legs out of the car.

And Kristina in the backseat.

Odum left the door open, obviously unbothered by the incessant dinging. "Here we are. Wild Bill Lake." Odum gave Jude a hard stare that dared him to speak.

"Yeah" was all Jude could muster. His mouth felt dry, like flannel. He was trying to keep his attention focused on Odum, but he was thinking about Kristina in the backseat. He'd been thinking about her quite a bit since his last vision, wondering if, in some sick way, she was involved with the missing children. It fit, in some odd way. She hadn't specifically been in his vision of Nathan's abduction, but it fit.

Now, seeing her in the back of Odum's car, it fit even more. Obviously Odum had, too. Jude swallowed hard, then stepped forward.

Odum grinned. "Well, might as well use the facilities while I'm here," he said, tilting his head toward the outhouse. He didn't wait for an answer or comment from Jude before walking away.

Jude looked into the car again, saw Kristina returning his gaze. He walked to the passenger side and slid into the front seat. He stared straight ahead, waiting for Kristina to say something. Odum's open door was still dinging, so Jude reached over to pull it shut.

Finally he broke the silence. "So do you have something to tell me?" He didn't want to turn around, didn't want to look at her through the metal partition.

"I can't really tell you anything you don't already know. I never have, anyway," Kristina said from behind the partition.

Thanks, Ms. Cryptic, he thought to himself. He realized she'd always spoken that way, and it had never really bothered him before. But it did now.

"Enough with the riddles. I want some answers. How could this happen?"

He heard her shift in the backseat. "Things aren't always what you think."

He sighed. What kind of answer had he expected from her? "I'm discovering that."

"So you've figured out where the boys are?" she asked.

He nodded, having lost his desire to speak. He just wanted to get this over with. He knew Nathan and Bradley were safe for the moment, but still . . . he wanted it to end. "How could you be involved in all of this?" he said, his voice breaking. "I mean, why?"

"I know you're hurting right now, Jude. But when you dance with the devil, you don't get to pick the music."

Jude snorted. She sounded like a Hallmark card gone bad.

"I think you've finally discovered it," she said.

"Discovered what?"

"It. What you're supposed to be doing. All the signs."

"And that is?"

"You're a prophet, Jude. Like Moses. Or Jonah. A messenger. God sent Moses to deliver messages to people, and Moses just said, 'I can't.' More or less, anyway. Jonah, too. You're no different. Up until recently, you've been saying you can't. But I think you're finally discovering you can."

He sat, letting her suggestion bounce around in his head. He thought about Rachel's recent prayers, followed by his own.

"Where you're sitting now, you don't get to talk to me about God."

Ahead of him, Jude watched Odum walking back from the toilet. Behind him, Kristina leaned forward in her seat and spoke softly, almost whispering. "We all have our parts, Jude."

Odum swung open the door. He peeled off his jacket and threw it onto the front seat next to Jude before getting back in. He turned to Jude. "I'm ready when you are," Odum said.

"We need to go up the road a bit," Jude said. "To the end."

Odum nodded. "The end of the road it is."

Even though she gripped the steering wheel as tightly as she could, Rachel felt her hands shaking. When she had been a young girl, one of her friends had a younger brother with palsy; that was how Rachel felt now. In her hands especially, but also throughout her entire body, she felt her muscles quivering.

Rachel tried a few deep breaths as she pulled to a stop in the darkness. The home was remote, dark. Terrifying. Time to calm her nerves. She had to do this, for Nathan, for Bradley, for Nicole. There was no way around it. Jude had his role; this was hers.

Rachel turned off the engine, pulled the door handle, and listened to her door screech open. The sudden sound of the door startled her, emphasizing how everything else in the area was so silent. Rachel closed the car door with another creak, then stood and listened. A few crickets and cicadas, but nothing else. Silence covered the home and surrounding woods in a thick, suffocating stillness.

Rachel looked toward the home. No lights glowed, inside or outside. No one had been in the home since daylight, she guessed. She hoped.

Go now, the voice inside told her.

Rachel took the keys to the rear of her car and opened the trunk. She looked at the home again. Still no movement or sound. She rummaged around in the trunk, squinting her eyes and cursing the feeble light bulb that was no help. Then, she spotted it. Most of the time Rachel called it a tire iron; tonight she called it a little bit of courage. The smooth, black iron of the tool felt cold in her hand.

She smiled. Cold, hard iron. That's what she was. Rachel climbed two steps to the front door and rang the doorbell. She cocked her head to the side, listening. She rang the doorbell again, then knocked. "Anybody home?"

Not a sound from inside.

Rachel gripped the tire iron tightly, looking around her. The home was in the countryside, with no neighbors nearby, but she still felt as if she needed to look. To make sure.

No one else was around, so she made the next move. She turned the tire iron around in her hand and put the blunt end through the glass of the front door.

Iron. Be strong as cold iron, she said to herself again as she swung open the door.

"You're not married, are you, Chief Odum?" Jude asked.

Odum chuckled. "Nope, never married."

"No kids?"

"No kids, either."

"So you've always lived alone?"

"Well, I don't suppose it would be any fun living with a cop. It isn't any fun for me."

"I can imagine."

Odum's face was bathed in the teal light emanating from the dash-board. It made him look tired, worn.

Odum turned an eye toward Jude. "You mind filling me in on what you know now?" he asked.

Jude looked to the backseat. Kristina nodded at him, encouraging him to continue.

Jude turned back to Odum and spoke again. "You remember I told you I knew about the boys because of a vision?"

"I remember."

"You didn't ask me about that vision."

"I don't much buy into that kind of thing."

"I told you it was a man I work with named Frank, but you never even asked me about him."

Odum remained silent.

"You know it's not really Frank. I know it's not really Frank. But we both know who it is, don't we?"

The vision came to Jude through the eyes of the Normal, through the eyes of the Hunter, tinged with the familiar hue of a film negative.

The Hunter and the Normal followed the car for a few blocks, hanging back. They could tell the woman driving the car hadn't seen them yet. She hadn't slowed down, and she actually California-ed a stop sign, only slowing down and rolling through the intersection. She must be in a hurry. Good.

They followed her, letting the adrenaline build in their bloodstream, enjoying the rush of power coursing through their veins. Yes, it was indeed good to hunt as the Normal. They were unstoppable.

Eventually they knew the time was right, knew the exact instant, and flipped on the lights. Up ahead, the woman driving the car saw the police cruiser behind her for the first time; they were close enough to see her in her rearview mirror, and they watched her reflection mouth a curse as she pulled over the car. Did she curse in front of the kids? Nah, she didn't look the kind to do such a thing; surely she had simply muttered it under her breath.

The Hunter and the Normal examined the neighborhood before getting out of the cruiser. This wasn't the best time of morning to be hunting, for sure. A lot of people would have already gone to work if they started at eight or eight-thirty; the nine o'clockers may not have left yet, but there would be fewer of them. Some stay-at-home moms would still be around. But chances were, most of them also had school-aged kids and would be en route to school.

Like the woman sitting in the car ahead of them. Yes, it was a bad time of day to hunt. But they could do it. They only had to go through the motions as the Normal, then get the woman and the Quarry out of there. Anyone casually looking out their window would see a police officer making a traffic stop. Nothing out of the ordinary.

They opened the door, slid out of the vehicle, and approached the woman's car. They sucked in a few large gulps of the autumn air, enjoying the sound of the gravel crunching underfoot. Their senses, all their senses, began to ramp up a few more cycles.

"Do you know why I stopped you today, ma'am?" the Normal's voice asked after the woman rolled down her window. They glanced into the backseat where the two Quarry sat. Both of them looked at the police uniform in wide-eyed wonder. Good, very good. They would use that wonder to their advantage. Their heightened senses began to pick up extra details. As one of the Quarry moved to wipe at his nose in the backseat, they heard the muscles of the arm contracting, the joint of the elbow swinging.

"Look, Officer, I know I didn't stop all the way at that sign back there—"

"You're right about that."

"—but I was just trying to get the kids to school, you know. Running a little late." She tilted her head toward the Quarry in the backseat.

"If you'd just step back to my vehicle, this won't take but a moment."

"I'm really sorry, Officer. Can't we just let this go with a warning?"

"Well now, who says you're going to get a ticket?" They smiled broadly at her. It wasn't a smile that was intended to put her at ease but to make her uncomfortable. They would get her back to the cruiser, there was no doubt about that, but they thought they might as well enjoy themselves in the process. She was nervous, scared, unsure. All emotions to be savored. They closed their eyes and inhaled the sick, sour scent of her fear, smiled, and stepped back. She opened the door and got out.

They turned to at the Quarry in and offered another grin. "You boys hang tight for a few minutes, okay?"

They followed the woman back to the cruiser as they watched the ions dancing in the air, illuminated in streaks of red and blue by the flashing lights. They sensed things no one else did. They weren't human; they were much more.

When they were inside the car, the woman tried another time to avoid a ticket. "Like I said, Officer, I'm really sorry," she said.

She still thought this was about a traffic ticket. She wasn't perceptive, extrasensory, like they were. "Oh, I'm sure you're sorry, ma'am," they said as they dug around in the breast pocket of their jacket. Their fingers touched the bottle of chloroform and the rag, then brought them out. Their other hand, the left hand, moved to the button on the armrest and locked the doors. Once the doors of the cruiser were locked, only the driver could unlock them. One of the advantages of hunting as the Normal, using the police cruiser.

They saw more of the whites of the woman's eyes now. She wasn't just scared, oh no, she'd gone way past that and on into terrified. They could hear her heart racing inside her chest, almost trying to pound its way out.

She tried to scream, but they were too fast and too strong. They had the chloroform-soaked cloth over her mouth and nose in an instant, and in her terrified state, her lungs betrayed her. She took in huge gulps of air, breathing the fumes. In a few short seconds she stopped struggling, then went limp in their hands. She'd be out for half an hour or so, which would give them more than enough time, but they still had to be careful. They liked to plan for all possible contingencies.

They scanned the houses up and down the street again, looking for activity. No one was outside. They opened the door to the car and jumped out, leaving the door hanging open, the *ding ding ding* of the door-ajar signal chirping like a lullaby. A fitting soundtrack for *accepting*.

Up ahead, a car approached, surely slowed by the flashing lights on the cruiser. No one sped by a traffic stop, even though it would be a good time to do so. After all, if officers had stopped another vehicle, they wouldn't be scoping other cars. Why didn't people realize that?

The Hunter and the Normal came to the door of the woman's car and bent down at the driver's side. Nothing to worry about, nothing in the least. Their back would block the driver's vision, giving him neither a clear view of their face nor the empty space behind the steering wheel.

As they bent down to the window, they looked into the backseat and smiled at the Quarry. Both of them. "How'd you boys like to ride in a police car?" they asked. Both boys looked back, unblinking.

The car passed down the road. Nothing out of the ordinary here. Just a traffic stop. Just an officer cleaning up the streets. That was what they did in the guise of the Normal: They cleaned the town of filth.

They pulled out the chloroform and the rag again, then opened the rear door of the car. "Tell you what," they said to the boys, "we're gonna have a good time. A real good time." They leaned into the backseat and marveled at how easy it was—how ridiculously easy. The seat belts held both Quarry in place, preventing them from protesting or escaping. And the Quarry were small, small enough to be carried back to the cruiser in one trip.

It wasn't a long drive to the house. Not a long drive at all.

Rachel gripped the tire iron tightly, so tightly she noticed her knuckles were starting to turn white. She relaxed her grip and then moved into the home. The moon had now risen, offering some silvery light through the windows. But it wasn't enough. Should she try turning on a light?

Rachel felt the familiar indentation on her lip and unconsciously bit it as she considered. She had to have a light, or she'd trip and break her neck. And if that happened, she wouldn't help anyone.

She looked at the wall near the door, found an old-style light switch. It wasn't a lever switch but a button switch: one to turn on the light, one to turn it off. Rachel held her breath and punched the button.

The porch light came on.

She turned off the porch light, then went to the next switch. This time a lamp in the corner illuminated the living room. Rachel stood silent, waiting. She willed her ears to hear any sound, any sound at all.

Nothing.

At the far side of the room, a closed door waited. Jude had said the door would be there, had explained what it would look like, but still, she had been doubtful. Until now. The door, an old barn door kind of thing that seemed out of place inside the home, looked exactly as Jude had described it to her. And what did that mean? Rachel nodded to herself. *It meant he was probably right about everything else, too.*

She grasped the tire iron as she opened the door to the basement.

Here, a string turned on a weak overhead light, barely lighting a path down the stairs. She hated basements, absolutely hated them. They made her claustrophobic.

Somewhere below, Rachel heard a noise. A rustling perhaps. Someone, or something, was in the basement. She swallowed hard and took the first step down.

Jude had to be careful, very careful. He was sitting next to a tanker of gasoline, and he had to light matches. He looked at Odum's face, still colored by the dash lights.

"I told you a lie, Chief Odum. Told you it was Frank, led you out here to get you away from your home." Jude stopped, closed his eyes, went on. "It's been happening for a long time now, hasn't it?" Jude had asked in what he hoped was a soft, sympathetic voice.

Odum stared at the road as he drove, saying nothing.

Jude continued. "When you first came here, you were very careful. You went to surrounding towns: Cody, Columbus, Billings, even Sheridan a couple of times."

Odum licked his lips, looked into the rearview mirror. Was he looking for some kind of cue from Kristina?

Jude glanced into the back, where Kristina sat staring straight ahead. Until she had showed up in Odum's car, he had never suspected she was involved, too. But when he saw her, it clicked. It made sense in some way, the two of them together.

Kristina acted as if she didn't notice Jude's gaze. No matter. It was too late now. He had shown his bottom card to both of them; no chance of folding now.

"But lately," Jude said, "it's been eating away at you. And today, you broke your first rule: you hit your own town. You weren't really planning on doing it, but when you saw both of the boys together, they just kind of pulled you along."

Jude stopped, and they drove in silence for several seconds. The pavement ended, and now dust began to rattle through the window next to Jude. He pushed the button to make sure the window was up all the way, but already he could feel a fine grit settling in the car's interior. The windows were locked, anyway.

"Now, I'm just guessing at this part," Jude said, "but you were the one who freed Sohler from the hospital, weren't you? It worked well, gave you a fall guy. Gave you the go-ahead to strike in your own town, because you could just hunt down Sohler, shoot him, be a hero to the world."

More silence, except for the rumbling tires on the gravel road.

"It did fit together rather well, didn't it?" Odum finally said. "I mean, when you led me to Sohler, that was quite providential. His own kids, can you believe that? His wife left him a few years ago, and, well." Odum licked his lips. "I guess Kenneth has been a bit unbalanced since then. Never sent his kids to school, never let 'em outside the house. A real sicko, huh?" Odum turned to look at Jude, actually seeming to enjoy himself.

Jude said nothing, so Odum continued. "You've surprised me, Mr. Gress, you surely have. Maybe there's something to your psychic vision thing after all. Luckily, though, I've prepared for that. I'm a man who likes to prepare."

Jude wasn't sure where Odum's gun came from, but he found himself looking down the barrel of it.

At the base of the stairs Rachel looked around the dark room and willed her eyes to adjust to the low light. A light, a lamp, there had to be something down here. In the corner she spotted another button switch, walked over, and pressed it.

A single overhead bulb gasped to life. She glanced around and saw built-in shelving on the walls, with a few boxes and jars here and there. On the dirt floor sat an old wooden worktable of some kind, and across the room, on the opposite wall, hung two large burlap bags with something inside. Something that was moving. And . . . was that sobbing she heard?

She started to speak, but her voice caught in her throat as she thought of what the boys had endured that morning: something nearly as bad as what Nicole had endured. Worse in some ways, because they were still conscious, terrified of what would happen to them next. Neither boy had spoken, and she realized why. They thought she was Odum.

Rachel made herself speak: "Nathan? Bradley?"

"Mommy?" she heard a bewildered voice ask. One of the bags moved, swaying on the hook.

"It's me, honey!" she said, and now her feet were carrying her across the room. She pulled the bag off the hook. Nathan was a big boy, and she wouldn't normally be able to lift her son so easily, but the adrenaline and the joy coursing through her veins made the bag as light as new snow. She sat the bag on the floor and fumbled with the knotted rope. It was a tight knot she couldn't unravel, and it forced a grunt of frustration from her lips. She thought of the tire iron she'd just put down. She picked it up and pushed the blunt, chiseled end into the burlap just below the knot until she had gouged a small hole. With some work she managed to rip a line down the bag along a stitched seam. Inside was Nathan, puffy-eyed and perhaps a bit pale, but as beautiful a sight as she had ever seen in her life.

"Mommy?" he said again quizzically, as if still unbelieving this was all happening.

"It's me, Nathan," she said. "You're gonna be just fine." She pulled him close, hugged him, and promised herself she'd never let him go again. "We're gonna get Bradley, and then we're all gonna go home, and everything is going to be just fine." It felt like a lie when she said it; the image of Nicole with tubes and wires sprouting from her body couldn't possibly be called *just fine*, but it needed to be said right now. For her, as much as for Nathan.

Nathan pulled away from her hug at the mention of Bradley. "I . . . I think Bradley's hurt, Momma."

Rachel stiffened. "What do you mean?" she said as she stood and pulled the other bag from the hook, then started working on it with the tire iron.

"We heard you up there, and Bradley said, 'I'm scared, I'm really scared,' cuz we thought it was . . . you know . . . the policeman coming back. And it was like he started choking or something."

Rachel worked open the bag, pulled out Bradley's limp body, and laid him on the floor. "Bradley?" she said. "Sweetie? You okay?" His skin felt cold and clammy, his eyes closed. He didn't respond. She put her ear down over his mouth, turning her head to look at his chest. This was what she had been taught to do in childhood CPR; she had signed up for the class a few years ago. She felt no breath coming from Bradley's mouth, saw no rising or falling in his chest.

He had stopped breathing.

Jude wondered how Odum intended to drive the car and keep the gun pointed his direction at the same time. But not for long. Odum pulled to the side of the road and put the car in park. "I'm a little tired of driving," Odum said with a smile. "How about you take over?" Jude nodded and opened his door; Odum did the same, keeping the gun pointed at Jude. "Stay right there," Odum commanded as he walked around the car to the passenger side where he waved with the gun, indicating Jude should move to the driver's side. Jude did as instructed. Odum and Jude slid back into the car at the same time, forming an odd mirror image of each other. Neither of them bothered with seat belts.

Odum waved at the road in front of them. "Anytime you're ready," he said.

Jude put the car in gear and eased out onto the road again.

They drove in silence for a few minutes. Jude tried to ignore the gun's muzzle just a few inches from him but couldn't. He cleared his throat. "You're not going to kill me, Chief Odum," Jude tried. "If you wanted to do that, you would have shot me already."

Odum laughed. "Well, well, an amateur psychologist. Actually, if you'll take a peek in the back, I think you'll see I made a stop on the way here."

Yes, Kristina was quite a surprise. Jude still hadn't figured out how or why she was involved in this whole mess, but he was quite sure the answer was about to be revealed to him. The answer, about to be revealed. Revelation. He smiled humorlessly. Those were nice, prophet-like words; Kristina would love them.

Jude reluctantly looked at Kristina in the rearview mirror. This time she returned his gaze, then slowly gave him a level shake of her head. She tilted her head to her right, indicating something on the seat next to her. Jude turned to look in the backseat, and saw what she was indicating: a shovel.

"The shovel?" Jude asked, a bit bewildered. "You mean the shovel?"

Odum snorted. "Of course I mean the shovel. Best they sell at Renton's Hardware. It's a little surprise for you, a lovely parting gift, as it were."

Jude focused his attention on the road ahead, watched the headlights tracing a path along the gravel roadway. "A parting gift?" he said.

"I don't know if you've ever tried to dig in these woods, Mr. Gress," he said. "Difficult. Lots of roots."

Jude continued to watch the road and stayed silent.

"I think you're starting to see," Odum said, "that I don't really like to dig. And maybe you're also starting to see why I haven't shot you yet."

Jude could tell Odum was looking his way more and more now, getting excited as he talked.

"How tall are you, Mr. Gress?"

"Just under six feet."

"Then a six-foot hole is what you'll be digging, if you get my drift."

Jude got the drift. Got it just fine.

Rachel let the memories of her CPR training take over. She checked Bradley's airways, tilted his head back, put her mouth over his, and exhaled.

"Mom? Is . . . is Bradley okay?" Nathan's voice sounded pinched, strained. She could tell this was scaring him, but there was no way around it. She needed to get Bradley breathing again. Rachel did the chest compressions, then stopped and placed her ear over Bradley's mouth again.

"Mom? I'm—"

"Sweetie, Mommy needs to concentrate right now, okay?" Still no breathing from Bradley. Tilt the head, three breaths. *This is like Jude,* her mind told her. Jude Allman, the guy who was famous for dying. And wasn't it ironic that it would all come to a scene like this?

Rachel moved to the chest compressions and, under her hands, suddenly pictured Jude. It was Bradley she was bringing back to life, of course, but her mind told her it was also Jude. That was her purpose, her reason.

Still no breathing. Nothing.

She exhaled more breaths into Bradley's mouth. How long should she keep this up? How long could Bradley go without breathing before he had some brain damage? *Like his mother,* she thought quickly, then pushed the thought from her mind. Three minutes was the figure that came to her mind. Three minutes. Had it been that long?

She went to the compressions again, and now she could hear Nathan starting to sob and lose control. But when she looked at Nathan, she dimly realized he wasn't the one sobbing. It was her; she was hearing herself bawling, losing control.

As she held her head over Bradley's mouth, listening, watching, her body betrayed her. The sobs became huge, wracking gasps that made her convulse. It was as if, in willing Bradley to breathe, just breathe, her own body wanted to suck in more air. But her body also wanted to shut down.

She collapsed her head on Bradley's chest. It couldn't happen like this. It *couldn't*. She couldn't come all this way, do all this, only to lose Bradley. She had promised Nicole.

Rachel felt Nathan's small hand on her back, rubbing. She turned and hugged him tightly again, letting herself cry. The image of Jude crying in Nathan's arms came to her mind, and she realized now that she'd been lying to herself all along. She was disturbed that Jude hadn't come to her and shared his problems, but she now saw that she wasn't the strong one in her family. It was Nathan who was strong, Nathan who gave the comfort. Nathan who was the center.

"It will be okay," she heard Nathan say. But she heard another voice say it in unison—a deeper, more resonant voice. Her internal voice of God. She realized her son, like the voice, was a gift from God. Her son. Her center.

"*Don't be afraid,*" God's voice and her son's voice told her at the same time. And she wasn't.

With that, Bradley's mouth opened to draw in a deep, long breath.

"I'm not getting much of a reaction out of you, Mr. Gress," Odum intoned. And as Jude thought about it, he could see the chief was indeed getting a bit upset; Odum had obviously expected a blubbering idiot who would beg for his life. Of course, Odum had no way of knowing he sat next to a man who was quite familiar with death and who was now unafraid of it.

Jude shrugged. "Not sure what you expected," he said as he looked across the seat. "But I'm more than willing to die for my son." Odum's coat, lying on the seat between them, caught his eye. Jude replayed a part of the vision in his head: the part where Odum slipped the bottle of chloroform and cloth inside a coat pocket.

Odum grinned while keeping his eyes on the road. "It's a nice thought, but after you dig your hole and occupy it, I still get to go

home, Mr. Gress. The Quarry—" Odum's voice shifted. "Your son—
is waiting at home for me."

Jude put his left hand on top of the steering wheel. With his right
hand he started exploring Odum's jacket on the seat between them,
knowing the darkness of the forest night would hide his actions: the
only light in the car was the soft glow of the dash displays. "Why do
you think I asked you to come up here, ten miles away from your
home?" Jude asked as he blindly slid his hand around the folds of the
coat. He felt a bulge, then worked his way around the lining and
found the pocket's opening. Inside, he felt the chloroform and cloth.

Odum went still, quiet. "What do you mean?"

Jude carefully grasped the bottle and cloth, slid them out of the
coat and behind his back. "By this time, Chief Odum, my son is
probably long gone from your house. My . . . his mother went there
while we came here. She's probably back at the police station now.
Your police station. And I'll bet what they find in your home will be
much more interesting than anything they found in Sohler's."

Odum's eyes rolled to white for a brief second, then focused. They
rolled again, focused. He let the gun drop to his side. "Well," he said
simply. And then, in a low whisper, he said something else Jude could
barely hear: "Switch."

Jude felt his nerves kick up another notch. Careful, he had to be
careful. In the backseat, Kristina stayed as eerily quiet as she had been
for the whole ride.

"I . . . I know about your childhood," Jude said in a hushed tone.

"Pull over here," Odum growled.

Jude pulled to the side of the road but tried to keep the conversation going. "Your mom committed suicide when you were young, a
horrible thing for you to go through. You blamed yourself for it, and
maybe even your father blamed you for it."

Odum said nothing. Jude wasn't sure if he should continue or not,
but he felt like Odum was out on a ledge; he needed to talk Odum
into backing off of it.

"It's not fair, I know," Jude continued. "It kinda made your father a bit crazy, didn't it? And he took it out on you. A horrible thing to live through, Chief Odum. But you did it. And believe it or not, I know what that's like. I think you can get help. We can just turn around and go back now."

Odum smiled, a demented, twisted smile. "A fine lecture, Mr. Gress. You *should* really think about becoming a psychologist some-time." Odum raised the barrel of the gun toward Jude again, and Jude swallowed hard.

"However," Odum said, "I think I'll just stick with Plan A right now." He reached over and twisted the key to shut off the car. "Howzabout you grab that shovel in back, Mr. Gress?"

Odum opened his door, then slid out; Jude followed suit, cupping the hidden chloroform and cloth behind him. Jude opened the back door to the car to reach for the shovel. He exchanged a look with Kristina, then slowly shook his head. Jude glanced up at Odum, whose eyes were now wide and wild.

"How about just you and me on this one?" Jude asked.

Odum smiled. "Of course just you and me, Mr. Gress. I wouldn't have it any other way. Don't even have to bring the shovel, if you'd rather dig with your hands."

Jude glared at Kristina as he grabbed the shovel; she reached out to touch his arm, but he pulled away.

"Something wrong, Mr. Gress?" Odum boomed.

"Nothing, nothing."

"After you, then," Odum said, giving a comical bow. They set out into the woods, stepping over low brush and downed timber as they moved. The air was cold, crisp, dark. The loamy ground beneath them crackled with leaves and larch needles.

"You've heard of Extreme Measures, haven't you, Mr. Gress?" Odum seemed almost jovial now, as if his whole world weren't falling down around him. Jude certainly hadn't expected this latest twist.

"Extreme measures? Sure, yeah. I guess so."

"Well, maybe you've heard of it, but I doubt you've ever experienced it before. This," Odum said as he waved the gun at the forest around him, "is even a bit more than that. Let's call it Beyond Extreme Measures, eh?"

Odum was babbling now, but Jude wasn't about to argue with him. No sense kicking a dog when it's cornered.

"Let's just keep that shovel down at your side, in case you're thinking of taking a swing," Odum said. "It doesn't matter how fast you can move, Mr. Gress. A .38 slug moves much faster."

Jude nodded and kept walking. He wasn't really thinking of swinging the shovel. He had something else in mind.

"I'd still like to know how you did it, Mr. Gress. How you figured it all out."

"I'm not real sure of that myself." That was the truth.

"I mean, knowing about my childhood and—"

Abruptly, Jude tripped and went facedown on the ground. He rolled onto his back, then clutched at his lower leg.

"What?" Odum asked.

Jude spoke through clenched teeth. "Twisted my ankle on a big root, I think. I . . . I think I might have hurt it pretty bad."

Odum pointed the gun at Jude's midsection. "Get up."

"I'm not sure if I can."

Odum cocked his gun. "You can if you don't want your guts ventilated," he said.

Jude rolled over again and made a show of getting up slowly. At the same time he filled his left hand with dirt from the forest floor; he kept the chloroform cloth clutched in his right hand. After he got to his feet, he turned toward Odum.

He acted before he had a chance to think about the danger of the situation. He knew he'd only have one chance, and he took it. Shifting into high gear, he threw the dirt at Odum's eyes and rushed him at the same time. The dirt worked: subconsciously Odum reached for his face, pulling the gun away from Jude.

Jude hit him hard and fast. Odum was larger, and at least twenty pounds heavier, but Jude had surprised him. He drove his shoulder into Odum's stomach as hard as he could, and he heard Odum's lungs reverse direction as his breath came out in one long *whoosh*. As they fell to the ground, Jude clamped the chloroform-soaked cloth over Odum's mouth.

Odum struggled for a few moments, trying to buck off Jude's body. But Jude held tight. Odum was strong, incredibly strong; Jude was glad he hadn't tried anything with the shovel. Odum would have eaten him for lunch.

Before long, Odum's body went limp, yet Jude kept the cloth over his face. He didn't want to fall for a fake flop, then let up his guard and have Odum overpower him. So, after about thirty seconds, when he was certain Odum was out, Jude relaxed. He looked around for the dropped gun, found it, then grabbed Odum by the shoulders and started dragging him.

It took about twenty minutes for Jude to get Odum's limp body back to the car. Odum had to be at least two hundred thirty pounds, and Jude wasn't used to dragging around that kind of dead weight. A few times he thought of leaving Odum, but he was too scared. He didn't want to let Odum out of his sight now. If he took his eyes off the monster, the monster might escape. And if the monster escaped, he might show up somewhere else.

Just before he reached the car, Jude set down Odum's body and pulled out the gun. While he knew there was no way he could use it on Kristina, he hoped she wouldn't know that.

He stalked toward the car and was surprised to see her still sitting in the back. He knocked on her door window with the barrel of the gun; she turned without seeming surprised, as if she had always expected him to be there. Quickly he opened the front door and stared at her through the metal partition.

"Can't really believe you're still here," he said.

She turned to look at him. "I'm not going anywhere," she said. "It's not my time yet."

Whatever that meant. No matter; now he remembered the cruiser's doors and windows were only operable by the driver so she wouldn't have escaped if she even wanted to. This made things easier: with the locked doors and partition, he didn't have to worry about Kristina doing anything in the backseat while he drove. The big question was, what should he do with Odum? He could maybe put Odum in the back with Kristina, but he didn't like that idea. This was Odum's car, and he was sure the chief knew how to retract the screen or unlock the doors. Plus, he was sure he didn't want both of them sitting together—behind him, no less—as he drove back to town.

Then an idea hit him: the handcuffs. He could handcuff Odum, put him in the front seat, and keep the gun on him.

Jude went back to retrieve Odum's unconscious body. He cuffed Odum, then dragged him to the car and struggled to push him into the front seat. Odum stirred in Jude's arms, waking from his chloroform-induced slumber.

Jude realized he'd left the cloth and the bottle out in the forest somewhere; there wasn't any way he was going to put Odum back to sleep, and there was even less chance of him winning a physical struggle. He patted down the officer, wanting to make sure he didn't have any other weapons.

Odum was clean.

Jude checked the cuffs one last time to make sure Odum was secure. He closed the door and went to the other side. As he slid in, Odum opened his eyes for the first time. He stared blearily as Jude started the vehicle and turned it around. Jude held the gun so Odum could see it; Odum stared at it but said nothing.

They drove in silence for a few minutes before Odum spoke. "Well, doesn't this just beat all?" he said.

Jude stayed silent. He glanced in the rearview mirror at Kristina; she returned his gaze, said nothing. Now wasn't the time to talk. They would have plenty of time to talk when they got back to Red Lodge.

Odum moved slowly, slurred a bit as he talked; the chloroform hadn't worn off all the way yet.

"Mr. Gress, I'd like to congratulate you on your psychic vision thing. Well done. Maybe you should go into business with Dionne Warwick." He chuckled. Jude said nothing; he was too tired, too drained to talk. And he was still afraid. Very afraid.

"But I bet there's one thing you didn't see coming tonight," Odum continued. "One very big thing."

Odum stopped. Obviously he was waiting for Jude to answer. Okay, Jude could humor the man. "What is that, Chief Odum?"

"This."

It happened so fast, Jude barely saw it. Odum's cuffed hands snapped out and grabbed the steering wheel, wresting control from Jude. Jude, in his surprise, dropped the pistol, putting both hands on the steering wheel. Odum was stronger, so much stronger, and the car was already off the road before Jude could react and get his foot to the brake.

A canyon, it's a canyon, Jude thought as the car sailed through the crisp autumn air. And yes, of course they were in a canyon. In a heartbeat Jude thought of Nathan and Rachel and mouthed the words, "Please, please, please . . ." He saw the rocky bottom approaching, and Jude had the sensation not so much that they were falling, but that the earth was rushing up to meet them.

Rachel was stunned when she walked into the hospital room. It couldn't be possible, couldn't be possible at all. Too much damage. The rational side of her brain told her this, let her know all the things it had categorized as possible and impossible.

And then the voice inside—in harmony with her son's voice—assured her of what was real.

The octopus Nicole was gone. The smiling, vibrant Nicole was back, sitting up in her bed. After a few days in intensive care, she had been transferred to a private room, and this was the first time Rachel had seen her since . . . since.

"Thanks for taking Bradley for a few days," Nicole said. Amazing. A little slurred speech, but no paralysis of any kind. Nicole Whittaker had taken a bullet to the brain, and now, just a few days later, she was sitting up and talking. *Miracles still happen*, the voice inside her said. Rachel smiled. Yes, miracles did indeed still happen.

"Bradley is welcome at our house any time. In an odd sort of way, since they went through the whole—" Rachel paused and searched for a word to describe what the boys and Nicole had endured, yet no such word existed—"the whole thing together, I think they've been kind of healing together, too." She smiled at Nicole. "Sounds crazy, I know."

"No, it doesn't," Nicole said. "It sounds perfectly sane to me."

"He's just down the hallway, in the play area with the nurse," Rachel said. "You wanna see him?"

A tear slid from Nicole's eye as she nodded. Rachel backed out into the hall again and waved at the nurses' station.

"They told me I should have been a vegetable," Nicole said. "And without Bradley, without him, I think I would have been."

Rachel nodded, sensing Nicole needed to get out something important.

"I don't really remember much. But I had the strangest dream," Nicole continued, wiping at her eyes. Rachel grabbed the box of tissues from the nightstand and handed it to her. "You ever have that dream where you're trying to run, but you can't seem to get out of slow motion? Like you're in molasses or something?"

Rachel smiled, nodded.

"Well, that's what was happening, and then I heard you."

Rachel stiffened. "Me?" she said.

Nicole dabbed at her eyes with the tissue. "Yeah. I remember exactly what you said: 'Nicole, he's okay. And we'll bring him back. Just hang on to that.' When I heard that, I could run. Somehow I knew I was going to be fine. Nutso, huh?"

Rachel took Nicole's hand between her own hands, cradling Nicole's palm as she had done just a few days before. "No," Rachel answered softly. "It sounds perfectly sane to me." They smiled at each other.

"So how's Boo Rad—er, Ron—doing?" Nicole asked.

"Well, for starters, his name isn't Ron. I have a long story when you get out of here," Rachel said. "But the short story is: he's fine. With you and him in the same hospital at the same time, I think we have a lot of doctors scratching their heads right now."

"Mommy?"

Rachel turned and saw Bradley standing at the doorway, accompanied by the nurse. His eyes were bright, joyous. He ran across the room to Nicole's bed, and Rachel helped him crawl up into bed next to his mother. Nicole hugged her son, long and hard, and Rachel knew what she was thinking at this very moment: *I'm not going to ever let him go.*

Jude opened his eyes, stared at the wall of the hospital room. He was in a bed. He was smiling.

He knew he'd been to the Other Side again, but this time had been entirely different. His heart still pounded with the joy of it, his lungs still held the crisp, living air. Most of all, his lips still tingled with the aftertaste of the Other Side: a taste like the sweetest, purest honey he had ever imagined.

A taste nothing like copper.

At the base of the bed, a doctor was intently studying charts on a clipboard. Jude cleared his throat, and the doctor looked up. Jude recognized the look in the doctor's eyes. It was a look he knew well, a look that said *my status has just left my quo.* A look Jude had seen on a few doctors' faces in his lifetime. Or should that be lifetimes?

"I . . . uh . . ." the doctor stammered. "You're alive. I mean, awake."

"Old habits die hard," Jude answered.

"What's that?"

"Nothing. Why's my bed up like this?"

The doctor seemed puzzled. Clearly this was not the first question he'd expected out of a resurrected patient. "I'm sorry, uh—"

"I mean, why is my bed up instead of down?"

"Oh. Well, your wife . . . she's been coming in, and she said you'd be more comfortable that way. That you preferred to sleep sitting up. And since there wasn't any clinical reason to keep you flat on your back . . ." Jude smiled. *Your wife.* Rachel wasn't his wife, of course— although the sound of the doctor saying the words sounded oddly sweet. Still, he made no move to correct the doctor. In an odd sort of way, he enjoyed the thought himself.

"You were in a serious accident," the doctor began. Jude recognized the beginning of the sermon, usually entitled something like *You're Here and You Shouldn't Be, and I'm Trying to Figure Out Why.* "When they brought you in, you were clinically—"

"Dead?" Jude finished.

"Yes. We couldn't detect a respiration, or any brain activity—"

A thought flashed into Jude's mind. Kristina. Kristina had been in the car with him. "What about, um, the other passengers?"

"Michael Odum? Dead on arrival, I'm afraid." The doctor looked at him uncomfortably, and Jude could tell the doctor desperately wanted to add *but then, so were you.* So Odum was dead. He somehow knew that would be the case.

"Actually, I meant Kristina."

The doctor's eyebrows furrowed. "I'm sorry?"

"Kristina. She was in the backseat."

The doctor put on a new look, the old *I don't know what you're talking about, but then, you did take a pretty good hit to the head* look. "I'm sorry, you're mistaken," the doctor said, finally getting to use a bit of condescension in his voice. "There wasn't anyone else in the car."

Jude blinked a couple of times. The familiar bloom of surfacing memories burst before his eyes in vivid color again, and he saw. He *saw.*

Rewind. Eight years old. The hospital morgue. The crisp, linen sheet rolls back, and the smiling face of a woman looks down at him.
Kristina.

Fast-forward. Kristina sits in his house. "Let's just say I won't be here very long," Kristina says.

Rewind. Sixteen years old. His hospital room. The nurse tells him there's something special about him, then serves him dinner.
Kristina.

Fast-forward. The Red Lodge Cafe. "I'm not here for me," Kristina says. "I'm here for you."

Rewind. Twenty-four years old. The hospital lobby. The woman opens the emergency door and lets him escape.

Kristina.

Fast-forward. Odum's car. "You're a prophet, Jude," Kristina says. "Like Moses. A messenger."

Play. Now. Thirty-two years old. Kristina's cryptic notes, scribbled on sticky papers: *Eight, sixteen, twenty-four . . . see a pattern here?* Yes. Crazy eights, signifying a new beginning, a resurrection. And the next number in that pattern was thirty-two. Jude's present age.

Jude looked back to the doctor.

"Are you okay?" the doctor asked. "You seem a little flushed. Experiencing any—"

"I'm fine, I'm fine," Jude said, although he wasn't. A door had been opened inside his head. "Could you hand me the phone there?"

The doctor kept his gaze fixed on Jude a few more moments, then moved to the phone. He handed it to Jude, and Jude immediately dialed. He still remembered the phone number.

"Thanks for calling the Stumble Inn. How can I help you?" the voice on the line said.

"Could I get room 305, please?"

A pause.

"I'm sorry, sir, could you say that again?"

"Room 305."

"Well, sir, we don't have a room 305. Could it be another room?"

Jude paused. "You're telling me there's no such room?"

"That's what I'm telling you. We only have two floors."

"Okay, thanks."

"Sorry I couldn't help, sir."

Jude smiled. "Actually, you have helped. Quite a bit." Jude hung up the phone and handed it back to the doctor.

"Out of curiosity," he said to the doctor, "what room am I in right now?"

"I was just thinking of that while you talked," the doctor said. "A strange coincidence that you're in patient room 305."

Of course. "Coincidence," Jude said with a smile. "That's me. Mr. Coincidence." Jude somehow knew inside that every time he had been in the hospital, he had always been in room 305. He didn't know the significance of the number, and maybe there was nothing horribly significant about the number itself. But it was a sign. One of those infamous signs Kristina had referred to, big as life and glaring in front of his face.

"One more thing," the doctor said. "I did some tests because, well—"

"Yeah?"

"Anyway, I'd like you to start taking an iron supplement."

"Why?"

"You're anemic. Happens more often to women, but sometimes in men, too. If you don't get your iron up, you might experience some disorientations—strange smells, maybe—"

"Strange tastes?"

"Yeah, I suppose. If it gets serious enough, it might even cause memory lapses."

Jude thought about it. The copper taste, the blackouts, the visions . . . could they all be symptoms of anemia? It seemed good old science was trying to explain everything for him now.

Trying.

Jude smiled and leaned back against his pillow. "Does this bed go back any farther? Like flat?"

"Sure it does," the doctor said. "You want to lie down?"

"Yeah. Yeah, I do."

Jude pulled on his first shoe, then reached down to tie it. He stopped, closed his eyes for a moment, concentrated on all the sounds filtering in around him. He heard a doctor being paged out in the hallway. A low cough from someone in the next room. A muffled television playing some atrocious sitcom. The squeaking of rubber shoes on the linoleum outside.

And then, a squealed "Daddy!" Jude opened his eyes, looked toward the door marked 305, saw his son standing in the doorway—*his* son, radiant and perfect—and smiled.

Nathan bounded across the floor and leaped into Jude's arms. Jude embraced him, drank in the smell and feel of having his son close, and knew he would do everything possible to hang on to those feelings forever.

Rachel appeared at the doorway and walked across the floor toward the bed. "How are you feeling?" she asked.

"Never better," he answered. And it wasn't just a fluff answer. It was the truth.

"We have a present for you, Daddy," Nathan said.

Jude held Nathan at arm's length and grinned, then looked at Rachel. She shrugged her shoulders and brought a wrapped gift out of the shopping bag she was holding.

Jude took the package, made a show of shaking it and trying to figure out what it was. "Is it a new car?" Jude asked.

"No!" Nathan squealed with delight.

"A big pot of spaghetti? Spaghetti's my favorite, you know."

"No, no!"

"How about—"

"Just open it, Daddy. You'll see."

Jude pulled off the ribbon and tore at the paper. Inside was a box kite. He stared at the kite a few moments, let the memories of a chilly Nebraska morning spent with his father blow across his mind. Then he fixed his eyes on Rachel. "Thank you."

She shrugged again. "You talked about flying one with your dad. Maybe Nathan should fly one with his."

Jude turned back to Nathan. "It's the second-best present I've ever been given," Jude said. "You remember the first best?"

"My hand?" Nathan whispered.

"You got it." Jude slipped on his other shoe and started to tie it.

"And look, Daddy, I got a present, too." Nathan reached into his pocket, fished out something, and held it up. It was a small wood carving of a frog with a crown on its head. A frog prince. "The other Mr. Janitor gave it to me."

Rachel jumped in. "Frank invited us over last night. You should see in his basement—it's filled with these incredible wood carvings, thousands of them. Must have taken him years."

Jude smiled. Frank's beloved work.

"About ready to go?" Rachel asked.

"Sure, sure. Just getting dressed, making myself presentable, you know."

"You up to having a few more visitors first?"

Jude narrowed his eyes as he looked at her. "Like who?"

Rachel walked back to the door of the room and motioned to someone out in the hall. A few moments later, Tiffany tentatively appeared in the doorway, holding Joey's hand. Tiffany whispered something into Joey's ear, and Joey walked across the room toward Jude. Joey had managed to put on some weight and already looked healthier.

"Thank you," he said to Jude in a faint, almost impossible-to-hear voice.

Jude felt tears streaming from his eyes as he hugged Joey. He pulled in Nathan for a hug, motioning for Tiffany to come over as well.

Rachel came to them, put her hand on Tiffany's back. "Um, *he* went under the radar for a few days," she said, obliquely referring to Sohler. "But it sounds like the police have picked up his trail in Minnesota. Anyway, the kids have been staying with us, and so has Bradley. One big, happy family."

"A big, happy family. I like the sound of that," Jude said, and smiled.

Rachel returned the smile, then changed the subject. "It's nuts out there," she said, motioning her head toward the door.

"I'm sure it is."

"You're the biggest thing to hit Montana since the Unabomber, judging from the size of the crowd."

Jude nodded, then stood up.

"There's just one more thing I've been wanting to ask you," Rachel said.

"Shoot."

"Did you . . . see anything?"

Jude knew what she was asking. A question he had once hated, because the only answer he had for it was a lie. But not now. "Yes," he said, the sweet, honeyed taste still on his lips.

"And?"

"And I have some work to do." He paused. "Some messages to deliver, you might say."

The corridor was usually empty, filled only with the reverberations of echoes and the shadows of footsteps. But even now, as Jude, Rachel, Nathan, Tiffany, and Joey walked down the corridor, Jude heard more than their footsteps: he heard the sounds of a large crowd, murmuring, clamoring, waiting for him outside in the hospital lobby.

They walked by a janitor mopping the floor. A woman. She was rather small, with chocolate eyes and light hazel skin. Maybe she was Indian. Or Hispanic. Or a light-skinned African American. Or a mix. Jude nodded to Kristina, and she nodded back.

A phalanx of police escorts waited, naturally, along with hundreds of other people, television equipment, cameras, and a thousand other details that blended into one giant sea of shape and color.

Jude smiled, looked at his family. *His* family. Then, he grasped the handles and pulled them, opening the doors and letting the sea of light and noise wash over him.

ACKNOWLEDGMENTS

Writing a book is a solitary project, but any writer soon finds out its publication is a community effort. I'd like to thank some of this book's community supporters:

My lovely wife (Nancy) and lovely daughter (Jillian): thanks for putting up with late nights and early mornings.

My immediate family (Mom, Dad, Shauna, Bob, Merle, Bob, Pam, Mike, David, Thomas) and extended family: thanks for the encouragement and enthusiasm.

My church family (Faith Chapel in Billings, Montana) and Friday Community Group: thanks for the support.

My network of friends and writers who offered input and advice at various stages of the journey (CJ Box, Justine Musk, James Beau-Seigneur, Eric Wilson, Robert Liparulo, Tim Mohr, Leslie Thomson, Brandilyn Collins, Kathryn Mackel, Melanie Wells, Creston Mapes, Chris Well, Tim Downs, members of the Zoetrope writing community, the Faith*in*Fiction online community, the RMFW Alpha Critique Group, and all my Volunteer Publicists): thanks for the inspiration.

My iPod and its playlists (especially the music of Better Than Ezra, the Pixies, Wilco, Foo Fighters, Hillsong, David Crowder Band, and Rich Mullins): thanks for the soundtrack.

My publishing team (everyone at Bethany House): thanks for making it all happen.

My editor, Dave Long: an extra-special thanks for discovering the manuscript and bringing it to life (ha, ha). Without you, it would still be a four hundred-page doorstop.

My God: thanks for always being a part of my life, even before I knew you.

And finally to you, my reader: thanks for being the most important part of the publishing process.

AUTHOR'S NOTE

Although Red Lodge, Montana, exists, the version that appears in this book is somewhat different from its real-life counterpart: I've taken liberties with geography, added nonexistent businesses and landmarks, and just plain made up details to suit the needs of the story. I hope the good people of Red Lodge will forgive me. The town of Bingham, Nebraska, Jude's hometown, is entirely fictional.

Finally, if you enjoyed this book, explore more of the Other Side at *www.tlhines.com*. Sign up as a Volunteer Publicist to get *Lazarus Expanded*, a free companion e-book with deleted scenes and extras, or win prizes such as a share of royalties and a role in my next novel.

ABOUT THE AUTHOR

Montana-based T.L. Hines's list of past jobs includes trimming Christmas trees, sorting seed potatoes, working the graveyard shift at a convenience store, and cleaning cadaver storage rooms. A graduate of the University of Montana (BA, English Lit), he has spent the last sixteen years as a copywriter and advertising agency owner/manager. He has also won three air-guitar contests in which he performed songs by ZZ Top. Contact him at *www.tlhines.com*.

Be the first *to know*

Want to be the first to know
what's new from
your favorite authors?

Want to know all about
exciting new writers?

Sign up for BethanyHouse newsletters at
www.bethanynewsletters.com
and you'll get regular updates via e-mail.
You can sign up for specific authors or
categories so you get only
the information you really want.

Sign up today

More Adrenaline-Pumping Fiction From Bethany House

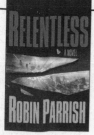

CAN DESTINY BE UNDONE?

Grant Borrows steps off the bus for an ordinary day of work, looks across the street, and sees…himself. In that single moment, the comfortable life he's known ends, and for reasons beyond his control he's hurtled into a race—both for the truth of his identity and ultimately for the survival of the world he's known. Soon he must discern who, if anyone, he can trust and how to hold onto that part of him that's never changed, that fragment of eternity he knows is called to stand strong against all odds.

Relentless by Robin Parrish

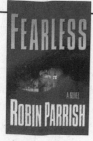

EXPLOSIVE SEQUEL TO *RELENTLESS*

After the events of *Relentless*, the world has changed. Hundreds of super-beings walk among. Esarth's inhabitants, an unexplained series of natural disasters have shaken the populace to its core, and fear fills the heart of every human being. But there is hope—the man known as Grant Borrows. After an extraordinary discovery in London, Grant realizes that the world's only hope may come from unraveling the truth about himself once and for all. But what he comes face-to-face with leaves even this most powerful of men shaken with fear....

Fearless by Robin Parrish

JASON BOYER JUST GOT AN INHERITANCE TO DIE FOR

Jason Boyer knew his father's business empire would pass to different hands—which suited him fine. The money was crooked and the power corrupt. But when an accident claims his father's life, everyone is stunned by the unveiling of a revised will. As Jason tries to handle the business more honestly than his father, he soon finds that standing for what's right may bring murderous consequences.

The Heir by Paul Robertson